PINK BALCONY
SILVER MOON

PINK BALCONY
SILVER MOON

A Sentimental Love Story

By
Narendra Simone
…*killing softly with his words.*

ISBN: 1496120507
ISBN 13: 9781496120502

This is a work of fiction. Names, characters, places, and incidents either are the product of the author's imagination or are used fictitiously, and any resemblance to any actual persons living or dead, events, or locales is entirely coincidental.

Prologue

The night moved on imperceptibly across the sky. Unlike the day, it made no sound and gave no sign, but passed unseen, unfelt, over the city, till the moon was ready to step forth. Then the eastern sky blanched and a small gathering of clouds opened their gates. Suddenly the edge of a silvery moon peered through the scattering clouds, hesitant for a moment, and then rose as if confident of its mission.

Moments later the moon was wading through the shallows of white clouds. Beyond a few high-rise, residential towers and distant trees was the great hollow of darkness, the Salish Sea, and the moonlight. The moon was there to put a cool hand of absolution on the snow-clad brow of the Olympic Mountains.

Sitting still on the balcony of his condo, Andrew Donavan reflected on his day. It was the first day of spring, the day of the year when the sun crosses the celestial equator moving northward. It was the last day for Andrew at the Department of English at the University of Victoria on Vancouver Island. This is where he had worked for the last several years as one of the forty faculty members engaged in teaching a range of English studies, from Old English to contemporary poetry, and modern literary theory to postcolonial literature, including Canadian and American Literature.

It was the day when Andrew knew that his life would never be the same again. His decision to leave the university was not entirely caused by, but its roots lay in an event that happened in 2009, three years back. One of his students, Yasuko Thanh, won the Journey Prize for her fictional novel, *Floating like the Dead*. Thinking back, he distinctly remembered two conflicting feelings he'd had. A sense of elation due to the shining success of one of his students, and despair for he was still struggling to find enough inspiration to write a prize-winning novel of his own. His dream of becoming a writer remained unfulfilled.

He had realized that something was missing in his life. Following this event, he descended into a life that was devoid of excitement and his passion of writing began to ebb like a receding tide. In a smoldering rage one day he tore up everything he had written and wiped the hard disk clean. He wanted a new start in life, a fresh start filled with creativity, vivid imagination and unbridled passion. But he didn't know how to find it.

He sighed and stared blankly at the sky. Spring nights were cold in Victoria. A million stars appeared on such a clear, cold night, and they lay scattered so far down the horizon that they seemed to mingle with their earthly friends of thousands of tiny lights that adorned the Parliament Building on the banks of the Inner Harbor. He traced Orion and part of the Big Dipper. And that is where his knowledge of the cosmic world ended. He stared at the stars and found a conglomeration of stars that looked like an open book. Ashamed by his own lack of creativity, he gave up. *How is it*, he mused, *that so many people have multiple talents and all my life I have done nothing but teach.*

Andrew was emotional, but not sentimental, although he was also timid and yielding, but only to a certain point. He could give way and accept a great deal even if it what was contrary to his convictions, but there was a certain barrier fixed by honesty, principle and his deepest convictions, which nothing would induce him to cross. He glanced at the framed photograph of his mother through the balcony sliding doors and a faint smile played on his lips. His mother had died too long ago for him to have more than an indistinct remembrance of her caress. But on troubled nights of disquiet, memories of her would stir the sense of love she once gave him.

His days were as empty of excitement as his soul was of fulfillment. He had found the island claustrophobic and the university atmosphere sedate and he often wondered what it would take to revive the joy in his heart he once felt when he was fifteen years of age. In the past few years, an awareness had descended upon him that perhaps the only way he could have the old exaltation again was to return where he had first felt it—Manali, the beautiful small town of Manali located in the Himachal Pradesh in the northern part of India.

Whenever he went to Rossland in the Kootenays to ski, it often, and in so many ways, reminded him of the exotic Manali where he had spent a year of his youth when he was fifteen. Somehow its lasting impression had remained in his heart. Such memories, though sweet, were also painful as they reminded him of how he had found and lost his first and perhaps his last love, for ever since he could not commit to a relationship. He was a loner, but finally the loneliness that up until now had offered sanctuary, was now corroding his soul.

In the middle of the night, on the balcony of his ninth-story Victoria Harbor-view condo on the Saghalie Road, he felt sad, as if his discontent was disintegrating his spirit. There was a slight chill in the air, adding to the misery of the earlier damp day, and he turned up his heavy sweater collar and then stuffed his hands in his pockets. He couldn't remember another time in his life when he had felt so low and apprehensive. Low, because frustration filled his heart, thick and ugly, making him feel increasingly unhappy; and apprehensive, because he was on his way back to Manali.

His mother had always said that to dream is to hope, and to hope is to live. And that is what he wanted: to live a meaningful life filled with hope. His mother's words ricocheted in his mind: It is not life that is the gift, but living it. Eclipsed between diminishing thoughts and rising hopes, he had always felt that there existed a space between living and surviving, synonymous with twilight, dwelling in the hearts of those left to wonder how to find a truly fulfilled life, one that defies destiny.

Lately his feelings had been charged with passion and surging desires like a rushing river, encouraging him to embrace change, for there was no hope of redemption in the stagnation that he had been experiencing for the past few years. How could one ignore such feelings when they are wrapped around one's soul like a creeper around a tree trunk, sapping his life? He heaved a great sigh and said, "I must surrender to my fate and go to Manali."

The full moon was steadily rising in the sky and the night was clear and filled with the silver hue. He had always loved a silvery moon. He wished that rather than muted brown, his balcony was painted some vivid color to reflect the sentiments evoked by the moon. The cherry blossoms of early spring sleepily awaited the daylight to show their magic. Andrew took a sip of the Remy Martin he'd poured and his cluttered mind slowly drifted into his past like a leaf caught in a whirlwind aimlessly rides the currents.

His mind drifted further back to Manali, and he remembered the blood-stained baseball bat and the day he contemplated killing his father.

BOOK I

The Will of God
Over Forty Years Ago (1970s)
Calgary, Alberta, Canada

ONE

Thomas Donavan, the only child of a real estate magnate, a family highly regarded in the upper echelons of elite society, was a graduate student at the University of Calgary where he was studying chemical engineering. Spoiled by his father he, unlike most other students, drove a brand-new, jet-black Porsche 911 and lived outside the university residence in an expensive house. No one knew if the house was rented or owned by Tom's father. Tom never discussed his parents.

It was a two-story, four-bedroom house with luxurious furnishings. A gardener attended its manicured gardens and a cleaning lady came everyday to keep the house immaculate. In the large living room with oak panel flooring, Tom's pride and joy was his state-of-the-art Bang & Olufsen surround-sound, home theater system. The walls were adorned by many Canadian artists' original paintings, including Robert Harris, William Raphael, George Andrew Reid, Robert Clow Todd and Frederick Verner. The esthetically pleasing surroundings appealed to Tom's senses.

Tom threw large parties at home that made him a lot of friends and gained him enormous popularity among the pretty girls in the university social circle. Local gourmet restaurants catered the parties and a bar with barman was present for each party. Rare wines as well as liquors flowed endlessly in the Hollywood-style party ambiance as a DJ managed the music. Tom's parties, as the popular saying goes, were to die for.

His father's wealth spoiled him by developing his expensive taste in cars, music and restaurants, but it did not alter two things. First, it did not interfere with his studies, for he had a bright mind and was a quick learner; and second, and this was an interesting point of gossip amongst his friends, he never got intimately involved with a girl. Whenever his friends asked why he didn't have a girlfriend, he would answer, "I dream of a woman who is like the ocean, her moods moving with the winds of change, but always calm within. She has to stand out in a crowd." At his response his friends always laughed and wished him luck.

Though a lot of people knew him, they knew very little about him. Apart from the obvious, apparent from his habits and rich lifestyle, that he belonged to a wealthy family, no one knew anything about his personal life. Thomas never discussed his family or his feelings with anyone. No one was ever invited to his parents' house.

The fact that his father was an alcoholic and wife-beater gnawed at his soul but he never uttered a word of this to anyone. Tom could never comprehend why a successful and educated man such as his father would resort to violence. When Tom was a little boy his father would beat his mother in front of him as if to prove a point. Tom wanted to help his mother but couldn't stand up to his father.

As a boy he became a loner, preferring to avoid rather than confront tense situations, and at the first opportunity moved out of his parents' house. From thereon it seemed as if he had erected a force field around him that no one could penetrate. Those who insisted on probing into his personal life were never again invited to his parties.

Although Tom's parties were always overflowing with costly wines, beers, cocktails and liquors, he never touched alcoholic drinks. Canada Dry on ice was his favorite drink at parties and restaurants. Although he knew the real reason for this was that he did not want to grow up to become like his father, his friends were told it was because of some complex medical reason. Those who were jealous of Tom's lifestyle took immense satisfaction in that, though a man of enormous wealth, Tom did not know the pleasures of wine and women.

Tom's friends often hinted that he ought to seek a career in the film industry due primarily to his looks. Standing at six feet, three inches, and weighing two hundred pounds, he was lean and muscular with not an ounce of fat on his tall body. He wore his golden blond hair not too long and not too short and, dancing with the slightest breeze, it would often cover the right side of his forehead and right eye. His hair was almost silky and the envy of all women who spent a small fortune on products to get the texture of Tom's hair.

Solidly built, he always walked with a spring in his step. There was always a certain degree of urgency in his every move, and he never stood idle, chitchatting with friends on frivolous matters. But perhaps his best features were his piercing, soft-blue eyes. They had the depth of both dreams and ambition. Yes, Thomas was an ambitious man with a determined mind to rise after graduation in the flourishing oil and gas industry of Alberta. He believed that the vast oil reserves of Canada, second only to those of Saudi Arabia, would one day be the major contributor to the increased prosperity of his country and he wanted to prosper with it. His destiny was entwined with the development of the oil sands of Alberta.

In the first year of his courses, Tom earned top marks in his class; in fact, no one could match or beat his grades in all the various engineering departments at the university. His popularity rose to an even higher level and every woman on campus wanted to befriend this handsome, wealthy and brainy man. All the girls and boys alike coveted invitations to his parties. But there were those, few as they might be in numbers, who disliked both Tom and his parties. Tom on occasion had been known to lose his temper, especially when someone was abusive to a girl or had a little too much to drink.

On one such an occasion a senior student who had imbibed too much insisted on kissing a first-year girl who resisted his advances. It was not violent, just unpleasant. The crowd found it rather amusing and teased the girl, encouraging her to not be such a prude. The girl wanted to leave the party, at which time the senior in question grabbed her by her shoulders and pushed her back into the sofa where she was sitting before. Suddenly Tom appeared on the scene, took the senior student by his neck, literally dragged him out of the house and threw him out on the street, yelling, "Get the hell out of here and don't ever come back".

While the other boys frowned at Tom's bellicose behavior and the girls admired his bravery, what Tom didn't know was that his aggressive ways would one day get him into deep trouble. Tom's was a complex personality possessed by a single-minded passion for success.

TWO

In the final year at the university and a few months prior to graduating with an engineering degree, something unexpected and somewhat remarkable happened in Tom's life. At one of his large weekend parties at his home, he noticed a rather unusual girl. She was quiet, the shy type, as she sat in a corner chatting with another girl, sipping a glass of red wine. Her hands with long slender fingers were wrapped around the goblet. She had large almond-shaped eyes with long eyelashes. With her head tilted to one side and her hair cascading down, she was intently listening to her friend. Her hair was a thick, soft brown and long, flowing all the way down to her lower back.

Dressed in a tight, white, satin blouse with a couple of top buttons undone, showing her sensual cleavage, and tight faded blue jeans, her slim and well-proportioned body showed her ability as an athlete. Surrounded by seemingly sun-deprived, light-colored bodies, her body complexion was in contrast a sun-drenched, light-brown tone, with shining and smooth skin. He noticed that many hungry eyes were devouring her.

He was mesmerized and could not take his eyes off her. He had never seen a more striking girl. He watched her from a distance for a while and then, unable to suppress an urge to get to know her, he finally approached her. As he made his way towards her, she looked at him with her large, liquid-brown eyes. She smiled, lighting up Tom's world.

"Hi," said Tom in a whisper, and felt surprised at hearing his weak voice, "my name is Tom."

"No kidding," she said, with a broadening smile, "everyone knows who you are. Thank you for inviting me to the party, it is beautiful," she said, with a slight accent that he could not immediately place.

"I have not seen you here before," he responded, pulling a chair up next to her, and added, "are you studying at the university or visiting a friend?"

Her smile vanished for a second and then with a peal of laughter, she articulated, "I've heard this about you. You're so funny."

Thomas looked puzzled by her remark but continued the conversation by saying, "Well, thank you, but I didn't say anything funny. I merely wanted to know—"

Interrupting, and wearing a mock look of disappointment on her face, she retorted, "Now I feel hurt. I have seen you everyday for almost four years. We are in the same courses; I am in your class."

Thomas frowned as if in deep thought, and tucking his chin down, he stared at his effervescent drink. Using his index finger, he stirred the ice in his drink. He wondered if she was indeed hurt by his remark or was she having fun with him? He murmured in an almost inaudible voice, "That cannot be possible. How could I have missed you all this time?"

"Oh, don't look so serious," she laughed again, "I was kidding. A lot of people don't notice me. In every class you always sit in the front row and I am almost always in the last row. I don't like attention."

"I do apologize for my rudeness," said Thomas, regaining his composure, "and you must allow me to make a proper apology. Let me buy you dinner tomorrow…"

"Sunita," she finished his sentence by introducing herself and adding, "and yes, dinner would be lovely."

"Sunita," he said softly as if the name deserved to be uttered with love.

"It means well behaved, and that is the way I also like my friends to be," she said, smiling broadly.

"Thank you, Sunita, and I will make sure that around you I am always on my best behavior. Shall we say eight o'clock tomorrow? Where do you live?"

The next evening they went out for dinner at a restaurant of his choice, an expensive steak house with a pricey menu. It appeared that she enjoyed both the company and the meal and insisted on returning the favor. The next meal out was at a restaurant of her choice, which was an inexpensive Indian place with a limited menu. Tom had never experienced Indian cuisine before and tears ran down his cheeks with every spicy bite he ate. He drank the whole water pitcher and crunched on every bit of ice left in it during his meal to soothe his burning tongue and throat. Sunita, though she felt sorry for him, laughed throughout the dinner.

Tom never knew before that he had an affinity for the exotic. As days melted into weeks, he learned from Sunita the history of India and its colorful past. He promised himself he'd go there for a holiday, for he wanted to see for himself the land of mystique and magic as Sunita had portrayed it through her stories. He also had a desire to see the land where Sunita was born and brought up as a child. Unbeknownst to him, this desire one day would prove to have disastrous consequences.

THREE

What started as an inadvertent friendship gradually began to develop into a casual relationship. Tom would often invite Sunita out for dinner and they would talk for hours about world politics, nature, plans for their careers and many other topics, but never about their families. Sunita was not the prying type and seemed comfortable in his company and enjoyed his friendship.

But one evening while they were having dinner at an Indian restaurant, curiosity got the better of her and she asked, "You never talk about your parents. They must be awfully rich for you to have a car and eat out so often. Do they live far from here?"

"You never mentioned your parents either!" he retorted rather abruptly, avoiding her question.

"I love my parents," she said with a touch of pride in her voice, "and you never asked about my family so I never mentioned it. My father has his own taxi and he works very hard to pay for my education. He still calls me by my childhood pet name, 'Sunny,' and always tells me that I am the sunshine of his life. He is so funny and I adore him. My mom is a traditional Indian housewife and keeps us all together as a family. She is a wonderful mother and I hope one day to be like her. She doesn't have a mean bone in her body. I have no siblings. And that's it. Now you know everything about my family. We're not rich like you. Does this make any difference in our friendship?"

He lowered his eyes and stared at his food for a moment. When he looked up and met her gaze, her questioning eyes were waiting for an answer. He answered in a soft voice, "Not in the least. It was never about the money. And I am glad to learn that you come from such a loving family."

"But your parents…" she let her remark hang in the air so he could finish her sentence, but as he sighed heavily, she continued, "your parents would not approve of our friendship because my family is not rich? Is that it? I can see some hesitation in your eyes."

Tom put his spoon down and looked outside the window as if searching for words to compose a suitable response. Sunita leaned forward and with an edge in her voice, and a challenge in her tone, asked, "Oh my god, don't tell me it is because I am of Indian descent? I know I was not born here, but I am educated and have grown up here."

"Slow down, you are making too many assumptions. We are just friends," he said evenly, but his face expressed grave concern. He continued, "We don't need our parents' approval to be friends with each other. It doesn't work that way in our society; besides, I don't even know what you are getting at."

"So do you think we would need their approval if we wanted to be more than just friends?" She could not believe what she had just asked but it was too late now for her to retract her question. Color rushed to her cheeks.

With his face turned, Tom was still gazing out the window. For a moment it appeared that he did not hear her question. Then Tom turned his face back to look into her eyes and responded, "If you really want to know then I will tell you. My mom died of a fall from the second floor balcony of our house when I was five years old. Police registered it as an accidental death but even as a boy I remember how my dad used to beat up my mom. I don't think it was an accident."

Sunita opened her mouth, wanting to say how sorry she was, but Tom raised both hands, indicating that he was not yet finished. He continued, "Less than a year after my mom died, my dad remarried. My stepmother was my mom's best friend." There was a pause as his face hardened and a shadow of sadness mixed with a hint of anger passed over his face. It seemed that he wanted to say more but, choked with emotion, he simply closed his eyes. He pushed his plate away as if he no longer had an appetite.

"Oh Tom, I am so sorry," she murmured. "I did not know. I am so stupid sometimes. It was none of my business. Can you forgive me?"

He let out another big sigh and said nothing.

"Let us get out of here and go for a walk. Would you like that?" She held his hands in hers and Tom lowered his face once again and this time kissed both her hands. She was stunned. There was so much passion in that kiss that she shuddered with a pleasant but strange sensation. The kiss was a better admission than words, saying I love you.

She looked into his eyes and there she saw no demands but sheer hunger for acceptance. His usual demeanor of a rich boy throwing around money dissolved, and his soul lay bare in front of her. Overwhelmed by this transformation and with a racing heart, Sunita leaned forward and kissed him on his lips.

They left the restaurant but instead of going for a walk, ended up at her dorm. She put on some soft instrumental Indian music that added mystique to the romance in the air. She removed his shirt and buried her face in his chest as he unbuttoned her dress. Their bodies glistened in the filtered moonlight and he kissed every part of her. The room was filled with soft moans and the moon continued to shine as if approving of their union.

FOUR

Tom's life took a different turn after that day. The two were seen together everywhere, at parties, in the classrooms, and in public places. They were inseparable. Tom seemed to have mellowed. He would laugh at people's jokes and even tell jokes of his own. Most of the girls at the university were envious and even jealous of Sunita for having won Tom's heart.

As final exams were approaching, the couple got serious about their studies and disappeared from the party and social scenes altogether. Sunita moved into Tom's house where they could effectively study together. While Tom was a hard worker and could cover a lot of ground in a day, Sunita was good at understanding the fundamentals and first principles of every subject, so together they made an excellent team.

It wasn't a surprise to anyone when both Tom and Sunita graduated with honors and were immediately offered employment by the largest oil corporation in Alberta.

They'd been living together now for a few months and his hunger for a family took hold of his soul. Repeating history, he took Sunita to the same restaurant where he had first confessed his love for her and, as the waiter opened the most expensive bottle of champagne, Tom got down on one knee, offering her a small open box with a glittering diamond. He asked, "Will you marry me?"

"Of course, I will," she cried joyfully. With smiling eyes, she continued, "I did wonder about the champagne because you don't drink."

"Oh, today I made an exception. It is an exceptional day," he answered.

Over dinner she suggested that it was ridiculous that they still had not yet met their respective parents and invited Tom to dinner at her parents' house. That Saturday they arrived together at a small house in a high-density urban development and were greeted by Sunita's parents. Sunita's mother had prepared a sumptuous Indian feast and she and Sunita's father showered Tom with affection. They treated him like their own son.

That night when they returned to their home, Sunita asked, "What do you think of my parents?"

"What can I say," sighed Tom, "you are one lucky person. They are unbelievable and I am so delighted to have met them."

"So let's meet with your parents and get the formalities over and done with so we can get married," she was quick to suggest.

"We don't need to meet and seek approval from my parents," he answered cryptically, "let's set a date and get married."

"I know you've had a hard time with your parents," she said, "but I'm afraid my parents would insist on meeting yours. They will be relatives when we're married and would like to get to know them."

"Sit down," said Tom politely and yet firmly and as she sat on a chair, he kneeled beside her and held her hands. "I have already told my parents about you and your family and they refuse to meet. They even refuse to talk about it. They don't approve. I am afraid if you keep on insisting and your parents were to visit mine then there would nothing but embarrassment all around."

"What are we going to do then?" she asked in a trembling voice, as if someone had just kicked down her sand castle.

"We are going to get married as planned," he responded in a firm voice. "We don't need my parents' approval. It is our life we are planning, Sunita, and the love of your parents is enough for both of us. Forget about my parents and don't allow them to meddle in our lives."

It took Sunita time to accept that she would never get to know Tom's parents. In a simple ceremony and against the wishes of Tom's parents, they did get married. The ceremony was arranged in a small temple followed by a reception at the local Indian restaurant. A few of Tom's friends turned up and Sunita's parents invited quite a few of their family and friends. The absence of Tom's parents, though noticed, was not discussed.

Thomas Donovan wanted to have children to celebrate his love for his wife; he believed that a creation from their undying commitment to each other would be emblematic of that everlasting love. So he was pleasantly surprised when Sunita told Tom that she was already pregnant when they married.

"Why on earth would you not share such wonderful news before?" he asked, showing his joy.

"I didn't want you to marry me for the wrong reason," said Sunita, savoring every moment of his excitement.

He considered himself truly blessed as the arrival of their first child endorsed that belief and if there was ever a doubt, it was wiped out by the first smile of the newborn. They named him Andrew Anand Donavan. He brought such happiness into their world that when his Indian mother gave him the middle name Anand, meaning 'happiness,' Thomas was simply delighted.

FIVE

Tom's dad, apparently ashamed of Tom's shameless act of marrying into an Indian and low-class family, disowned him and wrote him out of his will and estate. He blamed Canada's immigration policies and the government for allowing so many Indians to come and settle in his country. Thomas did not care about his dad's attitude or wealth and found all the support and happiness he needed through the love of his wife and son. They both worked hard and rose to highly successful executive positions in the same oil company. As it turned out, Tom had an uncanny ability to time the market and amassed a significant fortune from his investments.

To celebrate their five years of a successful rise on the executive corporate ladder, Thomas and Sunita bought a large house that looked more like a small estate in the Mount Royal area, one of the most prestigious residential communities located in the Elbow River Valley and one of the wealthiest neighborhoods in the southwest of Calgary. It was originally developed by the Canadian Pacific Railways and in those days was known as 'American Hill' due to the number of wealthy American entrepreneurs who built their homes there in the early 1900s.

Even with the couple's resounding successes, Thomas's dad could not accept Sunita into their family and made no effort to contact them even though they lived literally two blocks away. Sunita's parents were the only grandparents Andrew knew and enjoyed visiting. Whenever Andrew asked his dad about his parents he was told in a stern voice to go out and play with his friends. His mother did try to explain to him the differences between his dad and his dad's parents, but Andrew could not understand how a father could refuse to see his own son living two blocks away and for so many years. But then Andrew was only five and lived in the confines of his own little world.

In time, Thomas was turning into his father as he rose among those in the high society of oil executives of Calgary, where status was paramount. He drove an expensive Mercedes, became a member of a private golf club, bought a villa on the French Rivera, and made sure that his father heard about it. Sunita disliked his escalating vanity with their rising financial success but kept quiet about it. To her he was not the same man she knew when they were together at the university. In the business world he had developed a fierce competitive nature, a love of material objects, and a violent temper. But he never raised his voice or showed that temper toward his family. When at home he reveled in the love they shared.

Five years of blissful marriage and high living passed uneventfully but then, soon after Andrew turned five, their dreams came crashing down around them: Sunita was diagnosed with Lobular Carcinoma In Situ. Though it was considered a marker of increased risk of breast cancer rather than actual cancer, it did pose a serious threat of developing breast cancer. Thomas spared no expense to give her the best treatment, and doctors recommended Tamoxifen for prevention, but Sunita opted for a bilateral prophylactic mastectomy as a preventative removal of both breasts.

Tom disagreed with Sunita's choice and several weeks passed before Sunita could convince Tom of her decision. But when luck runs out the devil comes to play. Though she took the courageous yet drastic step of opting for a mastectomy, she made the decision rather late, and Infiltrating Lobular Carcinoma had spread cancer into other parts of her body. Panic struck her and once again she had to muster all the courage she possessed to prepare herself for chemotherapy. She bore the anguish of this treatment with mettle as she fought for her life. Her greatest strength was Thomas by her side. She often said, "Tom, promise me you will not cry. You must be brave for Andy. He will need you now more than ever."

"Don't talk like that," Tom would answer with a resolute voice, having total faith in modern medicine. "These are the best doctors one can have. They will not let us down. You will be fine, just hang in there."

Though overtly confident, Tom was distraught. He would often question the doctors and they would assure him that she was receiving the best treatment. They told him not to worry. But worry he did, as he complained once or twice to the medical board, asking them to assure him that everything possible was being done. He even threatened to sue them if he found negligence and willful misconduct in their treatment. His constant badgering and often harsh and dogmatic attitude seemed to have upset quite a few of the doctors and they started to avoid him.

Time passed and Tom became more aggressive toward the doctors. He began to lose confidence in their ability to save his Sunita. She should have been better by now. He also became fearful, as Sunita was the embodiment of his whole life. He couldn't let her go for without her he was doomed. He loved her, his first and last love, as he would often say, more than he ever loved anything.

As her strength diminished with the ferocity of the aggressive treatment, finally she caught an infection due to her reduced white blood cell count and one night went to sleep never to wake up again. The night she died, Tom lost his world. As he lay in his bed, he closed his eyes, half wishing he had not promised Sunita not to cry in front of Andrew; half wishing he had no tomorrow. Horrified by the thoughts that rose within him, he demanded, like the despairing man he was, "Is life without her worth living?" He could not restrain the tears that rolled down his cheeks. But as promised, Thomas never wept in front of Andrew.

SIX

Fueled by anger and grief, Tom engaged the best law firm in town to go after the hospitals and the doctors who were involved in his wife's diagnosis and treatment. He blamed them for negligence and malpractice. Fighting against the entire medical system, as Tom found out, was time consuming and exorbitantly expensive. But he persevered. His relentless crusade to find someone responsible for her untimely demise finally cost him his job and his personal wealth began to dwindle.

Tom's friends and Sunita's parents advised him to withdraw his case and let her go. None of his fight was going to bring Sunita back. But Tom remained convinced that justice was required for Sunita's soul to rest in peace. When he didn't like the progress of the first law firm, he fired them and brought in another. He didn't stop there. He started writing to the press and embarked upon a campaign to make the medical system admit to their mistakes and deficiencies.

The medical system was strong, undisturbed, and had deep pockets; plus, they were willing to fight Tom to protect their image. But at the same time the medical system didn't want such unnecessary publicity and without prejudicing their reputation, were willing to make an out of court settlement, just to get rid of Tom. Tom's new lawyer was happy, but not Tom. It wasn't the money that he was after; he wanted Sunita back or the medical system to admit their mistakes publicly. Tom was obsessed with making the medical system pay with the sacrifice of their good name.

Tom's lawyer tried to convince Tom that eventually the medical board would win, for in his wife's treatment, everything was done by the book, and whatever case Tom's lawyer had dreamed up was weak. They should take the money while they had a chance. Tom fired his second lawyer and appointed another one.

As court proceedings continued over the next several months, Tom finally realized that all his savings were gone and he could not go on fighting the medical system. He needed to find work to rebuild his life. He sold the house and Mercedes and downgraded to a condo and a Mazda, but still desperately needed a job.

One day Sunita's father came to see Tom. "You are going to lose," he said in a sad voice, "and not just the money, for you have already given away your house, car and job, but also little Andy. We cannot look after him day in day out. Oh, we love him, but he needs his father. When was the last time you hugged him?"

After this visit Tom sat down with a cup of coffee and pondered what he was going to do next. Whatever he decided, somehow he knew that in his plan Andy was not included. He could not bear to look into his face for the child reminded him of Sunita. There was so much of Sunita in Andrew that Tom could not endure his presence. He decided to send Andrew away. Yes, he determined, as he firmed up his decision, it was best for Andrew to grow up in the care of a boarding school.

To implement his plan, he needed money for St. Georges in Vancouver, where Andrew would go, an expensive private boarding school. Reluctantly but having no other choice, Tom dropped all charges and settled out of court and the compensation he received after paying his attorney's fees was enough for him to send Andrew to St. Georges.

Once Andrew left home, Tom turned his attention to rebuilding his life, or more accurately, his wealth. The two words were synonymous to him. The oil corporation he had worked for before rehired him and before long he was again climbing the corporate ladder. Tom was highly regarded by his employer and the industry for his entrepreneurial ability to grow companies through innovative business models. He would compete through cooperation and developed many unincorporated and equity-based joint ventures to contribute to the significant growth of the company where he worked.

One such joint venture, one of a kind, and perhaps the first one for Canada, was with the state-owned Oil and Natural Gas Corporation of India. It was part of a new initiative undertaken by Tom's department to expand Alberta's reach into new and potentially lucrative natural resources, and to do so, the new joint venture company was to be located in Manali, in Himachal Pradesh of India. Tom was appointed its new director and asked to relocate for a one-year assignment to set up and staff the office.

Tom saw this as an opportunity, not just for financial gain, as such positions were attractive, but more so to get away from Calgary for a while and find some solace in the pristine nature of the Himalayas. Himachal, meaning 'land of snowy mountains: Himalayas,' held yet another attraction for Tom, for it was the land where Sunita had come from. He wanted to discover her roots.

SEVEN

When Tom disclosed his plan of relocation over dinner with Sunita's parents, who, since Sunita had been gone, had been towers of strength for him, Sunita's father said, "Tom, ten years have passed since Andy was sent to St. Georges. He is a teenager now. Oh, we visit him as often as we can, but you have visited him only once a year. The poor kid always spends his summer holidays at camp."

"But it has been good for him," reasoned Tom, "his grades are good and he will one day have a great career and make a lot of money."

"There is more to life than money, *Beta*," said Sunita's mother, in a soft and amiable voice.

"What she is saying," said Sunita's father, nodding his head and at the same time gesturing at her with his hand, asking her to let him do the talking, "is that Andy has not known his father's love. Don't you think that it is about time he came home?"

"But wouldn't this be the most inappropriate time?" protested Tom. "There would be no school for him in Manali. It is a very remote town."

"We know where Manali is," insisted Sunita's father, "and we have done some research. There is a very good American International School that is not too far from where you will stay. But my wife and I have thought of something quite different."

Tom remained silent for he was sure that he was about to be enlightened with their scheme. Sunita's father continued, "We have dome some thinking and believe Andy could benefit from a gap year. Take him with you and let him explore Manali while he enjoys your company and experiences your love. Who knows, perhaps India is the place that will bring you two together. It is only for a year anyway, so upon your return we could then reevaluate where Andy ought to go next."

Tom wanted to resist the idea but a voice in the back of his head made him reconsider. Could this be fate that he was going to the place of Sunita's birth and perhaps it was her spirit that was pleading for him and Andrew to be together? He did not believe in fate but Sunita did and she was still alive in his heart.

Taking his silence as at least partial acceptance, Sunita's father drove his message home, saying, "Tom, think about it. You are making all this money for your son, the one you don't even talk to more than once a year. He is your only connection to Sunita and if you don't do the right thing now, you may end up losing him too. Take Andy with you."

"Let me sleep on it," said Tom, after a pause. "Perhaps you are right, but let me think it over and we'll talk again in a couple of days."

A couple of days later when they met again it was decided that Tom would go to Vancouver and discuss the idea with Andrew. Later that weekend, Tom arrived in Vancouver and went to see Andrew, presenting him with the idea of moving for a year to Manali and attending an American International school there.

Andrew resisted the idea of moving to India for he couldn't bear leaving behind all his friends, but then he knew he needed extraordinary willpower to make his case, because every time he saw the angst in his father's eyes, his will failed him. On one hand his suppressed anger towards his father for sending him away to a boarding school, and on the other his yearning to be at home with his only family, had always confounded him, and this time it was no different. He was utterly confused.

So it came about that a month later, at the age of fifteen, Andrew allowed his father to make all the necessary preparations to move to Manali and reconstruct their lives in the merciful shadows of the calm and peaceful western Himalayas.

Tom and Andrew took a flight from Calgary to London and from there to New Delhi. Tom wanted to fly from New Delhi to Bhuntar, the nearest airport located fifty kilometers from Manali, but unfortunately, only a one-plane airline called Jagson Airways operated there and it was considered highly unreliable and unsafe. So they flew to Chandigarh where they rented a car with a driver who drove them three hundred kilometers to reach Manali. It was an exhausting trip for both but as soon as they arrived at their bungalow and saw the awe-inspiring view surrounding them, their fatigue melted like butter on a hot pan.

Through the joint venture partner, Tom was provided the use of a beautiful bungalow on top of a hill surrounded by an expansive valley not too far from the majestic snowy mountains. The bungalow came with round-the-clock house help, a cook and a gardener, and it was originally built during the British Raj times. It seemed to have gone through many renovations, each adding more color and charm to its beauty. An octagonal-shaped building wrapped in a covered veranda, it had three bedrooms, a large open-plan sitting area, and also included a dining room and a small kitchen. Servants' quarters were built in a separate building, which also housed a larger kitchen, used by the cook to prepare meals and keep the smoke and smell out of the main bungalow.

It was early spring and Tom was thankful that the winter season had just ended. Stepping into this mystical land, Tom had felt the curious sensation that Manali was not just for wealthy Indian honeymooners; it was a place to make a journey into the very soul of nature and satisfy the quest under the colossal Himalayas for a spiritual awakening.

Tom felt that destiny or perhaps the spirit of Sunita had brought him to a place where he was meant to find real peace, and a meaningful life.

BOOK II

Loss of Innocence
Spring 1992
Manali, Himachal Pradesh
India

EIGHT

Over the past few decades Manali, with its quixotic beauty and salubrious climate, had become a key tourist destination for wealthy Indian holidaymakers and in particular, with the loss of Kashmir due to the continuing conflict, was popularized as a premier honeymoon destination. Manali, with the majesty of the world's tallest mountains, was equally successful in luring foreign tourists who were attracted by its culturally distinctive hill people and for specialized trekking with gateways to the Spiti and Leh Region.

The twentieth century seemed to be bringing a series of cultural and environmental changes to Manali, thanks to its increasing tourism and the recent discovery of a huge potential resource of oil and gas. Seeing it for the first time, Tom noted the prevailing ignorance towards the fragile ecology with regard to both respect for the native ethnicity and the preservation of nature's beauty. India had a long way to go to catch up with world-class environmental standards. But Tom knew that while a lot was left to be done, it was not going to be done in any hurry. Time had little value in India. A non-revenue generating initiative such as environmental control was not a popular issue, not in India, not anywhere.

Tom knew that Manali, at twice the altitude of Calgary, was going to be cooler but the cold never bothered him as he was quite used to the frigid temperatures of Alberta. But the challenge arose when it came to Andrew's education. Unlike what was told to him by Sunita's father, the nearest suitable school was located forty kilometers away in another town called Kullu. On Indian roads, forty kilometers was a perilous, long and time-consuming distance.

After a couple of days of settling in and recovering from the long flight, both Tom and Andrew went with a driver to check out the Cambridge International School located in Kullu. The Kullu Valley spreads out in its amazing and beautiful charm on both sides of the Beas River and runs eighty kilometers north to south of this river. Its awe-inspiring glens and mossy meadows are encircled by the rushing streams and meandering brooks, flung east and west. Andrew pointed at the snow-capped mountains and Tom, smiling at his enthusiasm, asked the driver to pull over by the roadside, where they got out for a better look at the valley.

Tom scanned the wide-open spaces and took a deep breath, rejuvenated by the exhilarating air of the Himalayas, and felt lucky to be standing in the variegated mountain scenery. In its colors, so similar, yet in its character, so different from Manali, where the Beas River was flanked by the Deodar and pine trees and fruit orchards with the sparkling clear water meandering through the town, Kullu Valley was recognized as the Switzerland of India.

Once having arrived, they were well received by the staff at the school and given a tour of the facility. The staff was enthusiastic and the facility was well equipped. There was no doubt that Andrew could enrich his experience by spending a year at the school. The school members explained that it was rather unusual for them to accept a student of Andrew's age but they were willing to make an exception. They were also willing to give extra attention to Andrew to help him catch up and integrate with their system. Tom thanked the staff and told them that he would let them know his decision in a day or two.

Upon their return to Manali, Tom, though quite impressed with the school, was not too sure about daily drive there and back. He thought that it was an arduous journey for a fifteen-year-old due to the many potholes and increasing tourist traffic, and besides, in winter and the monsoon season, it would be quite dangerous due to mudslides. He knew he had to accept the plan of the gap year, as suggested by Sunita's father.

After carefully thinking over the subject of Andrew's schooling, during dinner one evening Tom asked Andrew, "I've a proposition for you to consider regarding your schooling. Both you and I have gone through some rough times and haven't spent much time together. I guess we both deserve a break. I never thought I could live anywhere but Calgary, but I'm happy to be here and away from the fast-paced life. Work here is conducted at a quiet, leisurely pace."

Andrew grew impatient with Tom's monologue, drifting away from the subject, so interjected, "School, Dad?"

"Oh, yes," smiled Tom, "school indeed. What I really wanted to say was that Kullu is too far and the roads here are dangerous. So, if you like, why don't you take what your generation calls a gap year and devote your time to exploring the valley and maybe pick up some hobby like photography? I'm confident that upon our return next year you will be able to catch up. Lots of kids your age do it, so what do you think? You don't have to answer me now; you can take some time to think about it."

Andrew just about dropped his fork and responded excitedly, "Really? You mean it? Oh yeah, there is nothing to think about, I'll easily take a gap year. Photography in this part of the world would be absolutely amazing and I already have my Nikon D70 so I'm all set for it. Thanks. Gap year it is."

Tom smiled and nodded as if he had no doubt that his proposition would be readily accepted. He continued, "I will have a car and a driver at my disposal. But I only need him to take me to the office in the morning and at the end of the day bring me back home. In between you can have the car and the driver. He can take you around for sightseeing and photography."

"Thanks," exclaimed Andrew, and after a momentary pause added, "but what about weekends when both of us are at home?"

There was a shadow of sadness that flickered over Tom's face but he smiled and responded, "Over the weekends I was hoping that we could go trekking and maybe find a golf club where we could play together. Maybe you can make some new friends at the golf club."

Andrew nodded and in his excitement never noticed the momentary sadness in his father's face. Was it guilt for so many years of neglecting his son or was it because he once had a dream to visit this place with Sunita? In either case, Andrew did not see it for he was used to ignoring his father, as it was from him that he learned this trait.

NINE

Tom called the school and thanked them again for their support and notified them of his decision.

As days passed, Tom was getting to know his staff at the office located within the premises of the local center of the Oil & Natural Gas Commission, and there he was introduced to the General Manager and various senior project managers. Tom was the architect of the collaborative deal with ONGC and well suited to look after its logistic details. Two of the senior project managers of the ONGC were assigned to work with Tom as a part of the technology transfer process.

One of the senior project managers was called Dinesh and other Harish; they were in their early thirties, a few years younger than Tom, and suggested that if he preferred, he could call them Dick and Harry. Tom explained that because his in-laws were Indian, he was quite familiar and comfortable with the pronunciation of Indian names and preferred to call them Dinesh and Harish, and besides, he didn't want the trio to be labeled as Tom, Dick and Harry.

As weeks melted into months, Tom was hoping that after his one-year assignment maybe he could come back here on a frequent basis to see the progress of his efforts and his friends again. He loved their hospitality. Every time he saw them outside the work environment, they would receive him with such enthusiasm it was as if they were meeting again after a long absence. He had an open offer to come as often as he liked to their houses for dinners. Both had very pretty wives who were excellent cooks. Tom had developed quite a taste for Indian cuisine and always preferred homemade meals rather than those found at restaurants. But he made a point of staying most nights for dinner at home to spend time with Andrew.

Andrew was still distant and not willing to talk about the past ten years. Tom thought that perhaps time was the only solution and after a whole year together things would be different.

Tom had developed a close friendship with Dinesh and Harish who had brought in another of their colleagues from the engineering department to form a foursome to play bridge. They were all good bridge players and it almost became routine to hold bridge session at Tom's bungalow twice a week. There was something else that made bridge sessions enjoyable. Tom's Indian friends were also fond of whisky and often partook of that feature of Tom's hospitality. While Tom would stay with non-alcoholic drinks, his friends would go through four or five rounds of whisky and surprisingly, it never affected their ability to play bridge.

Andrew developed a routine himself. He would sleep in late and by the time he got up and had his breakfast, Tom had already left for work and the car and the driver would be back, waiting for him. After breakfast Andrew would ask the driver to take him around the Manali and Kullu area and he would shoot dozens of digital photos. He preferred to go to a café for lunch, as he also had developed a taste for Indian food, and around four or so he would be back home, giving the driver plenty of time to ferry Tom. They would always have dinner together and although earlier they usually ate in silence, now they were beginning to share their daily stories.

One day Andrew came up with an idea to photograph not just landscapes, for after months of taking pictures of the same mountains, it had started to wear thin on him, but to find people as his subjects. In every attractive, young woman he saw a little bit of his mother and it fascinated him. He asked the driver to take him into town and leave him there because he wanted to wander through its narrow streets and take pictures. The driver looked a little concerned and in a soft voice said, *"Chote Sahib."* He always addressed him as the Little Sir, and his father as *Bara Sahib,* which meant the Big Sir. He continued, *"Bara Sahib* has told me not to let you go anywhere on your own. I'll wait in the car for you."

"No, you won't," Andrew answered in a convincing tone and then, handing him a ten rupee note, added, "I won't tell Dad if you don't, you know what I mean?" The driver understood the language of money and vigorously shook his head in compliance. They drove to the old part of Manali that was approximately three kilometers away from the new Manali, and this was where Andrew wanted to find his subjects. After the driver dropped him off he pulled on his Calgary Flames cap and started to wander through the streets, asking people if he could take their picture. None said no and they all obliged with a smile.

TEN

Tourism and ethnicity blended perfectly in this old charming town to offer a unique cultural extravaganza that Andrew had never experienced before. Andrew was amazed to find restaurants with Israeli cuisine and music ranging from techno to soothing Indian instrumental tunes amidst the sweet incense of burning fragrance sticks; it was a perfect cross-cultural fusion.

He stopped at the German Baker to have a milkshake and a small cake, and from a window seat could see life outside on the road. He switched to zoom lens and snapped a few pictures of people in the street. He was so engrossed in his photography and enjoying his milkshake and cake so much that he almost missed sight of a girl that was standing just outside the window, twirling her long braided hair in her hands. Andrew watched her closely as she was looking away from him and he could only view her side profile. She looked young, perhaps the same age as him, but it was hard for him to guess, as Indian girls were so petite and with such smooth and tanned skin they often looked younger than their age. He realized that he was staring at her but something kept his gaze locked on her and he could not let go.

She was rather tall for an Indian girl and her bare arms showed her skin color as having almost a golden hue in the morning sunlight. She wore a bright peacock-blue satin blouse in which were embedded myriads of tiny mirrors that reflected sunlight every time she moved. Her tight blouse accentuated her breasts that looked ripe for her age. Her heavily pleated long skirt was of a turmeric color that beautifully contrasted with her blouse. Suddenly Andrew had this inexplicable urge to photograph her. He emptied his milkshake glass and hurried out of the bakery. Once outside, he could see her face. She was a stunning beauty with large dreamy eyes that were soft brown with long dark eyelashes that reminded Andrew of some exotic butterfly. Her full lips were naturally pink and she was not wearing makeup or jewelry.

Andrew approached her and with all the courage he could muster, he uttered in a soft voice, "Hello."

She looked up as she was startled by his approach and blinked her big eyes several times, looking like a nervous deer. Andrew explained, "I'm so sorry, I didn't mean to startle you. My name is Andrew."

As her eyebrows rose slightly in perplexity, her lips stretched into a shy thin smile and she whispered something in Hindi that he could not understood, and then swiftly she turned and ran off down the street. Andrew, with one hand outstretched as if trying to further explain, stood there like a statue as he watched those swinging hips disappearing at the bottom of the street. "Ah," he murmured to himself, "she would have been the perfect subject for my photographs."

He daydreamed for the remainder of the day and that evening when he sat down for dinner with his dad, he was unusually quiet. "What's the matter, you aren't saying much? Everything okay?"

"Hmm, I'm fine," answered Andrew, but he looked as if he was miles away. Concerned by this, Tom said, "Look, I know going out everyday must get boring. If you've made friends then feel free to invite them over and chill out over a movie or a board game. This is your house too."

"Thanks, but honestly, nothing is wrong. Actually, I had a good day today. I'm looking forward to going out tomorrow. How was your day? How are Dick and Harry?" Andrew enjoyed calling them Dick and Harry but not to their faces. Andrew particularly disliked Harry for he was always teasing Andrew and treating him like a little boy. There was also something sinister in his smile that frightened Andrew.

They talked about Tom's work and he had a few humorous stories to tell to Andrew as the evening passed uneventfully.

Andrew at the age of fifteen weighed one hundred and fifty pounds and stood almost six foot. He was big for his age and could easily pass for twenty years old or definitely the late teens. It had something to do with Tom being six foot three and weighing in at two hundred pounds with a large bone structure.

The next day Andrew put on his denim jeans and yellow T-shirt, unknowingly reflecting the color scheme of the girl's clothes he saw yesterday. He was back at the German Bakery with a milkshake and cake and eagerly searching for her in the street from his window seat. He didn't have to wait for long as she was still in the same clothes, having wandered to the bakery, and stood exactly at the same spot as yesterday. He decided to take a bold approach this time so he tapped on the window and gestured for her to come inside and join him. She gave him a big smile and then turned around and ignored him. But she did not run away, which he took as an encouraging sign.

ELEVEN

Andrew came outside and smiled at her, while she pretended to not see him. Feeling more embarrassed than irritated, he walked up closer to her and said, "Why did you run away yesterday, I was trying to say hello to you?"

She smiled shyly but still didn't respond. Andrew, who had brought a small piece of cake on a napkin, offered it to her and she shook her head vehemently from side to side. "Are you mad at me?" he asked, with his brow raised, and added, "why don't you say something, this is very awkward." Suddenly a thought occurred to him like lightning and in a deliberately slow voice, he said, "Do you understand English?"

She shook her head from side to side but slowly this time, as if forming a thought in her head, and then screwing her lips as if trying to form some difficult words, said, "Small, a few words only."

"Okay," Andrew answered as he sighed with relief for now the puzzle of her silence was solved. He next said, stretching out every word, "My-name-is-Andrew, what-is-yours?"

"Lalita," she said swiftly.

"Pretty name," he said, repeating Lalita in his heart, and aloud, he added, "where do you live, Lalita? Am I saying your name right, Lalita?"

She nodded and then looked to her right and tiptoeing on her feet to gain some extra height, raised her right arm high and pointed with her index finger towards the horizon.

"Could I come and see your house to take pictures there? You know, photos of you and your family," he asked, showing her his camera.

She tilted her head to one side and stared at him wide-eyed. Andrew knew a little Hindi taught to him by some Indian students at St. Georges, but was never confident of using it. *But this could be an opportune time to practice that skill*, he reasoned and this time repeated his question in Hindi. Her eyes lit up and she responded in Hindi, "You speak very good Hindi and you have funny-colored eyes, green!"

Andrew smiled and responded in Hindi again, "I speak very little Hindi, I'm afraid, and yes, I do have green-color eyes." They both laughed and with the laughter it seemed that the barrier there a moment ago had vanished. She explained to Andrew that she would love to see her photographs taken by him for she had never been photographed before, but she could not bring him to her house or her father would be very angry. Andrew suggested that he come around tomorrow morning and pick her up from somewhere near her house and they could drive down by the Beas River where he could take some photos. Reluctantly she agreed, for she could not resist the offer of riding in a car, something she had never experienced before.

Next day at dawn the valley greeted the sun by opening up its colorful heart. Andrew stayed in the warmth of his bed for a while. After his breakfast he asked the driver to take him to a small village that she had pointed out just on the fringes of the old part of town. As they drove down a small dirt road through a row of mud houses he spotted her standing outside a hut at the end of the road. He told the driver to drive right past her and then stop about twenty yards away at a bend in the road. A few minutes later she came running and Andrew opened the back door to let her in. As she slid in, the driver gave her a stern look and shouted in Hindi, "Get out, you filthy thing." She shrank into the car seat like a flower closes its petals at the end of a day.

Andrew held her hand to comfort her and shouted back at the driver, "What is the meaning of this? Drive! And I don't want to hear another word out of your mouth." The driver cursed under his breath and kept muttering something inaudible but now followed Andrew's instructions.

Once they were outside the town she directed them to a beautiful spot where they got out of the car and went for a walk along the riverbank. Andrew took a few photos but the lighting was not that great. Neither of them complained, as they were delighted to be in each other's company. They enjoyed the long walk together and Andrew again practiced his Hindi. When Andrew asked if she went to school she smiled. Questions about her siblings, parents and their line of work all met with the same response. Lalita smiled a lot and Andrew loved looking at her.

After a long two-hour walk and chatting, Andrew dropped her off near her house and on the way back home the driver said, *"Chote Sahib,* you must never see that girl again. She is a Dalit, you know, from the untouchable class. These people are dirty and we must not touch them."

"What rubbish," Andrew retorted, "keep your prejudices to yourself and if you ever utter a word about this to Dad, I will blame everything on you. So mind your own business and keep out of my affairs."

"But *Chote Sahib,* these Dalit people are thieves and cannot be trusted. They need to be treated harshly and kept in their place."

"That's enough!" Andrew shouted. "Just drive the car and do as you are told."

The driver remained silent the remainder of the journey, sulking.

TWELVE

The friendship of Andrew with Lalita that started in early spring remained reserved for a while, limited to chats and walks, as if a rose garden waiting for summer months to blossom. As they relaxed more in each other's company, they gradually progressed to a level of relationship that could only be described as comfortable. A level where they could hold each other's hand while walking and often laugh at frivolous things. There was a mutual attraction and a hint of love in their eyes.

Spring turned into summer and their relationship did blossom. Lalita could now speak many more English words and with much more ease than before, and Andrew's confidence in speaking Hindi grew. Throughout the summer months, Andrew and Lalita saw each other regularly for walks and photography sessions, but always covertly. The clandestine nature of their relationship added spice to their lives. Their days were filled with fun and their nights were restless.

They never went into town together and kept their friendship a secret from Tom. The driver was now a part of their game and handsomely rewarded by Andrew for his silence. One day Andrew came up with a plan to take pictures in better lighting as Tom had bought him a complete lighting set for still photography. But he did not know how to ask Lalita, for she was shy and he was afraid that she might misunderstand his intentions. He decided to wait for an opportune moment.

As the days melted away, their hearts developed a yearning. A yearning for more intimacy, but without crossing the line, for there was the danger that such an intimacy might damage their friendship. One late afternoon when the sun was low, they were holding hands, exultation in their souls, seemingly gliding effortlessly along the river path, their two long shadows trailing behind them.

They stopped to watch the river. It reflected the yearning in their hearts. The bushes shook, the grasses swayed, and then everything stood still in attentive immobility. She glanced up, her soft brown eyes, usually so sad and weary, lighting up and Andrew gently squeezed her hand. They both smiled but as color rose to her cheeks and, overcome by shyness, she withdrew her hand from his, their burning lips unquenched.

Breaking the awkward silence, Andrew asked, "Would you like to visit me at my house this Friday? I have a studio at home where the lighting would be perfect for photography."

She drew farther away, and the same a constrained smile appeared on her face, shy, suspicious, accusing. She shook her head no but her eyes were saying yes.

He determined not to grow impatient. "Just for a little while, please," pleaded Andrew, holding her hands again, "no photographs, if you don't want them."

There was an awkward pause that could prove pivotal to the delicate balance of their friendship. "Okay, just for a little while," consented Lalita.

What Lalita did not know was that veiled in that innocent invitation rested the summons of her death.

On Friday, the driver picked her up and dropped her at Andrew's bungalow at about eleven in the morning. Andrew told the driver to come back about three in the afternoon. Andrew had already converted his bedroom into his studio and had the lights set up correctly for portrait photography. He asked her if she would mind doing some poses lying in his bed. Lalita hesitated at first but then, trusting Andrew, agreed.

Lying on his bed in a tight red blouse and pleated white cotton skirt with one leg bent and the other straight, both her arms stretched over her head, she posed like a ballerina dancing in mid air. Andrew looked through the lens and then came over to the bed to smooth out a fold in her skirt and in doing so, accidently his hand caressed her leg. He realized that he was alone in his bedroom with the prettiest girl he had ever seen.

He stepped back and stood frozen for a moment. "Is this okay?" she asked, and then added, "I don't know about my hair. Would you like to style it?" Was it a polite invitation for Andrew to take the next step? She smiled. He leaned over her to fashion her hair and accidently his cheek caressed hers. Electricity passed between them and she raised her lips as if inviting him into her world. He lowered his head and kissed her lips and his body was charged with excitement.

Color rushed to his cheeks and he pressed his lips a little harder on hers, she responded by placing her hands on his chest. He lay next to her and cupped her face in his hands and kissed her deeply. Involuntary yet aggressive movements of their hands began to remove each other's clothing. They were not experienced but their bodies, burning with red-hot passion, somehow naturally knew what lay ahead and they surged towards it like a rising wave does towards the full moon.

Their bodies collided as their souls merged, seeking to become one, and in their quest to satisfy their hunger they found themselves above all prejudices. Breathing heavily, he held her in his strong arms as she moaned with pleasure. Their world was beautiful and they unashamedly explored every part of it. Time stood still as the sweetest moments of life passed between them.

Suddenly someone pushed the bedroom door wide open. "What the hell do you think you're doing? And you," Tom pointed a finger, trembling with rage, at her, "get the hell out of my house. Now. And if I ever see you again with my son I swear I'll kill you."

Shaking with fear, she hurriedly put her clothes on and ran through the open door, knocking over a chair in the process. Tom picked up the chair and righted it, and then sat in it. With angry eyes, he stared at Andrew and said, "You ought to be ashamed of yourself. I had not expected you to stoop so low. I trusted you and you took advantage of that. I shall not forgive you for this. If your mother was here she would have died of shame."

Andrew retorted, "Leave my mother out of it. I'm sorry you had to find us this way. But she is a good girl and she is my friend. I have known her for quite some time now."

"Have you lost all your senses? She is a Dalit, unclean." Andrew's voice rose with disappointment and anger and he added, "Do you even know what that means? People here don't even touch them. I found the driver wandering in town without you and he told me all about your stupidity. You leave her alone or I'll teach her family a lesson they will not forget the rest of their lives, you hear me? Now, you stay home and don't go anywhere till I tell you."

Andrew glared at his dad with burning eyes. A dark thought surged from his heart and clouded his mind.

THIRTEEN

The air was thick with tension as Andrew stared at his dad as his frustration and anger welled up. He said, "If you ever do anything to her, I'll never forgive you. We're friends and I don't care about her being Dalit or not. When did you develop such prejudices? Isn't she a person just like us?"

"You're far too young to know what you're doing," his voice mellowed. "Just trust me on this one. I'd lose my job if the local community were to find out that you're fraternizing with a Dalit girl. Besides, she is far too old for you to befriend; she is twenty-one, according to the driver."

Andrew was quiet now. *Twenty-one*, he mused. She did not look a day older than fifteen. Why didn't they discuss their ages, but what did it matter, he contemplated. He almost forgot that his dad was still sitting there awaiting a response from him. Finding him in deep thought that Tom took for remorse, he left the room for Andrew to dress and reflect on what he had done. "Oh God," he said under his breath, "what am I going to do to protect my son? Why could he not find a decent girl for a friend? A Dalit, oh, what would people at the office say if they found out?" He decided to talk with his Indian friends in the evening, in confidence of course, to seek their advice for they must know how to deal with such a situation to avoid further repercussions.

Andrew remained withdrawn and shut up in his room. He missed his mom, thinking she would have understood him if she was alive, as he cried silently. He remained in bed and refused to touch meals that the cook brought for him. Every time he closed his eyes he could sense Lalita's warm and soft body next to him. He must see her again, but maybe in a few days, when the dust had settled. He wondered what she must think of his dad who so rudely threw her out. He would apologize on his dad's behalf, he mused. Under the bed sheet, covering him from head to toe, he peered at the small screen of his digital camera and reviewed Lalita's pictures with her smiling face and brilliant eyes. Those soft brown eyes would be crying now, he feared. His eyelids heavy, he started to fall into a heavy sleep.

But then, on the edge of sleep, a dreadful feeling like he was just about to fall off the edge of a cliff jolted him back into wakefulness. His dream seemed real. His body stiffened in a sudden cramp, and he lay still, waiting with his eyes open for the phantom cramp to dissolve. He did not know for how long he lay on his back, staring at the ceiling, his mind still churning out the same disturbing thoughts and images. He daren't close his eyes. Then— gradually—it slowed, and his mind went numb then relaxed and he didn't know when, but his eyes closed, and sleep was at hand. Suddenly and once again, on the threshold of sleep, the jolt, the shock, the cramp that came over him. Once again, he was shaken awake from his peace, quiet, and oblivion.

With no further outbursts from his father, Andrew noticed that it was now dark outside and he could hear his father talking as he played bridge with his friends. He could not hear what they were saying but just their muffled voices and a lot of clinking of glasses. *They are drinking whisky again.* He pursed his lips in distaste. He didn't realize until that moment how much he hated his father's friends coming around every week and getting drunk at his father's expense.

Taking a few minutes' break from the game, Tom said, "You guys are drinking a lot tonight; slow down, I need to talk with you."

Harish, knocking back his whisky in one swift move, and putting his empty glass on the table gesturing for more, said excitedly, "We're celebrating tonight. Didn't you know that our friend here, Dinesh, has been promoted to be the new general manager, and me the new director? Tomorrow you will receive a formal circular about it. You will have two new project managers, but from now on we will be part of your executive team. All decisions from now on will be easy. We together will run this office and there's a lot of money in it for all of us. Come on, Tom, I know you never drink, but how about tonight? Just a little one for our sake?"

"That's great news, but sorry, I never touch the stuff," said Tom, and they all raised their refreshed glasses again and drank more. "What did you want to talk about?" asked Harish, slurring his words. And then in a questioning voice said, "You look rather upset, and if I'm not mistaken, even angry tonight. What's up?"

Tom hesitated but then told them what had happened that morning. As he recollected the story his voice rose and he could not hide his suppressed anger. He got up and opened up a new bottle of whisky and sat back down to refresh everyone's glasses, saying, "I've a good mind to go over to her house and have a word with her father. My driver told me that she lives with her father and has been corrupting my son. My god, he is fifteen and she is twenty-one, she should know better."

Harish had a large build, with thick, curly black hair and bulging eyes. Now, with bloodshot eyes and slurred speech, under the influence of alcohol, he said, "These Dalit people have been spoiled since the days of Mahatma Gandhi, who called them Harijan, children of God. I'll tell you what they are. They are bloody bastards, parasites. They ought to know their place. And when they forget their place it is our duty to remind them who they really are, the bleeding untouchables. They only understand one language and I think, Tom, if you want to stop them, then let us go teach them a lesson that they won't forget. You must act now to save your son from these bastards. Come on, have a little drink, you might need it tonight. I'm glad you told us, we can help you."

"I sure would like to stop these thugs," said Tom, gesturing with his hand for Harish not to pour him a drink. "I knew you guys would help me. Let's go and talk to them. I sure would like to give them piece of my mind."

Harish looked at Dinesh and it seemed they had a silent language between them as they both smiled broadly and then Harish announced, "Yeah, why not, let's talk to them, but we will do more than just talking. I know what she wants." He looked around and found Andrew's baseball bat that he picked up and took a couple of practice swings, as if feeling its weight, and then they all jumped in his car and headed for the small village by the old Manali town. Left behind on the table was a double whisky in a glass for Tom that he did not touch.

FOURTEEN

Late that night when Tom returned Andrew was fast asleep. Or so he thought. Tom leaned over Andrew's bed and caressed his hair gently and kissed his head. Andrew could smell alcohol on Tom's breath. As Tom turned away from Andrew's bed to leave his bedroom, Andrew opened one of his eyes and what he saw froze the blood in his veins. Tom, with his shoulders slouched and head hung low, seemed to be carrying the weight of the world on his shoulders and in his right arm he was loosely holding the baseball bat, on which Andrew could see thick stains of what looked like blood in the nightlight.

Andrew was fully awake now. Deep in his heart he felt the terror of what his father in his rage and drunken state may have done. He felt a rising fury in his own mind. He wanted to scream and ask his dad, what had he done? But the guilt over what he had done earlier that day, which he beginning to believe was the root cause of what his father did, overcame his courage and he lay there in bed immobilized by both fear and rage. Hot tears rolled down the sides of his face. He lay awake for what seemed like hours.

The next day Andrew, by his own choice, remained shut up in his room and ate his meals alone there. Finally Sunday morning arrived and Andrew came out of his room to find his father reading the weekend newspaper and drinking coffee. When Tom saw Andrew, he put his newspaper aside and said, "Would you like some breakfast, son?"

Andrew nodded his head affirmatively and sat across the small table from his father. "Look, Andrew, we should talk," said Tom.

"No, Dad, let me say something first," said Andrew. Without waiting for a response, he explained, "I'm so ashamed of what happened. I'm so sorry. I do like that girl but it was wrong of me to do what I did, we did. We didn't plan it that way and had no idea what we were doing. I don't know what else to say." In his heart Andrew had decided to clear the air between them by first admitting his mistakes and then maybe he could ask if he did see some blood on the baseball bat. Was there any violence towards her? Did his father and his friends hurt Lalita? Why did his father resort to alcohol?

"You don't have to say anything more," assured Tom, as he leaned forward and squeezed Andre's shoulder. "I acted harshly and I'm sorry too."

They both stood and embraced. The bitterness they'd had for the past couple of days between them melted away in seconds after their reconciliation. Forgiveness is a powerful force.

After they sat back down and Andrew finished his eggs and toast, he said, "Dad, I know you and your friends went out that night with my baseball bat. Did you hurt Lalita?"

There was a sudden twitch in Tom's face and he put his fork down. After a pause that seemed like an eternity to Andrew, Tom replied, "Nobody hit her."

"Thanks, Dad. I am sorry that I asked such a stupid question."

Andrew realized that in his disquieted state of mind the other night he must have imagined blood on the baseball bat and felt a sense of joy that everything was back to normal. After a few minutes elapsed, he said, "Dad, I do understand now the inappropriateness of what happened but I think it would be wrong of me not to go and see her and say I'm sorry for what happened to her. Would you be okay with it if I went over to her house to apologize, and if she no longer wants to see me, then I guess to also say goodbye to her. But Dad," he hesitated for a moment and then continued, "I must do this alone."

Tom diverted his gaze, picked up the newspaper, and then put it down again on the table. He gestured to the cook to bring some fresh coffee and then focused on Andrew, saying, "Look, I had to go and talk to her and her father for your sake, for our sake. I was upset and my friends were angry and things got a little out of hand. I'm not too sure what actually did transpire in the heat of the moment, but everything is settled now. It may be wise to let things be. You don't have to go there anymore; besides, I heard yesterday that they have left the village and moved on."

Tom got up and turned around to leave, since he did not want to go into details of what actually did transpire the night before. Some of it was a blur now and some of it he did not care to recall.

FIFTEEN

Andrew jumped to his feet and grabbed his dad's arm, forcing him to face him again.

"Moved on," said Andrew, in a perplexed tone, "moved on to where? They were here on Friday. They wouldn't just get up and leave, and besides, she wouldn't go away without saying goodbye to me. What do you mean when you said things got out of hand? What did you do? Did you threaten them; did you pay them off to leave town? What?" Andrew stood up and his voice showed the return of his suppressed anger and irritation and with color rising in his cheeks, he asked doggedly, "What exactly did you and your friends do to her, Dad?"

Tom picked up the newspaper and in an exasperated tone responded, "Let it go, Andrew. I am not proud of what happened yesterday but you'll understand it one day when you're older."

Andrew glared at his dad, turned around and ran out of the bungalow and kept on running, not knowing what to do next and where to go. Tom sent the driver after him and told him to keep an eye on him. He knew Andrew would need time to understand the way things are handled in India.

An hour later, wandering aimlessly on the road of the old Manali town, he saw his car following him. He stopped to let the driver catch up with him. Once inside the car, he asked, "Why did you squeal on me to Dad? Did I not pay you enough?"

"I'm sorry, *Chote Sahib*, but *Bara Sahib* was very angry when he caught me without you and wanted to know everything. I'm so sorry, Sahib; I'm a poor man and have a family, a wife, four children and aging parents. I need this job, *Sahib*. I had to tell *Bara Sahib* everything. Please forgive me."

"Okay, okay," Andrew said in an irritated voice, "now take me to Lalita's house. I just want to see if she is okay. We won't stay long and we'll go straight back to the bungalow afterwards so you don't have to lie for me."

When they reached her house it was locked up with no sign of life. Andrew asked around and finally one woman with resentment written all over her face, in a bitter tone, said, "A car with four people came and Lalita's father was beaten badly. I don't know their whereabouts. They have been driven away from their home by those bullies."

Andrew felt a pain in his heart as if someone was squeezing it. He asked the driver to take him to the city hospital in the new town. Once he reached the hospital he inquired about the girl and her father. The doctor in charge explained that he did treat the father for severe internal injuries and a broken arm. He could not say anything about the girl for he did not treat her. Andrew sighed and murmured, "At least they spared her, thank god."

The doctor could not explain where they might be. As Andrew started to leave, the doctor rubbed his chin as if contemplating something, and then said, "It is possible that maybe out of fear of further reprisals they fled. Beating Dalit people is a common occurrence and no one, including the police, pays any attention to their plight."

Andrew thanked the doctor and in the hope that this doctor might have some further information on the family, asked, "Isn't there anything on your records that could tell me about her family or where they might go?"

"No," said the doctor instantly and then after a moment's pause added, "strange thing though. The girl's father, the old man kept saying something about the same hand that was raised to beat him, one day would beg for his mercy."

Andrew sighed heavily and returned home. He and Tom did not talk to each other for the next few days. About a week later Andrew noticed a police officer in the next room talking with Tom. He moved closer to the door so he could hear the inspector. He heard him say, "Mr. Donavan, I believe you know why I am here. But this is an unofficial visit to give you both a warning and some advice. We have a serious complaint against you and your friends and I believe you know what I'm talking about. We would deal with you friends in our own way but we've a problem with you. This town survives on foreign tourists and we don't like foreigners to get into trouble here. My superiors have asked me to have a private word with you to strongly advise that if you could find your way to leave this country quickly and not ever come back to Manali then we will not bring any charges against you. Well, I won't take too much more of your time, but advise you to leave India this week, preferably in the next couple of days."

"Thank you, Mr. Tiwari," Tom responded, and the policeman left.

Andrew never received any explanation from his dad but it was obvious to him that his father was involved in beating up the poor man and that is why, two days after the police came, they were on a plane bound for London and then to Calgary.

BOOK III

Winter of Discontent
Winter 1992
British Columbia, Canada

SIXTEEN

U pon their return from India, the Senior Vice President of Tom's employer, unhappy with Tom's behavior there, and afraid of possible related implications, called him in for an urgent meeting. "Tom, we are restructuring our management team and I'm afraid we are going to let you go. We will compensate you adequately, of course." That was of little consequence to Tom for all it did was fire up Tom's entrepreneurial spirit, and instead of seeking employment elsewhere, he started exploring other business options.

But first he had to get Andrew back into school. Andrew hated every moment around his dad and wanted to get back to the St. George's boarding school in Vancouver. "Why don't you finish your schooling here in Calgary and after that attend the University of Calgary, to graduate with an engineering degree?" Tom suggested. "That is where your mother and I went. It is a great university and I have certain influence there."

But Andrew wanted to return to his family and to him his family was his friends and teachers at St. George's where he had spent ten years of his life and had all his education to date. "No thanks," he said in a low but firm voice, "it would be too difficult for me to fit into a new place. I would like to return to St. George's."

They both knew that a gulf now existed between them and Tom had hoped that it was temporary, and that with the passing of time and a change in his son's surroundings, all the bad memories would diminish, hopefully replaced by new experiences. He blamed the differences between them on Andrew's immaturity and adolescence.

Upon returning to St. George's, Andrew felt a sense of relief. Andrew recalled that when he had first moved to the boarding school he had found life both challenging and unbearable. The loss of his mother was a big blow and then the unfamiliar surroundings and strict lifestyle of a boarding school had made him retreat within himself. He remembered how he hated contact sports even though it was mandatory at the school that he participate in rugby, but with time he had gained the confidence of the school nurse, who understood his dilemma and on most occasions would give him sick leave.

Without letting his father know, Andrew changed the science courses that Tom had earlier selected for him to art courses. It was not based on rebellion, but rather that he wanted to follow his passion in languages. He was fascinated with English literature and once introduced to the nineteenth century writers he became fully absorbed in their works. Somerset Maugham, DH Lawrence, Hennery James, Edith Wharton, Leo Tolstoy, and Graham Green were just a few of the many whose

writings he found fascinating and spent most his free
time reading. He wanted to be a writer.

With the severance package Tom received, he started
up a pipeline services company providing specialized
synthetic coating for the buried oil and gas pipelines. It
was the first Canadian, and only company in Alberta that
had the technology and ability to provide both polyeth-
ylene and polypropylene external coatings for the buried
steel oil and gas lines, as well as transmission pipelines.

In a short period he had built this company from zero
profit to close to over twenty million dollars in profit,
employing over one hundred staff, and recently he had
floated the company on the Toronto Stock Exchange.
The markets were in his favor and he made what the
analysts called a killing by taking his company public.

Tom with his unprecedented success in the business
world had restored and even surpassed his previously
held prestigious social status in the oil and gas society
of Alberta and was once again rubbing shoulders with
the oil barons of the Province. The 'Oil Week' ran his
picture on the front page of the magazine with a feature
article on his company. Tom became a highly eligible
bachelor in the regional world of the rich and famous,
but he resisted any suggestion of remarrying. Deep
down in his heart he was a sentimentalist and could not
bear the thought of betraying the memories of his late
wife by bringing a new woman into the house.

Suppressed deep in his heart was a desire to do better
than his father did in business, specifically for two main
reasons. First, Tom thought that his success in business

would be a fitting tribute to his late wife, who against all odds was so committed to making a success of their relationship; and second, and perhaps unbeknownst to even him, he was still yearning for recognition from his father.

Meanwhile, the years came and went and time in Andrew's life drifted away from him. Finally the day came when he graduated with English Literature as his major. Although Tom came to attend the graduation and congratulated him, he did not look too pleased with his choice of subject.

SEVENTEEN

Tom had high hopes that if Andrew had graduated with a science major, he could have gone on to a business school or an engineering university, for he wanted to groom him as his successor to run the corporation. But seeds of hatred were planted in Andrew's heart a long time back and he involuntarily was inclined to do the opposite of everything his father wanted him to do to continue to fuel his dissatisfaction and maybe even his suppressed anger.

Soon after graduation, Andrew enrolled into an English Language degree program at the University of British Columbia, Vancouver. Andrew was willing to go anywhere but Calgary and he let his dad know his intentions. Tom once again swallowed his pride and let Andrew fulfill his dreams by continuing on the path of becoming an English teacher. Tom believed that once Andrew realized that the teaching profession was not going to give him the lifestyle he had been accustomed to, he would then return to school and maybe graduate this time with a business degree.

Tom was willing to wait for this since he knew that Andrew had the same stubborn streak and strong will as his mother.

While at school, Andrew never went to Calgary for summer vacation and instead chose to go to summer camps. While he was at the university, the lack of communication between him and his father continued, and they began to drift apart. Tom remained busy with his growing business and the only contact with his son was the infrequent phone conversations between them that he always initiated.

Four years after Andrew started his university program, he graduated with distinction. He enjoyed his time at the University for, unlike the boarding school, here no one at the University pressured him to participate in sports. He was free to make use of his free time in any way he wanted. While most other students partied and drank, Andrew retreated to his favorite pastime of reading nineteenth century writers. He dreamed of becoming a published writer one day, authoring novels of the same caliber as the old masters did. Now and then, when he felt inspired, he wrote poetry that often found its way into the university and local magazines.

Andrew remained one of the top students at the university and upon graduation had no problem securing a post-doctoral position at the University of Victoria on Vancouver Island. He chose to work for the university for two reasons: one, its scholarship; and second, his further detachment from mainland British Columbia, to put an even greater distance between him and Calgary. The latter suited him.

Andrew chose tragedy in English literature as the main subject for his Ph.D. program and focused on Othello as the key character. Weeks melted into months and months into two years and no sooner had he received his Ph.D. degree than he also secured a teaching position at the University of Victoria. He looked forward to having a life of his own where he did not have to depend on financial support from his father. He wanted a life free of his father's influence.

Growing up, Andrew was well provided for, especially when it came to financial matters, by his father. But he always felt that he was mortgaging his soul against every installment of money his father sent to him. He was looking forward to working as a teacher at the University of Victoria, enjoying the sense of freedom that one has when making one's own money.

He was convinced that financial security would bring a new sense of freedom and thus happiness. His salary was not going to be great but he was determined to curtail his expenses and keep his expectations within his means. The day he received his first paycheck he experienced a sense of exhilaration, for he no longer needed money from his father, and that further distanced him from his father and from what he'd hoped, his past, too.

Even though there were moments when he thought that perhaps he had been overreacting towards his father because of what had happened in Manali, and now that so much time had passed he ought to make mends with him, but somehow as soon as the desire for reconciliation appeared, a silent rebellion rose from within and stopped him from taking any initiative to commence appeasement.

Procrastination, though it did not resolve the situation between them, did somehow defer the urgency of contemplating any positive moves. Time like a serpent coiled itself around any reconciliatory measures and eventually smothered the life out of their relationship. Andrew and Tom continued to behave as strangers.

EIGHTEEN

Andrew now wanted to build a permanency to his detachment from his father and decided to buy a condo of his own in Victoria. As luck would have it, the timing was in his favor, since mortgage rates were low and developers were heavily discounting newly built condos, for sale almost at cost. Andrew engaged the services of a realtor to help him find a condo within his budget. The important thing was, as he explained to his realtor, that the condo must have a view of the water and it must be located on a higher floor to take full advantage of that view.

He was lucky; within a week after he visited about dozen places, he chose a brand new condo that was ready for him and met all his criteria. Within a week of making an offer he had completed all the formalities and moved in. The condo was in showroom condition, fully furnished, and that suited Andrew. But unbeknownst to Andrew, his luck was about to run out, for some of the recent flood of Chinese immigrants to Canada occupied the remainder of the condo building. It seemed that none of its residents had a need to mix outside their

Chinese circles. Andrew did not know how to integrate with them.

But there was something inside him that knew beyond every rational belief and irrational doubt that he was not meant to live alone. That his mother's prayers for him to have a happy life would not go in vain. Neither his mother nor he believed in Christianity, but there was a verse in Matthew that he liked that read, "Ask and it will be given to you; seek and you will find; knock and the door will be opened to you."

He did try to knock on a few doors in his building but none of the Chinese Canadians offered any suitable opportunity for him to socialize. He never did learn how to pick out a lucky fortune cookie.

Soon Andrew's need for companionship turned into loneliness. He tried making new friends among his fellow faculty members. But he was in for disappointment for the whole English department was riddled with internal politics. Although he was no threat to anyone's career progression since he was the youngest teacher, the older professors looked down on him and offered no encouragement or support in helping him feel comfortable at the University.

He tried to socialize with some of the members who had started their career only a few years before him by inviting them out for dinner or drinks but they always had an excuse. No one wanted to be associated with a novice. It seemed that without exception all the faculty were concerned with their teaching careers and after work went straight to their homes to their families, so socializing through any outdoor activities with them was out of the question.

That presented yet another difficulty Andrew could not overcome. He was the only faculty member who was not married; therefore, he was not allowed in the so-called inner circle of those who were. There were two types of groups within the English faculty, those that were married and the other, married with children. Both groups considered Andrew an outcast.

But one day Andrew's luck changed. An old university friend, who was known for his flamboyance and engaging personality, and was now currently teaching at the University of California in Los Angeles, visited Andrew for the weekend. The trait they had in common was that they both disliked their respective fathers. Over a bottle of malt while sitting at his condo, Andrew explained his dilemma. "Would you believe it, I have even tried going to a singles bar to see if I could meet some single girl who was in a similar predicament as I am. Mind you, I did that only once and without any luck. I was appalled by the whole charade of sitting in a dark bar drinking alone and hoping to pick up a lady."

"And what made you think that a lady, if indeed she were a lady, would go to a dark bar looking for guys?"

"I see what you mean," laughed Andrew, "and once I even subscribed to an online dating service. To be honest, it was at this juncture I realized that I might have reached the level of desperation, for I had started hunting for a life partner while all I really wanted was a friend. Anyway, how have you been?"

"Three marriages, three divorces," the friend answered. "So listen to the voice of experience, for I have the perfect solution for you."

""Really?" Andrew moved to the edge of his seat, pouring another round for his friend and himself. "Go on."

"What I am about to tell you," said Andrew's friend in a serious tone, "is a one hundred percent guaranteed solution to end all your pain, and once you follow my advice, all your problems, current and those of the past, will disappear forever like they never happened. Are you ready?"

Andrew nodded in eager anticipation, like a child on Christmas who has been told to close his eyes to receive his presents and not to open them till he is told.

NINETEEN

Andrew's friend heaved a heavy sigh as if getting ready to impart a monumental secret. "Commit suicide," said the friend nonchalantly, "after that no pain and no more desperation. All your problems solved, guaranteed."

Andrew was aghast and felt like throwing his friend out of his home. "I thought you were my friend?" said he, raising his voice. "Are you sick in your head? I expected better from you."

"So, that is not an option then," he responded, laughing. "That is great. I was worried for a moment that you might be becoming suicidal so just wanted to be sure. Good to know that you are not that stupid. Wonderful. Let us start looking at other options then, shall we?"

Andrew let out a sigh of relief and, shaking his head, responded, "You're something, you know that?" Then after a momentary pause he continued, "Well, I did join a music group to learn how to play the violin. No friends, but I can play and guess what? I now spend hours locked up here in my condo practicing the violin."

As Andrew paused, he reflected on his lonely life. He knew that his only salvation was the memory of the little time he had spent years ago with Lalita—his first love. He then told everything about his time with Lalita to his friend.

"Time out," said the visitor making the sign of a 'T' with his hands. "I need to visit the wash room. But I am glad you told me this. When I get back I will have the perfect solution for you. It is quite simple actually." He pushed himself off the sofa and went towards the wash-room on his unsteady legs.

Andrew wondered what other surprise his friend had for him. No more stupid ideas, he hoped. As he waited his minded drifted back to his childhood. From his early childhood, he had become something of a mystery, inscrutable, vague, his thoughts a well-kept secret. Of course, he never intended to be that way but after his mother died and his father could not bear to look at his face and sent him away to a faraway boarding school, as he reminded his father of his loss, and living in a society where he was a misfit, the obscurity was a part of his survival.

The truth was that he was never given the opportunity, as every young boy should be given, to have his father around as a role model, to know who he wanted to be when he grew up. So, he didn't know who he was, and truth be told, he was afraid of being recognized as who he wasn't. All the tears he had cried, birthdays he missed, family holidays he never had, all of that and more, told him who he could never be. He had missed out on so many things in his life, ordinary events and normal occasions, that by now he could not care less about what he had.

His friend returned from the washroom and reclaiming his seat and taking a sip of his drink, he said, "As it often happens, the answer to your problem has been staring you in your face. You, my friend, need what in California we call closure, and it will only happen if you go back and find that girl again in Manila."

"Manali," Andrew corrected.

"Whatever," said he, waving his hand in dismissal of the error. "Listen, you will not find a resolution grinding away your life here. Get back to her and have a talk. That is all you need to do. Live a little. Go tell her how you feel. You won't have any peace till you do so."

Andrew realized that he needed this talk with his friend. He was pleased to get these things off his chest. On Sunday, late afternoon, while his friend went out for a while, he sat in his favorite deep-cushioned chair by the window with a book, but could not read, as his mind kept going back to what his friend had said.

Another woman that Andrew could never get out of his mind nor did he ever want to, was his mother. He often wondered how his mother, living in a foreign country, married to a man outside her culture, letting go of her mother tongue, food, music, clothes and traditions, not only survived but also thrived, and created a place for herself in what must have been a strange world to her. She must have had something that was more than just courage; it was also acceptance, resilience, perseverance, spirit, and tenacity.

She wasn't the kind of woman you felt sorry for, exactly. Rather, looking into her fine, sad eyes, you felt a deep sorrow; the kind of melancholy you feel when you're in a beautiful place and the sun is setting.

And mostly, now, when he thought of her, he felt sorry for himself, because his mother had possessed something that he needed now. He didn't know what it was, didn't even have a name for it. All he knew was that she could've taught him something, if only he had not been so young and shy and afraid to ask. If she could leave India and build a life in Canada, then why couldn't he leave Canada and build his life in India? This thought exploded in his mind like a fire-cracker. "Yes, indeed, why not?" he muttered.

"I want to attempt that but am frightened by trivi-alities like what people might say," he affirmed through clenched teeth, as if arguing with himself. An odd smile played on his lips. "Yes, it is within my reach and I am letting it all slip away because I am suffering from incon-sequential anxieties; that's so ridiculous." He laughed silently at the thought that he was talking to himself. "What the hell am I afraid of? Taking a new step, losing my career...what? Is that what I fear most? But I am thinking too much. It's because I think that I do nothing. Or perhaps it is that I think because I do nothing?"

He hadn't realized that it had become dark outside and sitting in the dark, he had been arguing in his mind for over an hour. He switched on the lamp close to him, and the yellow shade threw a brilliant light upon his arms, and upon the armrest of his chair, and left the rest of the room in darkening shadows. When he looked up, pos-sibilities swam in his eyes as he realized that his beliefs and the life he craved were the truths by which he must choose to live.

TWENTY

Late that night Andrew was sitting on the balcony of his condo with his friend, enjoying a nightcap. As they listened to the muffled music coming from his sitting room through the slightly ajar double door, '*Hit the road, Jack…*' his friend's smile broadened. He said, "Not only millions loved his self-styled music, they also admired the courage Ray Charles showed in conquering his drug addiction and overcoming the guilt of feeling responsible for the accidental death of his younger brother. As a blind man, if he could win his battles against all odds, then what are you so concerned about?" Andrew pursed his lips in determination and his resolve became firm.

The next day Andrew walked into the office of the head of the department and placed his resignation on his desk. Dr. Smith looked at it, looked up again at Andrew, lowered his head to reconfirm, and then, shaking his head from side to side, said, "You are going to throw away a great career, make a big mistake."

Quietly, as a man caught in a half-truth that he no longer cared to sustain, Andrew admitted, "You're right. It is a mistake I am making by throwing away a great career."

He paused for a moment and then in an excited voice continued, "But don't you see, it is my first big mistake and within, rather than feeling sorry or sad, I feel exalted. Isn't it extraordinary? But then you wouldn't understand since you don't make any such mistakes, do you? You have been in the teaching profession for what? Thirty years? More?"

"I have no clue as to what you are going on about but I can see what a grave mistake you are making," repeated the professor.

Andrew cupped his hand around the back of his neck and rubbed it as if he was tense. With a low grunt, he said, "Did your parents want you to be a teacher?"

"Of course," he responded proudly, "they were both excellent teachers and they wanted me to follow in the same noble profession. And even if I say so myself, I have made a remarkable profession of it. You, too, could be the Head of the Department one day. Listen to me carefully." He left his chair and came around to stand next to Andrew for emphasis. "Of the forty faculty members that I have here, you are the youngest professor and the brightest member of the faculty. I am counting on you to take my position one day. Whatever is bothering you, we can talk about it, okay?"

"Don't," Andrew said, irritation in his voice, "don't patronize me. I know what I am doing and my decision to resign is final. Perhaps one day I will see you again, but for now I am done."

Dr. Smith's body stiffened and with a stern face he returned to his chair. Leaning back in it and with pursed lips he said, "I don't accept your resignation."

"You what?" Andrew gave a little laugh of disbelief. "I don't think you can do that. Anyway, whatever, I am out of here."

"You walk through that door then I will make sure that you are never welcome back at this University," said the white-bearded man with an unyielding determination.

"Suits me fine," said Andrew, and as he walked out of the office he slammed the door behind him. He looked at the garden for one last time, and a feeling of rejuvenation filled his soul. He smiled and walked to his office to collect his belongings.

He found an empty cardboard box and started to place in it his few possessions. He gazed around one last time as if to say goodbye to his past.

This was one of the greatest crises of his life. For years he had suppressed his soul, in a kind of mechanical despair, doing his duty and enduring the rest. Then his soul had been enticed out from its bondage. Now he was going to break free altogether, to have at least a few months or perhaps even longer devoted only to developing his own joy. He felt enthralled after deciding to give up his job, a career, a nice city, his house, even his own country. This, to a man of his values, meant a breaking of shackles, a severing of ties, a new birth.

There were moments when one's past comes back to one, as it will sometimes when you have not had a moment of peace, and it came in the shape of troubled and noisy dreams. And this reflection of life did not in the least resemble peace. Oh, no. It was the stillness of a relentless force exerted over a sphinx-like intention.

Andrew's life was at a juncture. His days were empty and his nights were restless.

He pondered his past and with his gaze fixed on the wall opposite to where he sat, he wondered where the past thirty-odd years had gone. No wife, no children, just the dull life of a steady job as an English professor at the university. He wondered if quitting a career job today and heading for a remote place in India where he had been only once before when he was a teenager was a wise choice? Of course not, that was the point, he mused. A thin smile flickered on his lips as he realized that he wanted to get away from the wise, disciplined and conformed life to live the impetuous life he once knew. He wanted to break free. He wanted to feel young again: wild and invincible.

He collected but a few things and placed the box in the trunk of his car and without glancing back, drove away from the university campus. On his way home he visited a management company and signed a contract for them to manage and find a tenant for his condo. He knew he could use the rental income, as his income from savings was decent but not substantial.

The world was suddenly reversed before him; his confusion began to dissolve right before his eyes. The grandeur of the thought that he would now trust in his own judgment struck him; suspicions that had lingered in his mind before that he was unloved, not needed and had a worthless life, the echo of those sentiments, with a last inward cry escaped his soul; he stood tall and proud in the presence of his new destiny. Yes, for a moment, doubt had possessed him, but it was now gone; he rose, grand and saintly, his head erect. Life was nothing if not lived in the moment. He understood that now.

BOOK IV

The Call of the Mountains
Spring 2012
Manali, Himachal Pradesh, India

TWENTY-ONE

The pendulum of the world swings through the same positions again and again. Summer passed and winter thereafter, and came and passed again. It is a cycle that remains unbreakable.

Twenty springs had passed since Andrew was forced to leave Manali and now at the age of thirty-five, he was one more time Manali-bound. He looked out the airplane window and saw below the snowy peaks of the Canadian Rockies, reminding him of snow-clad Himalayan Mountains and his time in Manali when he was fifteen years of age. The Air Canada flight for London left Vancouver on time and was heading for Heathrow where he was booked to take Air India to New Delhi, from where he intended to take the deluxe bus service to Manali. Taking the bus was not only a cheaper option but he also preferred it, as he had time to enjoy a ride through the country.

Men who are naturally loners live and love far more through sacrifices than through pleasures. That is what Andrew believed in, perhaps because he himself was a loner and had a lusterless life. Real life is a life of anguish; its image is in that nettle growing at the foot of a tree in a forest where no sun can reach it and yet it remains green. He remembered his past when he was a teenager in Manali; he'd seen smiles in the small town, few to be sure, but he knew that they would compensate for many a grief that emanated from his time spent in Canada.

He had no plans of mentioning his sudden move to India to his father. He knew his father would never approve of it; besides, all his life he had made his own decisions first and advised his father afterwards. After cancer had taken his mother from him, his father had never married again and as a single parent raised him. Andrew was grateful for that but not to the point that he would give up on his own life. He recognized his father's hopes and accomplishments for his son, but also felt strongly about living life according to his own dreams.

Staring at the jagged peaks of Rockies below drifting past him, he wondered what his would dad do when he found out that he had quit his job and gone back to Manali. Ever since they hastily left India twenty years ago, there had been a silent war between them and his current decision was not going to remedy that. As he left the West behind, he felt as if the promise of the East welcomed those who were lost.

When he first arrived on Vancouver Island he was elated, as he found a new kind of freedom provided by the Strait of Georgia, the stretch of water between the mainland west coast and the Island, which somehow detached him from his father's influence. While at the university teaching English, he had progressed faster than the other faculty members and became an associate professor at the early age of thirty-one. But after years of the same job day in and day out, it had begun to wear on his soul, as he yearned for exotic lands and perhaps in his heart of hearts, he never gave up the hope of one day meeting Lalita again. He often dreamt of her.

She would now be forty years old, he mused. Would he recognize her if he ever saw her again? Would she recognize him? Would she want to meet him after what his father did to her and her father? He wondered if he would eventually get his chance to apologize to her.

As the plane left Rockies behind and sped over the wide-open prairies, he thought of the night when his father caught him naked with Lalita. How nervous and afraid he was. He had felt ashamed but rebellious, ashamed for he felt he had let down his father in upholding his image of propriety, and rebellious because he wanted to live his life on his own terms. The more he pondered what had happened twenty years ago, the more he felt he must find Lalita to finally have an opportunity to apologize to her.

But what if she was married and had children of her own? Indian girls under parental pressure do marry early. Meeting 'Lalita the mother' with her own children could be difficult and might destroy his illusion of that petite beautiful form he had been carrying in his heart all these years. Nevertheless, he still would like to meet up even just to say he was sorry. His mind was in a whirl and he slowly drifted into a deep sleep as the plane quietly left the Canadian landscape behind and headed out over the open sea towards England.

The airhostess awakened him as they were serving breakfast and were about ninety minutes away from landing at Heathrow Airport. Finally the jet made a soft landing and taxied to terminal three. Andrew was relieved to find that he was departing from the same terminal, as he hated catching a bus between terminals. As he walked up to a departure screen to double-check his departure time, only an hour and a half away, to his horror he saw that his flight was leaving from terminal four. He rushed to the information desk to clarify and there it was explained to him that Air India flights had moved from terminal three to the newly refurbished terminal four.

He cursed under his breath and rushed downstairs to catch the bus to take him to terminal four. While waiting for the bus and then going through security again, he began to panic due to the short time allotted to him to catch the flight, but many other Canadians in the transit line up at the security booth understood his predicament and pushed him to the front of the line. He did manage to arrive at the gate in time to board his flight. He always preferred a window seat and once he settled down in one, he relaxed and started dreaming of Manali. He was on his way.

TWENTY-TWO

The Air India jet on its easterly approach glided in and touched down at the new state-of-the-art Indira Gandhi International Airport, formerly known as the Palam Airport, built originally in World War II by the British. The airport was bustling with the sea of humanity, claiming to serve close to thirty million passengers a year. Andrew could have easily believed it for he thought that they were all there the day he arrived. He struggled through the formalities of immigration and customs and made his way out to hail a taxi to take him to the bus station. Once he found the right bus and secured his window seat, he let out a sigh of relief.

Leaving the city limits and the maddening crowd behind, he viewed the green fields welcoming him back to India, the India he loved. He could not wait to see those majestic mountains, and although the journey was over five hundred kilometers and more than ten hours long, he felt refreshed as the bus headed north for the mountains.

He glanced around the bus and could have sworn that he was transported back to the sixties. Most of the passengers were young adults from various European countries wearing colorful clothes and some young ladies, covering their heads with headscarves, were all carrying heavy backpacks. A young blond man pulled out his guitar from its case and started strumming a tune. Just like in the hippie era, these young travellers too were seeking spiritual experiences in the mystique of the exotic Indian landscape.

Andrew looked at his violin case and wondered if the group would mind him joining the young guitar player. He guessed that the young crowd around him could be half his age and he felt out of place in even conceiving the idea of joining their musical soiree. But then an attractive young girl with a head full of tight curly golden locks, that could not have been more than twenty years old, spotted Andrew's violin case and smiled broadly at him. In a heavy French accent, she said, "Won't you join us, please?"

Andrew wanted to decline the offer but his heart encouraged him and hesitantly his hands moved to the violin case, unclipped it and he took out the violin. The crowd changed seats to let Andrew and the guitarist sit together and after a few minutes of tuning their instruments, they started to jam together. A couple of hours evaporated like minutes and Andrew could not remember the last time he had so much unbridled fun, when his mind and soul fused together and he enjoyed the simplest gifts of life.

When the bus reached Manali, he promised to look up the guitarist and the French girl again, and they told him where they were staying in Manali. Andrew stepped out of the bus and looked around. "Holy smokes," he said softly, "what have they done to this place?" The rising demand of tourism had resulted in many cafes, hotels and shops, and traffic on the Mall Road that seemed to have grown multifold. Nevertheless, it was still exotic in its colors, sounds, food, costumes, and languages, compared to Calgary or Victoria. He was happy to be in Manali. He hired a rickshaw to take him to his hotel about fifty meters away.

As the rickshaw puller grunted with every push on the pedals, Andrew took note of the area. The town looked as if each year of existence had slowly chipped away at the optimistic belief that everything would turn out all right in the end. He realized, as he looked around, that he might never have a fairy-tale ending. But familiar buildings in the aging streets and crumbling edifices offered their own comforting perspective. A life that seemed attainable.

Through his travel agent he had found himself a good deal at the Ibex Hotel in Manali that was situated on the Mall Road only fifty meters from the bus station. He was told that the location of this hotel was ideal as one could enjoy the evenings by strolling down the Mall Road to experience its busy market life and various funky cafes, and yet at the same time enjoy the surrounding dense forests and snow-capped peaks of the amazing Himalayas.

The hotel was clean, pleasant and staff friendly but turned out to be a little pricy. He decided to move to a cheaper hotel after a day or so. He took delight in everything around him and as soon as he got to his room and put his head on the pillow, he fell into a deep sleep that lasted all through the night.

TWENTY-THREE

He awoke fresh the next day and ravenous. The sun was shining on the tender green leaves of morning, and the woods stood tall in the vast open valley. He sat up in bed, looking dreamily out through the window, his arms folded across his chest.

Minutes later he was dressing and half-dreaming of life in an exotic land, a life away from the rat race of Canada: a life of freedom. He headed straight to the German bakery for breakfast. He was disappointed on two accounts. First, the bakery seemed to have become more like a hippy's joint with smokers and loud music; and second, the Mall Road has lost that blend of ethnicity he craved.

In the afternoon he talked to a local travel agent and asked about other hotels in the area. After listening to Andrew's requirements the travel agent said, "There is a small hotel called Drifters' Inn. TripAdvisor ranked it number one on their website. But the one I think you would like best is called 'Silver Moon, Pink Balcony.' It is said that on nights with a full moon, when standing on one's bright pink balcony, the moon glowing in the light reflected from the snowy peaks of the Himalayan Mountains appears as if it's made of silver."

Andrew loved full moons and liked the sound of 'Silver Moon, Pink Balcony.' He was about to say yes when the agent further added, "Very popular with Europeans, just booked a couple of days back some French tourists there."

So it was done and Andrew moved into his new small boutique hotel. And he was not disappointed; though it was small, it was charming and the staff was friendly. The room he had was a large room for a small, boutique hotel with ample furniture: in the corner on the right was a bed with a cushioned headrest; beside it, nearest the door, an ornate and painted chair. A small coffee table covered by a bright blue-, saffron- and turmeric-colored cloth stood in front of the chair.

Andrew walked up to the wall opposite to the bed. There, two maroon, crushed velvet-covered chairs sat on either side of a large window overlooking the street below and the lush green, vast valley beyond. He loved the awe-inspiring view. The window frame was adorned with white cotton lace fringe, perhaps a legacy of an old British decorative cottage design. On the side wall near the door was a heavily polished teakwood chest of drawers complementing the rest of the furnishings in the room. The paisley design in the muted, multi-colored wallpaper was applied on all the walls. Every sign of poetry and even romance was present in the room.

He loved the pink balconies of the small boutique hotel and couldn't wait for the full moon in the night ahead. He liked that the location was in old Manali with its old Manali charm and there he hoped to have a better chance of finding the whereabouts of Lalita. The village had a primitive air; it was rustic, and had the decorative simplicity the artists and poets were forever seeking.

Also, it was easier from his new hotel to take a few minutes' walk and get out into the country. From his balcony he had a glimpse of the river in the distance that brought back some sweet memories. That night when he went to bed in his new hotel he had a sleep the likes of which he hadn't enjoyed for a long time.

The next morning Andrew woke up early and, standing by his window, watched the fiery, red-hot globe emerging on the horizon in the eastern sky. It peaked above the distant mountains and seemed to stop for a while, as if observing the valley to which it was about to give life. Then, with measured speed and in effortless movement, it rose high over the mountains and gloriously proceeded on its path, giving light and life to the landscape below.

The mist hung over the waters, over the wide shallows of the river, and the sun, coming through the morning mist, made lovely whitish-yellow lights beneath the bluish haze, so that it seemed like the beginning of the world. A hawk soaring high in the cloudless sky reminded Andrew of the story of *Garuda*, as told to him by his mother, a mythological bird known as protector against all snakes or evil. It was like some strange symbol in the sky, and Andrew watched it almost hypnotized.

Andrew decided to go for a walk out in the country. Once he escaped the hustle of the town and was into the country, the initial shock he'd had at seeing the damage done to the town through modernization subsided and then everything he saw was suffused in this faint glow of old memories. It was as if his receptive faculties were afloat in a rich thick medium, like the fond de cuisson without which no good French chef will practice his culinary art. Yes, it was spring, with the Himachal valley bursting into bloom in acres and acres of silver fruit-blossoms, where a few weeks before were only dead boughs.

He had forgotten how lovely the little river was, with its shimmering, ever-changing wavelets. It seemed to him like a living companion while he wandered along the bank, and listened to its high, rushing voice, as if Lalita was crying out for him. He looked around and remembered those large dipping willows. He remembered the stone bridge. This is where he used to walk with Lalita. *Where is she now?*

He sat on a bench by the riverbank and closed his eyes. He felt a curious yet pleasant sensation in his heart. It was as if light fused in darkness and darkness fused in light, as in the rosy snow beneath the twilight. It was a magical moment and he was happy that he made the decision to run from the rat race of the western world to find this peaceful moment that somehow resonated only with the eastern civilizations. Perhaps it was because he was so well acquainted with the mysterious and mytho-logical stories of India his mother had told him when he was a little boy.

In the early afternoon he returned to old town and wandered through various shops of trinkets where the tourists were busily bartering over prices of handicrafts.

He had a leisurely lunch at a cafe and let the busyness of life go by him. He was content. As the evening approached a light rain fell. He didn't mind; he loved the rain.

He went for a stroll again through the woods. The drizzle of rain was like a veil over the world, mysterious, hushed, and crisp with the freshness of spring. He got cold as he hurried across the path by the river that meandered through the valley. The wood was silent, still and secret in the evening drizzle, full of the mystery of sleepy buds, half unsheathed flowers. In the dim twilight, pine trees glistened, dripping with tiny water drops as if they had washed off the last of the winter blues, and the green things on earth seemed to hum with gentle their life force.

Darkness had fallen and the moon was rising; but there was a peculiar breathlessness in the air. There were crowds of people in the street; foreign and Indian tourists alike were wandering in and out of various cafes; local people had come out for a walk; there was the smell of incense, marigolds, and jasmine in the air.

As the day had drained of its soft light of spring and the pleasant night grew luminous in moonlight, he felt more melancholy than usual. Back in his room he peered out his window and saw a large and shining white shard of glass from a shattered cosmic window lingering in the sky, frail yet prodigiously influential.

Soon he sank into deep thought, or more accurately speaking, into a complete mindlessness. It was perhaps the best sleep he'd had for a long time. He was home.

City born, he loved the country life.

TWENTY-FOUR

Several days had passed and Andrew, living in some kind of bliss, had neither attempted to start writing a novel nor had he actively looked for Lalita, something he had promised to do upon arrival in Manali. He was content listening to the sounds of exotic languages in the street, watching the colorful attire of various peoples, smelling the sweet scents of spring flowers and wallowing in the daily magic of Himalayan sunrises and silvery moonlit nights.

No, he had not forgotten Lalita. There was always a yearning in his heart to once again take her in his arms and if nothing else, then say goodbye to her, and even tell her how he had missed her, but he had to find her first. With days passing and spring yielding to summer, a special form of misery had begun to oppress him of late. There was nothing poignant, nothing acute about it; but there was a feeling of permanence, a sense of eternity about it; it brought a foretaste of hopeless years of this cold leaden misery. Towards evening this sensation usually began to weigh on him more heavily.

"With this idiotic physical weakness, depending on the moon or sunsets or sunrises or something, one can't help doing something stupid. You'll find Lalita and seek her forgiveness no matter what the consequences," he muttered bitterly. He knew exactly where Lalita's house was but every time he contemplated walking up to it his courage failed him. It was as if there was a glass wall between him and the house and to crash through that wall would mean shattering lives, and illusions. A married Indian woman, especially from a poor village background, living under the strict, traditional culture may not be accustomed to receiving a visit from an old lover. *Then again, no woman of any culture would without raising a few serious concerns,* he mused.

One morning as he finished his breakfast and a second cup of coffee, he chastised himself for being such a coward. *You are not going to accomplish anything if you are going to bury your head in the sand,* he upbraided himself. He felt a sensation rising from the pit of his stomach and almost physically dislodging him from his chair to take a step outside the café and head for Lalita's house. And before he knew it he was doing exactly that. With legs heavy with lethargy, he walked down the street and after a short walk of twenty minutes, he was standing right across the street from her house.

His heart began to race and his body started to tingle. He could not believe that after twenty years of absence, he was about to face Lalita again. *What will I say to her?* "Hello, I'm Andrew, and I have come to apologize for what my dad did to you and your father twenty years ago," he ruminated. What if she never divulged to her husband what happened to her all those years ago? *It would be absurd and could very well be injurious to unearth old secrets in front of her husband*, he meditated. Maybe he should first find out if she was a married woman, and perhaps he should try to arrange for her to come out to meet him at a café rather than barging unannounced into her house? Somehow this idea became fixed in his mind and he decided to knock at the neighbors' door and ask a few questions about Lalita.

He crossed the street and went up to the front door of Lalita's next-door neighbor's house. After a few minutes and as he was just about to give up and return to his hotel, an old woman opened the door and stared at him with inquiring eyes. She was a diminutive, withered old woman in her late seventies, with sharp malignant eyes and a sharp little nose. Her colorless, somewhat grizzled hair was thickly smeared with oil, and she wore an old sari of faded colors. Around her thin, short neck of shriveled, hanging flesh, was a necklace made of black leather and blue beads, and, even though it was summer, to protect herself from the cold mountain air, she wore a sweater filled with holes and yellow with age. The old woman coughed in the cool air.

Andrew cleared his throat and asked in his broken Hindi, "Excuse me, but do you know if Lalita still lives next door?"

"Why don't you knock at the door and ask for yourself," she answered, in a harsh tone.

"I don't want to surprise her," said Andrew, not knowing what else to say.

"You won't," she said abruptly, "because no one lives next door. The house has been empty for several years now."

"Are you sure?"

"I know what I know," she said curtly. Andrew thought that perhaps she was thinking of him as a wealthy tourist looking in the poorer neighborhood for a lady of the night. Several seconds passed; he even pictured a sneer in her eyes, as though she had already guessed everything. He felt that he was losing his mind, frightened that if she were to look like that and not say a word for another half minute, he would just turn around and run.

TWENTY-FIVE

Suddenly the essence of what he had just heard struck him. His assumption that Lalita would always be here was wrong; she was gone. And it seemed to him all at once that he was turned to stone, that it was like a dream in which one is being pursued, nearly caught, to be killed, and he is rooted to the spot and cannot even move his arms. *This cannot be*, he said to himself, *Lalita was supposed to be here*. The beating of his heart became pain. The bright summer sun shone straight in his eyes, so that it hurt to keep them open, and he felt his head spinning, much like a man in a fever is apt to feel when he comes out into the street on a bright sunny day.

Andrew muttered a soft thank you and she shut the door loudly. As if in a trance, he perfunctorily tried a couple of more houses and every time received the same answer. "Never heard of anyone called Lalita." People seemed almost hostile at seeing his presence in the neighborhood. Strangers were never welcome or trusted in the poor neighborhood of Dalits.

The house was still there but no one had heard of Lalita or her father. The exterior of the mud house was dark and marked with cracks, covered in dust like a broken and forgotten toy abandoned in a sandbox. The roof sagged with old age and neglect and leaned heavily on tilting walls, much as an old woman with a burdened back rests precariously on her cane. An uninhabitable dwelling, he could see it for what it was now.

She had disappeared from the village and from his life. He stood in the middle of the street wondering what to do next, like a lost traveller in a strange city. He couldn't remember when he started walking back to his hotel. When he reached the street, in trepidation he looked back...at Lalita's old house...and at once averted his eyes. He was conscious of a terrible inner turmoil.

After twenty years of waiting he was convinced of finding salvation through seeking forgiveness for his father's sins, for his cowardice. He had such high expectations of seeing her again and asking for her forgiveness, had hoped that he could find peace and perhaps even the ice between him and his father would melt. Once the wrong his father did was undone, he could have eased the guilt he had been fostering in his heart for so long.

An hour or so later a little clarity returned to his head. There were other ways he could find out her whereabouts. Perhaps the police would know. After a short deliberation he decided against it in case there was a case still pending against his father. He remembered the snippets of conversation he'd heard the police officer have with his father, advising him to leave and never come back to Manali.

He sat outside at a roadside café and noticed the sudden appearance at his feet of what looked like a child no more than six years old holding a small box filled with shoe polish tins and brushes. "Shoeshine, *Sahib*," he asked. Andrew resented the intrusion; he cherished his solitude as his last freedom in life. But then looking at the angelic, half-starved face he mellowed.

"Okay," said Andrew, forcing a thin smile.

A couple of minutes or so later, after finishing shining his shoes, the boy with his little head wobbling like a Russian wooden doll said, "Five dollars, *Sahib*."

"What?" Andrew, knowing that he was being ripped off, laughed at the vivacity of the boy and took out his wallet. Suddenly and out of nowhere a tall man appeared and, thrusting a five-rupee note into the little boy's hand, shouted, "Run away now, you little scoundrel, and don't give a bad name to India!" And then turning to Andrew, he said politely, "Don't mind these kids, they'll try anything to make extra cash for their family."

"You didn't have to do that. I knew it was too much but I was happy to help him by giving him five dollars," Andrew replied, puzzled by the man's reaction.

"Don't worry about it," said the stranger, "enjoy your day."

As he started to leave, Andrew stood up from his seat, saying, "Please let me pay you."

"It was nothing, forget about it."

"At least let me buy you a coffee. I could do with some company too."

The stranger thought for a moment and then extending his hand, said, "Ajit Kumar."

"Andrew Donavan," responded Andrew, shaking his hand and then gesturing to the waiter for another coffee.

Suddenly Andrew realized that Ajit was staring at him as if he knew him. Andrew tried but could not recollect if he was someone he knew twenty years ago.

TWENTY-SIX

Ajit raised his brows as if contemplating something to say and then in a manner as if he has known Andrew for a long time, said, "If you don't mind my saying so, looks like you are not having a good day. Something I could help you with?"

Andrew, sipping his coffee, considered this friendly and fascinating stranger. Perhaps in his early twenties, Ajit was almost six feet tall, slimly built with large, almond-shaped soft brown eyes. He wore his black hair long, and high on the bridge of his nose were round-rimmed glasses. He looked like an Indian version of what John Lennon looked like in his later days.

"I don't think so," said Andrew softly, "well, not unless you are psychologist."

"That I am," said Ajit, putting his coffee cup back on the table and looking straight into Andrew's eyes, "fresh out of university. Brand new with hardly any mileage."

Andrew laughed at his candor. "I'm going to be just fine. It's just that, well, you know," Andrew hesitated, "nothing time can't heal."

"Ah, you believe in philosophy. I'll tell you what you really need," responded the new friend. "You need a consultation with a practicing Buddhist. They have a great philosophy on life."

"Really?" Andrew began to enjoy the company of his newfound friend. "And you are going to tell me next that you can refer me to an excellent Buddhist philosopher?"

He answered, "You are looking at one."

"Buddhist philosopher and psychologist?"

"At your service." He took his jacket off and draped it over the back of his chair. "We could start with a simple step. Okay?"

"Okay, why not. Let's do it."

"Describe your father." He nodded after asking his question, exuding confidence.

"I don't know you well enough to talk with you about my family." Andrew wondered if he was being duped.

"Indulge me," insisted Ajit, readjusting his position to sit tall in his chair.

"You want me to physically describe my father?" inquired Andrew, now the one with eyebrows raised.

"Yeah. You know, how tall he is, what his complexion is like, what color eyes, then go into little more detail, like how he talks, how he smiles and was there a time when you looked up to him. Go on."

"Okay," said Andrew, with more amusement this time than puzzlement. "Well, in Canada he is commonplace in complexion, in features, in manners, and in voice. Nothing distinctive there, well, not that I can think of."

"You are really trying, aren't you?" said Ajit, shaking his head from side to side. "Come on, try a little harder. Describe his build."

"Okay," he repeated, and sighed. "He is tall and strong. His eyes, blue, are remarkably cold, and he can make those eyes as sharp as a knife. On his lips, the sense is of something stealthy—a smile—not a smile—I remember it, but I can't explain."

"Come on," encouraged Ajit, "you're doing so well. Keep going."

"This smile, it is almost lifeless, well, most of the time. It is only after he says something that the smile intensifies, but just for an instant. It always seems to come at the end of his speeches, as if to make the meaning of the commonest phrases appear absolutely inexplicable. Oh, people tend to listen to him, or perhaps they listen to his wealth. He commands veneration or maybe more accurately, recognition in his circle of friends, yet he inspires neither love nor fear, nor even respect. He inspires uneasiness. That's it. Uneasiness. Not a definite mistrust—just unease—nothing more. That is how I see him, and have always known him."

"Hmm, well, that tells me a lot about you and your father. You want to know my findings?"

"Not sure that I do but go ahead," said Andrew, laughing.

"You are not totally sure but think that you don't like your father; but you do desperately want him to love you, and you want this to happen without your doing anything about it. That's about it in a nutshell. Oh, one more thing. On the philosophical side, you are in search of truth, something that would present to you all the answers to your problems. You know, like what is wrong, why your life is the way it is, that kind of truth."

"Now wait a minute," resisted Andrew, while fascinated by the amazing deduction made by this young man, "when nothing else matters, people search for truth. They believe it will free them. But the truth is, and you can take this to the bank, that there is no truth. For truths and lies, rights and wrongs, are what we like to believe as distinctive and far apart. But actually they are not. In fact, they are so intermingled that at times it is hard to make a distinction between them."

"I think you have something there," said Ajit contemplatively, "but I am afraid you have got your thoughts a little mixed up. It is not the truth you are talking about, as we are surrounded by the truth; it is instead faith, or rather the lack of it is, that you are seeking."

As Ajit looked at his watch, Andrew realized that he had kept the young man for quite a while, so he stood up, shook his hand and said, "Thank you. You were very helpful and I hope we meet again."

Ajit simply nodded, put on his jacket and left. Andrew now knew why he liked this country so much. He learned more in an hour about himself than he had in the past ten years.

TWENTY-SEVEN

Though he was happy to find a new friend in Ajit, it was with a heavy heart that he returned to his hotel and went to sleep in the middle of the day. He wanted to awake anew, in a world of hope and promise, to restart his life, unencumbered and fresh.

Days melted into weeks and almost a month had passed as Andrew met with Ajit frequently to discuss and learn Indian philosophy. He let time slip away and hoped that somewhere and somehow one day he would find a way to locate Lalita. But in the meantime he diverted his attention to focus on why he came to Manali: to find the inspiration to write a novel. He started spending time in cafes and reading local newspapers in the hopes of finding a subject that would appeal to him. He enjoyed talking with the locals and tourists alike, discussing what brought them to Manali. He knew he had several more months until winter, so he took it easy and leisurely took notes on people and events around him, as he started to enjoy the local ambiance.

One day when he woke up and left his hotel for a walk, he suddenly stopped in the street as if struck by déjà vu. He dropped down on a nearby bench for a few moments and then rose back again to his feet, looking around in wonder as though surprised at finding himself in this place, and went towards his favorite cafe. He was pale, his eyes glowed, he was exhausted, but he seemed suddenly to breathe more easily.

Though restless, he felt he had cast off that fearful burden that had so long been weighing upon him, and all at once had a sense of relief and peace in his soul. He realized that for over a month he had not given a single thought to his past life in Canada. "Lord," he prayed, "show me my path—I renounce that accursed Canadian dream of mine."

Then his sole respite was to walk along the Mall Road, backwards and forwards, blotting out the surrounding sounds of traffic, feeling safe in the silence and solitude of the Himalayan Mountains. He allowed his mind's eye to dwell on whatever bright visions of twenty years ago rose before it—and, certainly, they were many and glowing; to let his heart be lightened. An inner voice told a tale that recounted the magical moments of the few months when he was here twenty years ago—a tale his imagination recreated, and narrated continuously; quickened with the aroma of spices, the colors of flowers, the commotion of life surrounding him.

It had happened to him before wandering the streets of Manali, not to notice the name of streets or the faces of people passing by, and he was accustomed to walk like that. This was is his small happy world in which he was comfortable being lost. But there was at first sight something so strange about the man in front of him, that gradually his attention was riveted upon him, at first reluctantly and, as it were, resentfully, and then more and more intently. He felt a sudden desire to find out what it was that was so strange about this man.

He walked along quietly and sedately, without hurry, to avoid awakening suspicion. He scarcely looked at the passersby, tried to escape looking at their faces at all, and to be as inconspicuous as possible. Glancing out of the corner of his eye in the direction of the man, he remained puzzled. He tried to remember but could not place him. *Could he be one of the help who worked at their bungalow as a gardener or a cook?* he wondered. Then suddenly his mind cleared and he knew exactly who he was. He hurried his steps and caught up with him. He touched the man's arm and he turned to face Andrew.

"*Arre, Chote Sahib*," the old man, who had served as the driver when Andrew was fifteen, exclaimed in typical Indian fashion and then, quickly putting his hands together, said politely, "*Namaste, Sahib*. You look exactly like the *Bara Sahib*." His grey hair was unkempt and his back was slightly bent, maybe under the burden of carrying the responsibility of taking care of his big family.

"How are you?" asked Andrew, in an excited voice, putting one of his hands on his shoulder as a sign of affection. He added, "How is your family?"

"Everything is fine, with God's help. How is *Bara Sahib*?"

"He is good," he answered, and then inquired, "Are you still working?"

"Oh, yes, *Sahib*. But if you like I could quit and work for you. You're the *Bara Sahib* now."

"Oh no, I'm just visiting for a short while and don't need a driver. But it is so good to see you. Would you like some tea?"

"*Arre Sahib*, it is an honor that you asked. It is not our place to sit with you to have tea but thank you so much. Have you been to see your old villa?"

"No," said Andrew. "To tell you the truth, after my mother passed away, the villa we lived in here was my first real home. And though it's been nearly twenty years since I last saw it, I was too happy there to revisit it as a stranger, its memories still live in me. My time in that villa was one of the happiest and the unhappiest." Andrew gave a little laugh and in a contemplative tone added, "But then, isn't that what life is all about?"

The driver simply nodded his head in compliance and said nothing. Andrew felt a little annoyed with their stupid traditions of class and status. He would have liked to sit over a cup of tea and ask him dozens of questions. He said, "Look, I hate to ask you this but did you ever see Lalita again? You remember that Dalit girl twenty years ago that caused so much trouble with my father, don't you?"

A frown wrinkled his face as he wiped his face with one of his hands. He nodded, as if considering how much to reveal. Then in a soft voice he said, "Oh, yes *Sahib*. Only a few days after you and your father left India she was back here with her father. Her father was pretty badly beaten up with a broken arm and other injuries. There was someone with them. He was some activist with political connections. They managed to register their case with the police, who arrested your father's friends for questioning. But apparently no charges were filed. All those ONGC engineers have powerful connections. The case was closed due to insufficient evidence and lack of eyewitnesses. There is no justice for Dalits."

"Perhaps you are wrong," said Andrew in a contemplative voice, "perhaps there is some justice. Oh, I know twenty years have passed but it is never too late for justice to be served." Andrew noticed that none of his response made any impression on the old man so he persevered. "I would like to see Lalita to apologize to her and make amends. I'll explain everything to her, and hope she will understand. Do you know where she lives?"

"Oh, I sure do know where she lives, and she is quite safe now," said the driver with an edge of sarcasm in his voice that did not escape Andrew's attention.

TWENTY-EIGHT

Andrew looked at him with his brows raised in question. When the driver did not respond, he asked, "Well, do tell." He continued, "Is she in town? Where is she? No one lives at that old house anymore, right?"

"She is with her gods. She went a long time ago, *Sahib*."

Suddenly his breathing stopped as the revelation pierced his heart. "When?" asked Andrew in a weak voice, not believing what he'd just heard. "What happened? Was she sick?"

"Sick," said the driver, his voice now dripping with acerbity, "no, *Sahib*, she was not sick. She was murdered. Her beaten body was found at the bottom of an abandoned well about a year after you and your father left."

"Murdered." He repeated, "Lalita was murdered?" He almost choked with rage as soon as a thought crossed his mind—he was responsible for what happened to her. A curse rose from the bottom of his soul. He was crushed and even humiliated. He could have laughed at himself in his anger.... A dull animal rage boiled within him. She was not just a friend. She was more than that.

"But…" The driver let his statement linger in the air, indicating he was not certain if he should add more to his unfinished thought.

"But what?" Andrew said instinctively, as he realized that the driver had more to say.

"But now it is causing a lot of stink. Some people are insistent even after all these years."

"What do you mean by stink? Are you sure you won't have some tea?"

He ignored the second question and answered the first, "Well, times are changing, *Sahib*. In your time here no one cared about Lalita and what happened to her and why police sought to suppress the case. But now, about a year ago, some activists from the 'Movement for the Annihilation of Cast' visited this area and one of its members or friends is trying to reopen the case to bring your father's friends to justice."

Andrew suddenly felt weak and light headed. Color drained from his cheeks and he let out a faint cry. He grabbed the driver's arm for support. *My Lalita*, he thought, *I will never see her again. This cannot be true.*

"Are you okay, *Sahib*?" asked the driver in a concerned voice and then looking around suggested, "would you like to sit down on the bench?"

After a few deep breaths, Andrew regained his composure and in a faint voice answered, "I'm all right. You said Lalita was murdered. Are you sure about that or was that gossip? Could it have been a suicide?"

"Oh, no. I'm quite sure, *Sahib*. Remember, her body was severely beaten. She was murdered. I'm sorry. I know you were friends with Lalita. I am so sorry to be the one to give you this news. I am sure you came here for a holiday and not to be bothered by what happened to a Dalit girl. I am sorry, *Sahib*."

Andrew did not detect in his voice the kind of hatred and bitterness he had before when uttering her name. He looked at him quizzically and said, "You don't seem to mind talking about her. Do you still think that Dalit are an untouchable class?"

"Oh *Sahib*," he said, as his neck wobbled like a bobble-head doll, it seemed something only Indians could do with ease. "I'm an ignorant and uneducated man. What do I know? The government is telling us that the Dalit are now educated and smart people and the law protects them. Only three years ago a Dalit from the Bahujan Samaj Party was elected as the Chief Minister of our country's biggest state, Uttar Pradesh. Time is changing us, *Sahib*, our culture is very different now than it was twenty years ago when you were here."

Andrew wanted to find out everything that had happened in the past twenty years but the driver apologized, as he had to leave for his work.

After saying goodbye, Andrew had a terrible longing for some distraction, but he did not know what to do, what to attempt. A new, overwhelming sensation was gaining more and more mastery over him; this was an immeasurable, almost physical, repulsion for everything surrounding him, an obstinate, malignant feeling of hatred. Suddenly, an utterly unexpected and exceedingly simple question perplexed and bitterly confounded him—was he responsible for her murder?

Andrew leaned against a stone wall overlooking the vast valley, reflecting on what he had just learned. A million questions whirled around in his head, none more prominent than the one that shook his very core—did she die because of him? Then something strange happened. He didn't know what made him do it but he walked into a bar and ordered a beer.

He looked at the glassful of beer on the table in front of him, and gulped it down with relish, as though quenching a flame in his breast. But in another minute the beer had gone to his head, and a faint and even pleasant shiver ran down his spine. He ordered another.

TWENTY-NINE

The next day when he woke up with a massive hangover he could not remember how many beers he drank the previous evening, or what time or how he got to his hotel room. Yesterday evening was a blur. He found it hard to fix his mind on anything. He longed to forget himself altogether, to forget everything, and then to wake up and begin life anew.

He had never expected that he would ever wake up feeling like that. Although uncertain about the time he spent in the bar, he remembered every detail of the previous day, of his encounter with his old driver, and he knew that a novel experience had befallen him, with an impression unlike anything he had known before.

He now realized that the dream that had fired his imagination was hopelessly unattainable—so unattainable that he felt positively sick, and he hastened to suppress what he had learned about Lalita. As he stood in front of the bathroom mirror and shaved, his brows were knitted, his lips compressed, his eyes feverish. He stared at his own reflection, and there was restlessness in his movements.

"I will never be able to apologize to my Lalita again." As he said this to himself, he was suddenly overwhelmed with confusion and turned pale. Again that awful sensation he had known of late passed with deadly chill over his soul. Again it became plain to him that he had wasted most of his life chasing dreams that were unattainable. *What is the point of living a life that no one cares about?* The anguish of this thought was such that for a moment he almost forgot himself. He showered, changed, and not looking at anyone in the lobby walked towards the hotel front entrance.

A few minutes later he found himself sitting in a café sipping a large, black coffee. The events of the previous evening slowly began to take shape in his mind. Perhaps all was not lost. He wondered if it was his destiny to be here, acknowledging that the timing of his visit when people were trying to reopen Lalita's case was uncanny. Could this be the story, his and that of Lalita's, he was supposed to write?

The rise of Dalit against thousands of years of prejudice against the untouchables could be a fascinating subject and he also had a personal interest in finding how and why Lalita was murdered. He from his experience at the University of Victoria knew that to ascertain what is happening politically in the region, one has to go to the cafes where students hang out. He decided to ask Ajit so when he met him later that day he asked, "I would like to write a book about the Dalit people and their struggle, but not based on historical facts, more related to what is going on now, you know, something specific, something current."

"Really?" responded Ajit, failing to hide the curiosity in his voice. "Whatever happened to uncovering the truth about your father?"

"I think it is a lost cause anyway. I have had a hard time getting close to my father because he once did something for which I am not sure he is sorry, and I am certain he will never suffer for the pain he inflicted."

"He will suffer if he is sorry for his victim. Pain and suffering are always inevitable for those of great intelligence and an open heart. I don't think your father is a bad man. Perhaps you ought to give him a chance. The really great men must, I think, experience a great sadness," he added.

"Ajit," said Andrew, assuming a serious look, "before you start peering down into my heart again, all I can tell you is that I am very interested in researching the Dalit situation in modern India. Someone suggested that I ought to talk with students, perhaps at Bob Dylan's Café. What do you think? Is that a good idea?"

"The one in the heart of old Manali where they play Bob Dylan's songs?" answered Ajit. "Ah, it is a hangout, yes, a place for interesting people. But now it is more popular with the tourists than the locals. The local crowd is at the new Green Forest Café on the Hadimba temple on old Manali road, only a few hundred meters from the temple. Unfortunately you won't find cakes and cookies there, it serves Tibetan soups, veggie dumplings and some great Indian snacks."

"Perfect, sounds like my kind of place. I guess I will start there," said Andrew.

"You want me to come along?" asked Ajit.

"No, this is something I have to do myself. The locals may not trust you on the subject of the Dalit, you know what I mean?"

"I've a better idea," suggested Ajit. "I'll take you right into the heart of the action and introduce you to a couple of my friends that are activists and raising awareness to support the Dalits' cause."

Andrew looked closely at Ajit and found no reason to distrust him, saying, "You're full of surprises."

"It is a small world."

"Did I hear you right that these activists are your friends?"

"Well, more friends than activists," he answered with a grin on his face. "These friends are young people with great ideological thoughts."

Andrew let out a sigh and in a contemplative voice said, "Whatever happened to the great race of India, the wonder that it once was?"

Ajit pursed his lips. "Some of these mighty and influential people descend from the Indian race that was once called *Suryavanshi* or 'Worshippers of the Sun.' They might better be called 'Worshippers of the Darkness.' Their souls are dark."

"Isn't there a legacy of the great ones that may remind people of what they were, what they could be?"

"Sure," answered Ajit, combing his hair back with his fingers, "it is in the form of generations-old festivals. My favorite is the annual festival of light, *Diwali*, that is celebrated to dispel the darkness of the past, offering the promise of an illuminated future; the whole story of mankind could be symbolized by such a tradition. Don't you have such celebrations in Canada?"

"Well, we do, but perhaps not quite the way you put it. We do celebrate Christmas but perhaps not with the same spirit as you celebrate *Diwali*, for everything in Canada seems to be so over commercialized. My mother used to tell me the story of *Diwali* and I wish she had celebrated it."

Ajit remained quiet as if pondering what Andrew just said.

"When are we going, then, to this Green Forest Café?" asked Andrew, breaking Ajit's trance.

"What? Oh, yeah. Meet me tomorrow morning at ten at the Green Forest Café and I'll bring my friends to introduce them to you."

THIRTY

The next morning Andrew looked at his watch and saw it was about ten minutes to ten so he quickened his pace. At about ten as he entered the Green Forest Café, he saw a few small groups scattered around the café eating and drinking and engaged in animated discussions. Finally he noticed Ajit with two of his friends sitting in a far corner. Ajit saw him too and waved for him to come.

Ajit made the introductions, "Meet Dr. Andrew Donavan, an English professor from Canada seeking to write a book about the Dalit movement." Then he turned towards his friends, "This is Jyoti and this is Sunil Sharma."

Andrew shook hands with Sunil and then extended a hand to Jyoti, but she folded her hands in traditional Indian greeting and said, "*Namaste.*"

Her slightly bowed head with half-closed eyes behind her folded hands suddenly stopped Andrew's world. She possessed an unquestionable uniformity of Indian style, broken only—and surprisingly—by two equally unexpected features: the sea-green eyes and bleached barley complexion. There was something in that face that gripped Andrew's heart. Momentarily everything faded from his focus, the surrounding din diminished and all he could see was the face of the young girl.

Jyoti was remarkably good looking; she was tall, strikingly well-proportioned, strong and self-reliant—the latter quality was apparent in every gesture, though it did not in the least detract from the grace of her movements. She reminded him of someone but he couldn't quite put a finger on it. Her hair was dark brown, there was a proud light in her sea-green eyes and yet at times a look of extraordinary kindness.

She was of lighter complexion compared to other Indians he had seen, but it seemed to catch the sun easily as evident in her face, which was radiant and fresh. Her mouth was rather small; the full pink lower lip projected a little as did her chin; it was the only irregularity in her beautiful face, but it gave it a peculiarly individual and almost haughty expression. Her face was always more serious and thoughtful than mischievous; but how well her smiles, how well her youthful, lighthearted, irresponsible laughter suited her face.

She sighed, and he noticed the secret pain that was on her lips, the smile of the slave who briefly rebels. Epiphany? He could not be sure for it was a sudden realization of truth, something he could feel but not express.

He wondered if she felt anything in her heart for he found her looking closely at his face. Unbeknownst to him she felt something compelling in his eyes. Sometimes he was handsome: sometimes as he looked sideways, downwards, and the light fell on him, he had the silent, enduring beauty of a stone-carved Ajanta statue, with his rather full eyes, and the strong arched brows, compressed mouth; that feature revealed his soul's immobility, a timelessness at which the Buddha aims, and which Ajanta statues express sometimes without ever aiming at it; something familiar.

Due to the eons of acquiescence in her race, instead of individual opinion, Jyoti felt a sudden, strange leap of sympathy for him, a leap mingled with compassion, and tinged with respect, amounting almost to affection.

"Is this a staring match?" Sunil asked, peering into their faces. Sunil was a strong-built, athletic-looking man with long hair typical of the sixties era, with large brown eyes and a goatee. His biceps were hardly contained in his tight-fitted sport shirt, and his large hands were wrapped around a coffee mug. He had a dark face, with stern features and a heavy brow; his eyes and gathered brows looked full of ire; he was at the peak of youth, but had not reached maturity; perhaps he was twenty-five.

Andrew blinked several times as if waking up from a deep trance and stuttered, "What? Oh, no. I'm sorry. I was just…"

Jyoti smiled for she noticed that Andrew had kind eyes, and a voice that told the quiet tale of its never having been raised.

"Just what, Dr. Donavan? You were staring at her for a long time, is something the matter?" Sunil's voice was soft but resolute as if it were more of a warning than a complaint.

"Andrew," he said, repeated, "please, call me Andrew, and I'm sorry, I wasn't really staring at you," directing his attention to her he continued, "I was miles away. I have been talking with Ajit and find India fascinating. I have also been researching the plight of the Dalit people and I understand you two are sympathetic to their cause. So I have a question to ask you, I mean all of you, okay?"

"Sure, go right ahead." It was Ajit who spoke this time, taking control of the situation, while the others looked on in silent compliance with suppressed smiles. The feeling was that of amusement rather than threatening. Ajit looked oldest of the three with the same long hair as that of Sunil but with a tall and lanky body. His features were feminine in nature and his voice was more of a whisper than one that carried excitement. He was a little darker in complexion compared to the other two, and that somehow added an air of maturity to him.

"Well, what I was thinking about," he paused for a moment before articulating his thoughts, and then expounded, "is that lately I've been reading a lot about reform in India and it seems that the past twenty years have been very progressive. And I don't mean just in the field of trade and commerce but also in human rights. Let me give you an example. Well, a good one would be the rights of the untouchable class. My question is that is it propaganda for political benefit or do you in your everyday life see such improvements around you?"

Andrew had chosen the question with an obvious interest. He realized that the more he could learn about the Dalit, the greater chance he would have of locating Lalita's murderer. It was an outside bet, but he was willing to try anything, save bringing the police system into it. But his innocent question had touched a nerve, as the faces of his listeners stiffened. *Remarkable,* he thought, *all three had the same reaction.* He wondered if he had said something wrong, perhaps touched on a subject that might be considered taboo.

THIRTY-ONE

At the prolonged silence, the feeling that something had gone terribly wrong grew in Andrew's mind. Fixing his eyes on Ajit, he looked at him as if appealing for his help. These were his friends and he must know, Andrew thought, what could be wrong with his inquiry. Before Andrew could contemplate his next move, Sunil broke the silence.

"The subject of the Dalit just popped into your head randomly, did it?" Sunil's expression of curiosity was still on his face but his voice was guarded.

"Would you rather talk about something else?" asked Andrew diplomatically for he did not want to upset anyone in case his question was inappropriate.

"No, let us talk about the Dalit problem, what is it that you want to know?" asked Jyoti, keeping a sharp eye on him.

"Just what I asked," said Andrew, now feeling a little awkward. "I just thought that India was making strides in modernizing its culture and wanted to learn the opinions of the young people."

"No offence, but you obviously know very little about Dalit and their centuries-old continuing fight against oppression," said the girl in a challenging tone.

"But," Andrew protested, "the untouchable class that before could not even mix with the rest of the society is now finding opportunity in politics and the business world. True?"

"When you approached us through Ajit, I was hoping you'd be different," she sighed and added, "you buy the book based on its cover, don't you?"

"Well," Andrew liked the way she presented her argument, wrapped in mystery and intrigue, and persisted, "I'm a good listener and a perpetual learner, so enlighten me."

Sunil spoke again, "No doubt, as you say, Professor, progress has been made but it is painfully slow and comes at a heavy price."

Andrew raised his brows for he felt Sunil had more to say. After a brief moment Sunil continued, "The ugliness of the whole thing is that when people cannot accept something even though logic dictates its appropriateness, then they resort to violence. And the traditionalists with their narrow-minded outlook always fall for the mob-mentality approach and pursue the path of destruction without questioning its validity."

"I'm afraid you lost me," said Andrew, shaking his head.

"The violence against the Dalit that Sunil is talking about," Jyoti interjected in an excited voice, "is a systemic violence including forced labor, denial of access to water and other public amenities, and sexual abuse. Oh, sure, the government passed a law in 1989, called the Prevention of Atrocities Act, to curb and punish violence against the Dalit, which is especially rampant in rural areas, but in practice the act has suffered from a near-complete failure in implementation. Policemen have displayed a consistent unwillingness to register offenses under the act. This reluctance stems partially from ignorance and also from peer protection."

Andrew could not believe his luck that with a simple question he had sparked quite a lively debate. These young people were motivated, informed, and believed in their argument. He wanted to pursue this further, so articulated, "Aren't there leaders," he asked with genuine concern, "who would step forward to support your cause? After all, all you need is one charismatic leader."

Jyoti laughed and her laughter was soft and musical like pearls from a broken strand falling and resonating on a marble floor. Once her laughter subsided she said, "This is a historical fight that goes back over two thousand years, it is not going to be resolved by a singular leader and government act. The earliest known historical person to have raised voice to protect the Dalit was Buddha and you don't find a more charismatic leader than that. Even he could not succeed, could he?"

Andrew had a delightful time talking with them and spent another hour discussing several other subjects. Jyoti asked him about his career as a teacher and listened intently to his response. She talked about her dream to become a professor one day. Andrew asked if they could all meet again and talk about the Dalit, they agreed and Jyoti asked if he could talk more about his experiences as a teacher. So, it was agreed that they would meet again in a couple of days.

Andrew had a restless night as every time he tried to construct a beautiful image of Jyoti in his mind the battered body of Lalita floating face down in a deep well replaced it. How frightened she must have been. How could people be such animals to murder such an innocent and fragile girl so brutally? He felt a rage within him as if someone had violated his family.

Two days later when they met again she came alone. She was in a bottle-green blouse and tight denim jeans with her thick soft-brown bangs bouncing on her forehead. Standing at five feet six, she was tall for an Indian girl and a powerhouse of unlimited energy. Andrew felt a curious attraction towards her that had more to do with admiration of her youth and beauty than a sexual attraction.

"Where are your friends?" asked Andrew, failing to hide his excitement at meeting her alone.

"Sunil comes from a wealthy family and his father doesn't like him mixing with us radicals. So, we are lucky if we see him once or twice a month. Ajit is a great friend but he is so wrapped around philosophy and psychology that I am sure he doesn't even know what day of the week it is. He is rather absent minded. They might join us later but for now you will have to put up with me."

Andrew stole a look from the corner of his eye and found her smiling. Her smile was half mysterious and half mischievous and he wondered if there was a covert message in her statement.

THIRTY-TWO

Andrew glanced around and found that some of the people in the café were shooting unfriendly looks in their direction. He could not determine if those surly looks were meant for him or Jyoti or perhaps because they were together in public. Suppressing his smile as he stirred a spoonful of sugar in his coffee, he said, "I'm glad you could make it."

They talked for twenty minutes about the teaching profession in Canada, when Andrew maneuvered the discussion towards the Dalit movement and said, "You know, I would like to develop a plot for my book based on some real cases and not write a book of boring historical facts."

"That sounds like a good idea, what do you have in mind?"

"I'm curious about an old case. A girl called Lalita was murdered some twenty years back right here in this town and I believe someone is fighting to reopen her case. Do you know anything about it?"

"You're kidding me, right?" she said, and a flicker of a smile appeared on her face. "You know it is us, well, mainly me, don't you?" Suddenly the expression on her face transformed from curiosity to fear and she added, "Who are you? You are not a professor; you are some kind of international police, aren't you?"

Andrew's jaw dropped but he stared at her in amazement. He swallowed and then articulated, "No, I am not in any branch of the police force. I am or was a professor of English. I had no idea that you were involved in the case. Honest to god it never occurred to me, your being so young and all. I was imagining some sixty-year-old with a ponytail and round-rimmed glasses. Honest."

She relaxed and they both laughed and then out of curiosity, she asked, "With some support from a big Dalit movement group in New Delhi, Sunil, Ajit and I are the beginning of a small activist group in Manali who are against the oppression of Dalit people. We are small but it is only a beginning and we intend to grow. But tell me, why this particular case? Have people heard about it in Canada?"

He fell silent now and was breathing slowly. She did not know what he was thinking, but she let the silence give him time to collect his thoughts. After a long pause, he said, "I've a particular interest in understanding what kind of people in the modern world behave like animals in murdering an innocent girl all because thousands of years ago a primitive society set up some basic rules about a cast system."

"Ah," said she, as if having a sudden epiphany. "You've no idea how deep it goes. They were not allowed to let their shadows fall upon a non-Dalit caste member and they were required to sweep the ground where they walked to remove the 'contamination' of their footfalls.

Dalit were forbidden to worship in temples or draw water from the same wells as Hindus, and they usually lived in segregated neighborhoods outside the main village. In the Indian countryside, the Dalit villages are usually a separate enclave a kilometer or so outside the main village."

"This is pure ignorance and it is hard to fathom that progressive India would believe in such nonsense."

"Old habits die hard and people would rather die or kill than break old traditions," said she in a contemplative mood. "To give you a little background, Dalit status has often been historically associated with occupations regarded as ritually impure, such as leatherwork, butchering, or removal of rubbish, animal carcasses, and waste. Dalit people work as manual laborers cleaning streets, latrines, and sewers. Engaging in these activities was considered to be polluting to the individual, and this pollution was considered contagious. As a result, Dalit were commonly segregated, and banned from full participation in Hindu social life. They could not enter a temple or a school, and were required to stay outside the village. While the city folks still frown on the Dalit, it is the rural people who would not give a second thought to killing a Dalit."

"How come you're so passionate about this subject? I mean, you could have picked so many other causes to fight for rather than at such a young age take on something that could be life threatening, especially in a small hill town like Manali?"

"Complicated age-old traditional and cultural values stem from our greed for more," she pronounced in a contemplative voice. "The pressures of modern life offer complicated choices—one cannot forget the sadness of yesterday and the injustice of the present…all we know and live for is the promise of a bright future."

"What're you saying," said Andrew in an exasperated voice, "did I miss something?"

"You haven't figured it out yet?" she said with a mischievous smile on her face. "I'll tell you, but promise not to jump up and leave the café?"

He narrowed his brow as if to sharpen his focus in deciphering the meaning of what she just said. A light dawned. "No way," he said as his eyes widened in surprise, "You don't say. I never could have guessed it." He thought for a moment on what he'd just said and then wondered if she would take it the wrong way so hurriedly corrected himself. "I don't mean it that way; I mean it in a good sort of way. I mean, it is simply marvelous."

When she gave him a peculiar glance he felt he might have blown his chances of working closely with Jyoti.

THIRTY-THREE

Jyoti let out a peal of laughter and flashed her pearly teeth, saying, "Well, it isn't written on our foreheads that we're Dalit. After all, we collectively are human beings differentiated mainly by our deeds, isn't that true? Once I have educated myself, dress and behave properly then it is no one's business to know to which caste I belong. Education is what will eventually bring about acceptance on both sides."

Andrew sat back and wondered if that was what he found attractive about her. *Lalita was a Dalit and Jyoti is Dalit too.* In India he had opportunity to meet only two women and both turned out to be Dalit. *What are the chances?* he mused. Perhaps his destiny was entwined with the cause of Dalits? Perhaps that was why he was back in India? She broke his reverie. "What was that wise crack about being so young? How old are you? You look to be in your late twenties and here you are travelling around the world."

"I'm in my early thirties, actually," he said, and wondered if that was stretching the truth just a little bit.

"Well, I'm in my early twenties so we are not that far apart," said she, soon to be twenty-one. She volunteered,

"Are you interested in sightseeing? I could show you around. Manali is a beautiful place."

Andrew found an inexplicable attraction towards this girl that he felt was both pleasant and baffling. Perhaps it was because he'd had little experience with female companionship and felt awkward articulating on a one-on-one basis.

"I would be delighted," he said in a voice that showed moderate and guarded enthusiasm and then, shifting in his chair abruptly, as if a sudden thought occurred to him, he added, "but if it is all the same to you then I would much rather stay here and talk over a cup of coffee. You see, as a teenager I lived in Manali for a year and have seen a lot of the countryside."

"When?" she asked, staring at him.

"Sorry," he fidgeted, "when what?" He felt that somehow he had given her a cause for concern.

"When were you here last?" she asked in a level tone.

"About twenty years ago, when I was fifteen," he responded matter-of-factly. Suddenly he realized his mistake and wondered if she would catch the lie told earlier about his being in his early thirties. It seemed she didn't.

"You mean when the Dalit girl Lalita was murdered?" she asked in a sharp voice. "And now you are interested in writing a story about Lalita. Who are you and what do you really want?"

Andrew felt he didn't really know Jyoti well enough to share his secrets. It was too early, as he decided, to tell Jyoti about what his father and his friends did to Lalita. He could not condone what his father did but his father had nothing to do with Lalita's murder. He felt convinced that sharing information about what happened to Lalita at his father's hands would only confuse Jyoti and then she may not be as cooperative in giving him information on the Dalit movement. And he needed her to get to the truth of what really happened to Lalita. He believed that writing Lalita's story and sharing it with the world would be the right thing to do to bring justice to her and to her people.

He leaned forward to meet her stare and responded in a confident voice, "I am a person just like you who cares about oppressed people. There must have been hundreds if not thousands of Dalit women who were unjustifiably treated during my one-year stay in India, but Lalita was the only one from this town, so obviously I have an interest in her story. I am only here for a few months and during my stay here, if I could be of some help to you, to your cause, then I would be delighted. But if you think I am getting in your way then please forgive this intrusion and I shall not be bothering you anymore."

He could see a softening of her stance in her eyes as she lowered her head and then in an amiable tone said, "I am sorry. In my business it is hard to know who to trust. I am so sorry. Let us start again. How do you think you could help?"

"You and your organization need to learn from history and then make the best use of evolving technology." Andrew didn't have any specific help to offer but wondered if by talking with Jyoti he could spark some bright ideas within her. He always found young and passionate people creative. Besides, she was the one who was closely involved in fighting for the Dalit cause.

"History," murmured Jyoti, as she scratched her head. "It was decades ago when Gandhi Ji organized a *'Harijan Yatra'* to help the Dalit population and raise awareness amongst the masses. Are you suggesting that we should do something similar? A protest march?"

As Andrew searched for an answer Jyoti's friend Sunil entered the café. He pulled up a chair and gesturing to the waiter for tea, asked, "What schemes are you two cooking up? I hope you don't mind me barging in? I can't stay long." He had addressed his latter comments to Andrew, who in response simply smiled.

"Andrew thinks we ought to learn from history and make use of recent advancements," suggested Jyoti.

"And how does one go about doing that? We've all the energy but obviously lack the experience and technology. Would you help us?" said Sunil.

"I would be happy to but for your sake I should remain in the background," said Andrew, feeling a rush from this exciting opportunity and yet fearful of repercussions, since the local police may still have on record his family name. They let his father go but he was not sure that somewhere there was not a file on him.

What he did not know was that by accepting Sunil's offer, he had invited the wrath of a much bigger and life threatening enemy than the local corrupt police. His life now hung in the balance.

THIRTY-FOUR

Andrew wondered if in the small town of Manali there were plain-clothed police that kept an eye on foreigners and their activities. He wondered if he was one of their targets. Blinking twice as if to discard those thoughts, he looked at Jyoti and Sunil and said, "Tell me what you are up against? I mean specifically."

"Anti-Dalit prejudices exist in fringe groups," said Sunil, as he smiled at the waiter who brought over his tea. "These fringe groups, such as the extremist militia Ranvir Sena, are largely run by upper-caste landlords. They oppose equal treatment of Dalit and have resorted to violent means to suppress the Dalit. I know you are interested in writing the story of Lalita but I am not sure if groups such as Ranvir Sena were behind the murder of Lalita; but they support and encourage the continuing violence." He gave a side-glance to Jyoti and took a sip of his hot tea.

Andrew scratched his head as if encouraging his mind to figure out a way to apply western technology to the centuries-old war of prejudice. Seeing that both Sunil and Jyoti were waiting for his response, he offered, "It is heroic for small groups like yours to put up a fight for such a worthy cause, but in reality you cannot take the whole system on all by yourself. These organized people you describe may be far too powerful for you to tackle. You know, David and Goliath."

Jyoti, with a smile of determination, said, "Given ample time, Professor, even the tallest peaks of mighty mountains may be reduced to small islands in a lake, and the sea bottom may rise to create some of the tallest mountains. This is not some miracle to happen, this has already happened on our planet. We will not quit our fight."

"You are personally involved," Andrew said, looking at Jyoti, "that may land you in trouble, for you might be seeking revenge and not justice. Don't seek vengeance, for it is a kind of darkness that in its generosity offers one its cloak of secrecy as security but it never offers a promise of deliverance when the morning comes."

"What do you suggest then?" asked Jyoti in a slightly irritated voice, "forgive and forget? Even the deepest wounds heal with time but their scars never leave. They remain as reminders for the victims not to forget the acrimony and violence involved. And if one cannot forget then why on earth does the world expect for one to forgive? Forgive and forget is not a model for a symbiotic relationship."

"No, I didn't say that, but vengeance will never give you the lasting results you seek," said Andrew contemplatively.

"Forgiveness is the first step towards reaching redemption. I give you that. But what if I am not seeking redemption through forgiveness but justice through revenge? What then? Tell me, what then?" Jyoti's voice was quivering with rising rage.

Andrew remained quiet, wondering if this conversation was doing more harm than good in guiding Jyoti and her friends, and hoping to build a friendship with them. After several moments of silence he decided to try a different approach and changed tactics, "It is okay to have dreams but one must appreciate reality."

"Dreams? I'm afraid I don't have dreams for I don't believe in them. Besides, one has to be asleep to dream. I," she said in an excited tone, "I have visions."

Andrew realized that Jyoti and her friends weren't just youths with unrealistic expectations, they were on a path that perhaps destiny chose for them. They were committed and passionate about what they wanted to accomplish. He searched his options as to what would people of Jyoti's type were doing elsewhere in the world to fight for their rights and, remembering a few relevant cases, ventured, "If you are going to fight this war effectively then you need to resort to the most powerful weapon created by the west and it's available globally for free."

Jyoti and Sunil looked at each other in puzzlement and then it was Jyoti who said, "You lost me."

"Social media. If there is one thing that even the world's toughest dictators and governments are having a hard time fighting, it is the public opinion of the west. Don't get me wrong, it has nothing to do with east versus west, it is a simple question of commerce. In today's globalization every growing country needs aid from the World Bank and the support of the International Monetary Fund. And if you could demonstrate to the western world the human rights abuse and oppression based on prejudices on an aggressive basis at the people's level then you can gain an upper hand in your battle and could well be on the path to a resolution."

Sunil and Jyoti both nodded their heads but their eyes showed either lack of understanding or the lack of conviction. "We have our own email addresses as well as Facebook and Twitter accounts but would need your help to take us to the next level," suggested Jyoti.

"I have already agreed to work with you," said Andrew, "but what we ought to do as the next step—" Before Andrew could finish his sentence there was a mighty crash as a brick came through the window where they were sitting. Shards of glass were all over their table and one pierced the left side of Sunil's face. Blood trickled down from the side of his face and onto the table. Andrew quickly grabbed several paper napkins and tried to put pressure on the wound. Jyoti and Andrew suffered minor cuts on their forearms.

"Let's take Sunil to the hospital," cried Andrew, and helping Sunil stand up, they rushed outside to hail a taxi.

Sunil was discharged after a few stitches and the doctor attended to the minor cuts on all three of them.

THIRTY-FIVE

The next day when they got together it was Jyoti who turned up with Ajit, and the owner of the Green Forest Café supervising the installation of a new window stopped them at the door and in a firm voice said, "Sorry, I cannot allow you political activists in here anymore, bad for my business."

"I'll pay for the damages if we were responsible," offered Andrew.

"Just don't come here anymore," said the café owner, and stood in the doorway blocking their way.

"We'll go somewhere else," said Ajit, "who wants bricks with coffee anyway."

Down the street they went into another café and after settling in a booth and while waiting for a waiter, Andrew asked, "How is Sunil and where is he?"

Jyoti and Ajit looked at each other and it was Ajit who answered, "His father does not approve of what we do so he is laying low for a while. Sunil has a good heart but weak spirit. His dad controls his world."

Ajit continued, "Professor, I know we perhaps are proud and young and foolish but it doesn't have to be your war. There would be no shame in it if you wanted to pull out."

Andrew smiled and countered, "Proud young people are proud young people. And proud old ones are—well, what I am. I believe you would help me more than I would be helping you by letting me work with you. We can help each other. I am no fan of bricks flying through windows but no, I don't scare that easily, so I am in."

Andrew looked at Jyoti and her eyes were sad and her face was mellow. Andrew smiled and said, "Are you concerned about Sunil? Is there anything I could do or get you?"

"Thank you, I should like some tea," was the sole rejoinder.

Ajit noticed her abrupt answer and distant mood so interjected, "Come out of your reverie. What is it that's bugging you?"

Jyoti let out a big sigh and responded, "It makes me mad, you know. I want to wake up my country. I want to shake it out of its nightmare. I want to bring it out into a new awakening. To where the mind is without fear and the head is held high. To where the world is not divided by walls of small-mindedness. Where good feelings emanate from the depths of truth. Where our hearts and souls are free. Where we are no longer lost in the desolate desert of old traditions. Where the mind is led forward into ever-widening thought and action. I want to wake up my country to see that heaven."

"Wow, slow down," said Ajit raising his hands up, "you're asking just a little too much of an old country. Have patience."

Andrew joined in, "I would have thought that decades of British influence would have brought India out of the darkness of its old traditions and into the light of the civilized world."

Andrew suddenly realized that his statement could be offensive and almost expected a rebuff for this hardly anticipated opinion, but, on the contrary, waking out of her scowling abstraction, Jyoti turned her eyes towards him, and the frustration seemed to clear from her brow. "You talk of the British?" said she impatiently. "Did you expect the British to think of anything more than trade and commerce? You think they came here to reform our society? You disappoint me, Professor." She searched Andrew's face with eyes that Andrew noticed were dark, irate, and piercing.

Andrew was about to respond in his defense but then suddenly paused in his reflection and, closing his eyes, lowered his head. Ajit came to the rescue with, "I know the misconception people carry about the British influence in India. But it is not the British that are to be questioned; it is the Indian society that is to be blamed. You see, in Indian society all men are divided into ordinary and extraordinary, not rich and poor, educated and ignorant, and civilized and uncouth.

"Ordinary men have to live in submission, have no right to transgress the law, because, don't you see, they are simply ordinary. But extraordinary, ah, they are a different breed. The extraordinary men have a right to commit any crime and to transgress the law in any way, just because they are extraordinary. These extraordinary men consider their prejudices to be their privileges and none gives them greater status than their odium towards the Dalit. Our extraordinary fight is against these extraordinary men."

Suddenly Ajit stopped and saw Andrew and Jyoti's gazes transfixed on him and he laughed loudly. "Ah, but it is all too boring, isn't it. I'd rather talk about you and your father." He directed his next question towards Andrew, "Tell me, based on what you and I discussed a few days back, are you getting any closer to bridging the gap between you and your father?"

Andrew was not prepared to open up the subject of his father in front of Jyoti but at the same time was tempted to get Ajit's views and thoughts on the subject. Andrew leaned forward and said, "Perhaps it would be more pleasant to talk about my mother?"

"The choice is all yours, Professor," laughed Ajit softly.

Tempted by the offer of access to Ajit's brilliant mind and eager to get his opinion, Andrew decided to go to the heart of his question and said, "One day I heard my mother say, in a movie theater, dark and inappropriate, and apropos of nothing: *I made a mistake; don't blame your father when you grow up.* And the curious thing was that I believed it on the spot and have believed it ever since, though she could tell me nothing more—not what was the mistake, not what made her say it, not what it really meant, nor anything else about it. It is one of those puzzles where the harder you try to solve it, the more impossible you find it to solve. What do you make of it?"

"I think it's rather easy to see what she may have meant," said Ajit, assuming his usual philosophical aura.

Jyoti's mood seemed to lighten with this change of subject.

Both Jyoti and Andrew stared at his face with different expressions on their faces: Jyoti, hoping that Ajit wouldn't say anything to offend; and Andrew, hoping to learn what his mother was trying to say. Ajit suddenly laughed, saying, "Don't look so serious, you two. It could be as simple as she was saying that she as a wife misread him but you as a son should see him in a different light, meaning you ought to see your father through your eyes and not those of your mother's. Your mother exhibited unusual courage to convey such sentiments to a child. I wish I had a mother like that."

"If you did," said Jyoti, "you two would bore each other with your philosophical speeches." And though none of them saw humor in her statement they all laughed just the same.

THIRTY-SIX

June advanced to July: a bright serene July it was; days of summer blue sky, placid sunshine, and indulgent western breezes filled the hours of its duration.

It was a clear clean morning with birds triumphantly singing. If only he could stay here forever. If only there weren't the other ghastly world of money and career. If only he could make this town a part of his world. He was aware that sooner or later he had to return to Canada, to his world of teaching and surviving while his soul continued to demand, screamed for a life of meaning, not a mere existence.

He was getting closer to both Ajit and Jyoti but didn't feel that the time was right to bring up the subject of Lalita again. But Lalita was the reason he was there and Lalita he must pursue. His whole reason for being in Manali was to find out what happened to her and tell her story to the world. Was the presence of Jyoti in his life now erasing the pain of the memories of Lalita? he mused. The question was difficult; the answer to it he did not want to know.

That day he stayed in his room and got back to writing more of his thoughts on the changing perspectives of India.

In the evening as Andrew walked along the stone wall, he found Jyoti sitting on a bench and pensively watching a sunset as it reddened the summits with so ravishing a glow that it was impossible not to feel a deep sense that our souls are forever entwined with nature and sway in harmony with the ebbs and eddies of the tides of time. Did the lost illusions of her girlhood return to her? Did the woman suffer from an inward turmoil? He fancied that he had the ability to perceive the anguish in her soul and so he said, "Some evenings are truly hard to bear, aren't they?"

"You read my soul, Professor," she answered, "but tell me, how does an English teacher have such a skill?"

"We have more in common than you think," he replied.

"Surely you are not implying some deep philosophy like our joys and sorrows vibrate in unison and souls echo each other's sentiments and are in harmony at twilight?"

There was a momentary hesitation for he could not explain to her that he somehow knew that she would be here; her gesture yesterday had promised it. For several days an explanation seemed to float between them; a silent world of understanding and acceptance. What his timidity had thus far delayed was now a perfect understanding between them, her inviting smile having overcome that gap. Perhaps this is how such nebulous relationships turn into perfect friendships. He felt both a growing sincere friendship and subtle rigidity on her unyielding opinions;

as if she was saying she could give him her life, but not her convictions. He loved it. But he could not reveal such thoughts for fear of being misunderstood, so with a nervous laugh, he said, "I love the way you celebrate your independence and it is so good to see how fiercely you fight for it. Your freedom is so pure."

The beautiful freedom of a woman was infinitely more wonderful than any pleasures in life. The only unfortunate thing was that men lagged so far behind women in the matter. Unlike a man who could only reveal himself by pouring out his soul, a woman could yield to a man without yielding her inner self. Control and boundaries, these were not easily understood by men.

She smiled, without answering. Little did he know that most people of this town would give their right arm to have the life he had in Canada. The misery of the poor world can be the adventure of the rich world.

"You seem to have such a lot behind you," she said, "money, career, family, a modern and civilized society. Why would you give up that world for this?"

"I would like to make all the rest of the world disappear," he said, "and live right here in this town, surrounded by friends like you."

Silent moments followed one another as they both contemplated the budding friendship.

He now realized why he was so very much at one with her, in his mind and hers, but bodily they were nonexistent to one another, and neither could bear to clearly express their feelings. They were so close, and yet utterly out of touch with each other's worlds. Andrew believed that what the eye doesn't see and the mind doesn't know, doesn't exist. It was all a dream; or rather, it was like the simulacrum of reality. He let out a deep sigh reflecting the state of deep confusion in his mind.

Perhaps it was the sunset, perhaps it was her sad eyes that made him want to pour his heart out and be totally open to her. She smiled and her smile radiated benevolence. They wandered together for a while and then Andrew invited her for a coffee. Sitting in a quiet corner and after he stirred his coffee, tasted it, and added one more cube of sugar, he said, "I'm going to tell you something." He gave her a look that said, "Please don't be mad at me."

She simply raised her brows. He said, "Little by little, getting to know each other, two people fall into a sort of unison, they vibrate so intricately with one another. That's the real secret of a good friendship, not having coffees and lunches; at least not the simple acts of socializing. You and I are interwoven in a somewhat complex friendship. If we can manage to stick to that for a while then I am confident that we ought to be able to simplify the complexities of our friendship."

"And you have a reason to believe this?" asked Jyoti, tentatively.

"The reason I say this is because I am convinced that fate has given us an opportunity to be together. I want nothing for myself but would like you to give our friendship a chance to blossom into something extraordinary."

No sooner had he made his appeal of friendship than he felt awkward, as blurting out his emotions so openly must have sounded absurd to her. Her eyes narrowed a little, with irony, perhaps with impudence. It seemed as if her woman's instinct sensed it. His heart sank.

THIRTY-SEVEN

He looked at her with expectant eyes and wondered what she was thinking. She was to give consent to weave a steady friendship with him, all one fabric, but perhaps brocaded with the occasional flower of an adventure. But how could she know what she would feel after he left? How could one ever know? How could one say yes to such an appeal? He was a tourist and this was an adventure. It might be important to some of these tourists, while they were experience the mystique of what they call the '*Indian Experience,*' that they then ask, what does this mean? Why should that flimsy definition pin one down? Of course, it was nonsense because any such friendships are predictable and always change, disappearing like the seasons.

A little smile, mocking or teasing him, yet gentle, came into her eyes for a moment then faded, and her face became expressionless. After a few moments of pleasant silence she said, "I am actually quite happy. I have come to the brink of eternity from which nothing can now vanish—no hope, no happiness, and no vision of our friendship. We are all together now and that is all that matters."

She had a peculiar, childish wistfulness at times, and with this an intangible aloofness that pierced his heart. It seemed to him he could never know her. There was a certain feeling of the remote about her, an estrangement between her and all natural daily things, as if she were of an unknown race that can never tell its own story. This feeling moved Andrew's pity to its deepest, leaving him helpless. This same foreignness, revealed in other ways, made him wish to run away from her. It was as if she would sacrifice him rather than renounce her fight for the rights of the Dalit. There was something in her he could never understand, so that never, never could he say he was a close friend of hers, as she often conveyed nothing more than an image of a simple acquaintance.

Andrew just sat there contemplating her answer and a sudden sadness overcame him. "If I have made things more difficult," she said, her eyes welling up and voice harsh with pain, "you will forgive me."

Her complex statements startled him. This was one of the cruel cuts that close friendship gives. Andrew stiffened himself; he smiled as he looked at her child-ish, plaintive lips, and her large eyes haunted with pain. "Forgive you?" he repeated. "Forgive you for a few days of perfect happiness; the only real happiness I have ever known." He tightened his fingers on his knee. He felt himself stinging with a piercing joy; but also restrained from holding her hands, as some of the customers in the cafe were looking at him with curiosity. He leaned back, and closed his eyes momentarily. He wanted this moment of togetherness to last. He could sense she was staring at him. He opened his eyes, leaned forward and said, "You make me very happy and I care for you. I don't want to see you get hurt, especially because of my involvement in your work."

Seized with compassion for the shipwreck of their lives, he turned back to memories of their recent pure past, yielding to meditations, which seemed mutual. She expressed neither fear, nor regrets, nor desire; but at a given hour her tenderness reappeared like a fire suddenly lit.

He was touched by her words, in which the depth of her personal feelings mingled with the warmth of affection, a combination that gives to women so great a power of persuasion; they know how to give meaning to the keenest arguments.

Their few exclamatory words revealed the mutuality of friendship in which they took sanctuary from their common sufferings. When language failed, silence faithfully served their disquiet hearts; together they luxuriated in the comfort of contemplative stillness, they met in the folds of this moment, they plunged separately with their burdened souls into the river and came out as pure as their souls could wish, with nothing but love to bind them. They entered the unfathomable gulf separately, they returned to the surface together, asking each other by a look, "How could we have missed the obvious before, for it was always present, staring us in the face?"

She gave him a poignant glance, which was like the cry of a child when his wound is touched; she was humbled but beguiled too. His reward was in that glance; to refresh her heart, to have given her comfort, what encouragement for him to pursue the journey upon which he had embarked.

He was a firm believer in the possible leading us to know the probable. The tears in her voice were the reward of what must be called a usurious speculation of love.

THIRTY-EIGHT

The next day Andrew was out for a walk when he sensed that someone was following him. It was one of those awkward feelings that you want to put down to paranoia but then prudence demanded satisfaction of an action. Andrew's knowledge of how to cope with such a situation was limited to what he had learned from various movies, but then movies did not relate to reality. While he contemplated his next move the man following him suddenly quickened his pace, and came right by his side, blocking his path, saying, "Do you have a light?"

A cigarette was hanging between his thick lips and his bloodshot eyes had a cold stare. His hairy chest appeared in an open collar bright-red shirt with the top three buttons undone. like some one had thrown an old carpet over a balcony to air. He was wearing a heavy gold chain around his neck and his thick hairy arms were adorned with a gold watch and silver bracelet around the wrist.

"I don't smoke," said Andrew, taking a step back. He somehow knew this was going to go beyond a confrontation. He wondered if he should shout for help or simply run. But for the time being he remained glued to the spot where he was standing.

The stranger's thick eyebrows were close together, making him look like a Cyclops. He ran his thick fingers through jet-black curly hair and in a sarcastic voice said, "Go home to your rock & roll, this is not your fight. I don't want to hurt you but if I see you messing around with those young kids again then the next time it won't be a brick flying in through a window, but rather somebody is going to find your body floating down the Beas River. You understand me?"

Andrew heard him but there was something in his threat, maybe the choice of words, which reminded him of Lalita's body floating in a well. He wondered if it was just a coincidence or was this man actually referencing Lalita's murder?

"What? You've nothing to say now? Good. Now be a good tourist and enjoy Manali for a couple more days and then go home. Okay? And leave these kids alone; they are bad news. Find your own kind to play with."

He took out a lighter and lit his cigarette, took a deep drag and blew a large cloud of blue smoke in Andrew's face and then laughing aloud, left him standing there alone. Andrew thought of reporting the incidence to the local police but then decided against it. He wanted to stay off their radar.

It was a beautiful crisp morning and the air was clean and refreshing. Andrew awoke with every molecule in his body resonating with a curious sense of elation. Jyoti had accepted his invitation to have lunch with him. Casual coffee chats were exactly that—casual. Having lunch with Jyoti without her friends was the next step. The next step to what, he was not too sure, but it seemed a natural progression for a wonderful friendship.

He had asked her to meet him at the Hotel New Adarsh restaurant, which was famous for its Himalayan delicacy, trout. Another reason he chose this restaurant was that it was considered expensive by both locals and tourists alike, and therefore allowed him some privacy. He spent the morning lazily reading Times of India over a light breakfast and a couple of cups of coffee. He didn't want to dwell on the fact that she so readily had accepted his offer to have lunch. He knew that Indians are fascinated by foreigners and will seize every opportunity to hear the history of their country. But there was more to it than that when Jyoti had tilted her head to one side, chewing on the end of a pencil in contemplation, and in a hardly audible voice had said, "I feel drawn to say yes and look forward to it."

A curious way of accepting his offer, he had mused. It was more mysterious than romantic, he admitted, but maybe it was the message in her sparkling sea-green eyes that he could not interpret well. Every time he gazed into her eyes, his heart was seared with an unknown and unaccountable pain, for her eyes were haunted and in them one could read the tragedy of her race persecuted by thousands of years of oppression.

He knew he was drawn towards her but in a way that was not sexual but more like a powerful magnet draws a small piece of metal—a forceful attraction. Could this be the influence of his half-Indian blood where love is expected to grow after the relationship is established? He smiled at his incongruous logic and shook his head from side to side in self-denial.

He arrived about ten minutes early at the restaurant to secure a table in a quiet corner. He ordered a Mango Lassi, a kind of Indian milkshake made from yogurt and mango pulp that he found both exotic and delicious, and a far cry from his usual Budweiser back in Victoria. A few minutes later Jyoti arrived and, hanging her bag on the back of her chair, apologized, "I'm so sorry, I just couldn't get rid of this friend. How're you?"

"Not to worry, you're not all that late. Would you join me with a Lassi?"

"Oh, no, thanks. They're great but have too many calories; you know what I mean? I'd be happy with some green tea."

Andrew ordered Jasmine green tea. When tea arrived and as she closed her eyes and scrunched up her full lips to carefully take the first sip, she looked like an angel kissing a dew-soaked blossom.

THIRTY-NINE

ndrew found himself staring at her and as she opened her eyes she said, "What? Something on my face?"

She always touched his heart, and he found himself unable to find the right look or the right word, while inwardly he bubbled with fervor, and a longing to express his feelings, although he wasn't quite sure what those feelings were.

"Oh, I'm sorry," said Andrew hurriedly and added, to hide his embarrassment, "I didn't mean to stare at you. It is just that I find that I…you are beautiful." He pursed his lips as if trying to come up with the appropriate word to express his feelings towards her. He couldn't say love, it was simply going too far; besides, he could not be sure if that word would have appropriately expressed his emotions. He was fifteen years older than her and, though attracted, he didn't have sexual feelings towards her.

She gave one of those little girl laughs and with a mischievous smile on her lips said, "You find me beautiful? I see. I bet you say that to all the girls you meet?"

"No, no," he said with color rising in his face. "It is ridiculous. I find I'm so flustered when I'm with you. Oh, sure, you're beautiful, but that was not what I was trying to say."

She laughed this time a little louder and he noticed that the owner of the restaurant was giving them a stern look. He said in a low voice, "Let's order some lunch, the guy behind the counter is giving us dirty looks."

She suppressed another laugh and simply nodded her compliance. He ordered the lunch for both and as they ate she said, "You never told me your middle name?"

"It is Anand," he said.

"Anand," she repeated as her eyes widened in surprise and she, putting down her knife and fork, said, "that is an Indian name?"

"Well, sure it is," he said matter-of-factly. "I'm half-Indian. My mother was Indian."

"Wow," she exclaimed, "why did you not tell me this before? We have known each other for so long and you kept that a secret. I never would have guessed it. You don't look at all like an Indian. But that explains why I feel such an affinity towards you."

"That's it," he shouted, "that's the very word I was thinking of earlier. I too feel that I've known you all my life."

She gave another one of her contagious laughs and said, "Ah shucks, you sure know how to make a girl feel more like a pet than a beautiful person." She gave him a playful glare and asked, "So, tell me about your mother, was she very beautiful?"

Andrew waited for the waiter to serve some fresh tea and clear away the dirty plates. He put a little sugar in his tea and stirring it, in a contemplative mood, said, "She was a very beautiful woman and rather extraordinary. Her love was special, unselfish and unconditional. She didn't say much but her eyes were very expressive and almost like yours, but of a different color. She died very young of cancer."

"Oh, I'm so sorry, Andrew, I didn't know," she responded, her voice laced with concern.

"Well, thank you, but it was a long time ago. At first I found her loss unbearable but later accepted it as my destiny, for I considered myself lucky to have such a special love, even for such a short time," said Andrew in a tone that was soothing and convincing. When no rejoinder came from Jyoti, he added, "I've been blessed with the kind of love that most sons can't even imagine. She gave me everything that I ever wanted so I learned to shed no tears, for my mother deserves celebration and not commiseration."

Andrew chuckled and said, "Listen to me going on about it. What about your mother, you never told me anything about your parents?"

"Didn't I tell you that I was raised by my grandfather? I never knew my parents. My grandfather tells me that they both died of some illness when I was only a baby."

"No, you didn't tell me any of this before. I'm so sorry that you never had the love of your parents. Is your grandfather here with you? I would like to meet him."

Again he questioned, but this time only in thought, *What is driving her? From where does she get her strength?*

"My grandfather, I call him Baba. He was determined to send me to a good school not the one where only Dalit kids go. But he had no money and I started my schooling at a Dalit school. The atmosphere was relaxed as we were all equal but the education was substandard, one inexperienced teacher and no resources. Suddenly one day Baba moved me to a normal school where I was the only Dalit student. It was a nightmare. Other students constantly tormented me because of my lower cast, and inferior status in society and my teachers never reprimanded any of the students who took pleasure in taunting me."

"It must have been terrible for you, how old were you?"

"I was six years old. It was a very strange sensation to an inexperienced young girl, especially someone like me, you know, an untouchable, to feel alone in the world."

"I admire your courage," said Andrew. "How did you manage all those years at that school?"

"The sense of adventure counteracted the negative reactions, but then the ache of fear often distracted me; and the fear with me became overwhelming when I had no friends. I will always remember that awful feeling of being utterly alone. I convinced myself to give up my dreams and run back to the Dalit school, back to my own kind."

Jyoti's voice was low and her eyes sad; at that moment, she looked as if she was miles away.

FORTY

This new revelation made Andrew feel a little closer to her. Andrew waited for Jyoti to resume speaking and seeing that she needed some sort of response, he asked, "But are you happy now that you stayed?" Andrew could almost feel her palpable fear. "I mean, you suffered while you were at the school without any friends, was it all worth it living in fear all your young life? I am curious as to how you, as a young girl, found such huge courage in those adverse conditions?"

"We as Dalit have learned to overcome our fears; otherwise, that woman whose body was found floating in the well would have died in vain, and how many more will continue to die if fear is to push people like me back into the safety of my Baba and of my own kind. No, I've learned to persevere, no matter what the cost, and that includes my life, if necessary."

She leaned back in her chair and for a moment looked lost, as if reliving her past, and then said, "He lives in New Delhi. My Baba. I was brought up by my grandfather in the big city of New Delhi where there is less hardship being a Dalit. My grandfather worked very hard, including working as a porter at the Railway Station and janitor at the Sheraton Hotel, to make enough money to send me to school and later for my university education. I graduated this year but found it difficult to get a job in New Delhi, and then a friend told me about a temporary teaching position here in Manali. So, here I am in a part-time teaching position and hoping to become a full-time and permanent staff teacher so I can look after my Baba in his old age. New Delhi is too expensive so this place suits me very well and I think Baba would be happy here too."

"Wow, you've thought of everything and left the big city life for a mountain village, that takes some courage too," he said, with a smile. "I wish I had clarity of mind like you do."

"Sometimes the excitement of my mind craves the bright lights of New Delhi and the tranquil calm of my spirit desires the stillness of Manali mountains, the flowing Beas River and the silence of green pastures. Seeking solutions to such dilemmas often penalizes most by falsely offering hope in procrastination. But thank heaven that I am blessed with a clear vision because in such a conflicted state, I know that neither mind nor spirit are the right places to search for the truth, as the right answer lies within the heart, where emotion takes predominance over prudence. My Baba does not understand any of it but somehow I'm convinced that my life is here, this is where I am needed. Does that make any sense?"

"Perfectly," said Andrew instantly. "Now I can see why you have such confidence."

"If I could be assured of your understanding and support then all the confidence I need to fight society would follow," she said, in a tone as if asking for assurance. Taking his silence as a sign of that assurance, she added, "Every perpetrator is a victim of his circumstance; that is understandable but not necessarily forgivable. His just punishment is not merely an apology from our government to his victims, and not to be viewed as a means of redemption. To receive redemption he has to face his day of judgment, and that is coming from movements like ours. We're not waiting for government policies and laws to deliver justice to us or to offer redemption to our oppressors."

"You are too advanced for your age. If you are asking me for advice then all I could tell you is let your education empower you and subsequently fill you with the passion needed to follow your cause. One needs passion to live as it fills the future with promise and not obsession, for obsession is naïve, like the feeling of invincibility of youth like I see in some of your friends. Be careful of rash decisions."

Andrew dispensed advice but it was he who could learn a few lessons from her courageous and eventful life. Even before he had met her, Andrew had this curious feeling that a part of him was missing and it was out there somewhere, had always been there.

Jyoti's presence was the warm cocoon in which his soul could live safe and sheltered; the atmosphere without which he would miss out on a big part of his life. Although this relationship had existed for only a few days, it was thanks to Jyoti that not one bitter memory, one undeserved injustice, darkened these days, when the remembrance of wrongs was so acute.

Jyoti smiled at his concerned advice and responded, "I don't get you, you know." She said this half seriously and half with mischievous intent. "I think under that 'what you see is what you get' façade, you are a very complex person. Don't be offended, I mean it as a compliment."

How could he be offended by anything she said? The ease of her manner and eagerness with which she said things about him freed him from the uneasy restraint of his crippling shyness, and this drew him to her. He felt as if he was talking to an old friend and not a stranger, even though that is who she was as he had met her only a few days back by introducing himself. A little sadness appeared in her eyes, yet her smiling face did not escape him; he felt an ache in his heart, wanting to offer her help, but he was aware that she did not know him well enough for that. He simply hoped that she would see more of him and get to know him better.

Feeling sentimental and emotionally attached, he said, "Jyoti, do you see, I mean, do you feel something between us? I hope you don't mind if I ask you—"

Andrew abruptly stopped, swallowed hard and poised himself to ask the question he had been meaning to ask for such a long time.

FORTY-ONE

Jyoti with an apprehensive look on her face quickly interrupted him, "I suppose there is one special friend in the life of each of us who seems not to be a separate person, however foreign and different, but an extension, an interpretation, of one's self, the very sense of one's heart. Such a special friend I have found in you, so please don't say anything and enjoy what we already have—a great companionship. Isn't that enough? Besides, soon you will be going back to Canada and it is quite likely that we will never see each other again. Right?"

He looked at her for a moment, nearly smiling. Then he quickly laid both his hands on her hands. Quickly he took them away again, as though ashamed of his spontaneous tenderness. This tenderness he felt for her caused his conscious mind to struggle with an undefined attraction, almost on the periphery of sensual desire, and his mind clouded over in utter confusion. He looked back at her again and said in a hurried tone, "I'm sorry. I don't know what came over me. It is just that I care for you."

The restaurant was almost empty now and the weather outside had suddenly changed for the worse. After a short while, though, the thunder had ceased outside, but the rain, which had abated, suddenly came streaming down, with a last streak of lightning and the muttering rumble of the departing storm. Andrew was uneasy. He knew eventually they would be again traveling their separate paths, a truth that he had only just realized inside himself and it had plunged him back into this somber mood.

He looked through the window and stared at the heavy rain, like a steel curtain, and had a sudden desire to rush out into it, to run away. *This is childish*, he thought. Why was he so obsessed with her? He had the friendship of Ajit and Sunil and could easily make other friends. And a strange feeling that he had not experienced before came over him and made it impossible for him to leave. He looked back at Jyoti and said, "I don't normally behave like this. I am too old to act like a lost teenager. Could we start again? All I want is your friendship. You know, a little time here and there to have a coffee together and sometimes a walk. I promise you I will be on my best behavior from now on."

Jyoti smiled and nodded. The rain beat down relentlessly outside. Andrew suggested after the meal that they have tea and Jyoti, looking at the rain outside, nodded in the affirmative. Watching the downpour they drank their tea in silence. He poured more hot tea from the teapot into his cup. He gestured with the teapot, asking if she wanted more and she shook her head. A yellow ray of intermittent sun shone over the trees and the golden hue of the late afternoon light glowed on her silent, abstracted face. He waited, but she said nothing.

The rain had ceased. There was a wet, heavy, perfumed stillness. Evening was approaching. He looked at her in wonder, feeling her devil of a will. She was silent, in the silence of imbecilic obstinacy.

Jyoti wanted to walk home alone and after thanking Andrew for lunch, went home realizing the depth of the sadness in her heart. It was as if her whole world was being twisted and she was entangled within. She adored Baba but always felt that somewhere in her growing up the burden Baba carried of her responsibility was transformed into her carrying the burden of looking after him. He was now her responsibility.

Her knees were weak as she walked. In her heart she was filled with mixed and confusing emotions, as if vulnerable and helpless. She could not make any commitments to distract from her path.

She liked Andrew. It was not the passion that was new to her; it was something else. It was the yearning. She knew she had always feared it, for it left her helpless; she feared it still, lest if she pursued her feelings for him, then she would lose herself, and she did not want to be effaced, a dependent, like a lost child. She knew she could fight it.

She had a self-will in her breast that could have fought the full, soft, heaving feeling of her heart and crushed it. She could even now do it, or so it seemed, and she could then take up her passion with her own will. Ah yes, to be passionate about a worthy cause like the rights of Dalit, one cannot afford the luxury of pleasant distractions. She knew that and she knew what the aim in her life was, for she was completely committed to it.

And she knew the thought of their separation was latent in both their minds, and at last she was sad. She had to enjoy whatever moments of joy were there in her journey for time drops these like fine old feathers.

FORTY-TWO

Andrew had barely made it out of his hotel lobby when he saw Jyoti rushing towards him. "Ajit is in hospital," Jyoti said, as though in despair, wringing her hands in excitement and distress. Her pale cheeks flushed; there was a look of anguish in her eyes. It was clear that she was stirred to the very depths, that she was longing to speak, to champion, to express something. A sort of insatiable compassion, if one may so express it, was reflected in every feature of her face.

"What happened," asked Andrew, gesturing for her to sit down on an outside bench.

"Someone abducted him, beat him up badly and burned him in several places with cigarettes."

"Who did this, could he talk? What did he say?"

"He said that the moment one quits mourning one's past, he is reborn. And when one does not allow fears to cast shadows on one's life, one then finds the key to living. He is more committed now than before to fight for Dalits."

"Yeah, that is what Ajit would say. He is an incredible young man." After a pause he added, "Is he going to be all right? I think I should go and see him at the hospital." Andrew couldn't help reflecting on his misadventure of receiving a harsh warning from that ugly stranger and somehow felt half relieved and half ashamed that no one had beat him up badly.

"Oh, yes, he should be out in a few days. First the brick through the window and now this, I wonder who is doing this?" she asked, not as a direct question but more as an inquiry.

He felt guilty for not sharing his warning with Ajit and Jyoti as perhaps it could have saved Ajit from his misfortune. Jyoti had to rush off to work and gave Andrew directions to the hospital.

A few minutes later when Andrew found Ajit there, he was horrified to see all the bruises on Ajit's face. "Are you okay?" asked Andrew.

"Nothing broken."

"Did you see who did this to you?"

"No, it was too dark and it happened too fast."

Andrew told Ajit of his encounter with the man who had warned Andrew not to continue his friendship with Ajit and friends and leave town as soon as possible.

"I see," said Ajit with a crooked smile, "and are you going to leave us soon then?"

"No. I am not going to leave. But perhaps it is the same man. I can identify him, if that helps."

"Oh, no, that won't help because no one is about to do anything," Ajit said with a sigh, "certainly not the police. For all I know they could have done it for money. But you should take that warning seriously. You could be the next person on their list."

"I don't think they would dare touch me. Canadian authorities would come down like a ton of bricks on local authorities if any harm were to come to me," said Andrew without any conviction for he knew it was a lie.

"You don't believe that, do you?"

"No, not really. But the real reason is that I feel that I belong here. You know, with you guys. It is like providence. I believe in your cause and I want to be a part of your struggle. No, I feel what you feel, Ajit."

"I see," said Ajit. Then he expounded, "I see it because I live it. You haven't experienced the pain and poverty of the Dalits. I appreciate your empathy but you can't feel what I feel."

Andrew, hearing this, hesitated, and Ajit seemed to take his silence as failing to understand his sentiments, so continued. "Let me put it this way: If I were to turn up in Vancouver Island, that is where you are from, right, and said I understand the suffering of the First Nation Indians, then would you see me as a genuinely concerned person or thank me for my concern and advise me not to miss a visit to Butchart Gardens while I was there? Professor, neither did God send you here nor did He ever mean to make the Dalit suffer. It is all caused by us and what is worse is that we do it in His name."

Andrew knew he could never win an argument against Ajit. He promised to come back and see him.

FORTY-THREE

Strolling leisurely down by the Beas River on a day that seemed to be almost like the end of summer, Jyoti looked at Andrew and, with an inquisitive look on her face, said, "You don't have to answer if you don't want to but what was it like for you losing your mother at such an early age? Do you miss her? I don't even remember my mother."

"No, I don't mind talking about my mother," said Andrew, enjoying the closeness of a wonderful friend. "I lost my mother when I was a little boy, and I've been waiting ever since as if expecting her to come back. Isn't that the weirdest thought? She was cremated on a stormy day. Calgary is known for its electric and violent storms. Such a storm was present on that day and I remember the sound of the rain that came down in sheets. I felt as if all of nature was sad at her untimely departure. The wind swept through the Bow valley and the consoling sky around us was black with swirling clouds, and the rain was quite persistent. I don't know if you can understand this but I didn't feel sad. I felt expectant. It was as if she would come back one day. Isn't this crazy?"

He looked straight at Jyoti, and she at him. They seemed to have formed an alliance in that look: she was the other half of his consciousness, he of hers.

"And what about you?" asked Andrew. "You can share the secrets of your early life with me. Your secrets will always be safe with me, you know."

Jyoti laughed, and he did not detect any bitterness of spirit. She was not laughing at him but at karma. She believed in karma. The blood suffused her face and neck. With a question like that he had her so much on edge she was inclined to answer, "So be it." Instead, she went back over her own history: it consisted of petty discords in contemptible surroundings, then of her dreams and fancies, finally—Andrew. "In my life," she said, with a fine, grating discord in her tone, "I might say always, real life has seemed just outside my reach, just beyond the stupid, ugly place where I exist. I seem to have been hedged in by sad circumstances, able to glimpse outside them now and then, just to see what I am missing—the real life others lead."

"How could you say that?" Andrew responded. "Most people do nothing with their life and waste it. What you are doing is exceptional and gives real meaning to life, makes it all worthwhile, doesn't it?" Andrew let a pause give her time to focus and then he added, "If you want, I suggest you share with me everything you know about Lalita so together we can bring her oppressors to justice."

Jyoti frowned, studying his face for a moment, and then answered, "I wish I could help you but I don't know much. This town, its police, everyone I talked to hushed up about her. I don't know if it is fear or money that has silenced them. There is nothing to tell."

Andrew pondered what she said and muttered under his breath, "Then I think I know where to start."

"I'm sorry, what did you say?"

"I said I wouldn't know either where to start," said Andrew quickly, to keep Jyoti from harm's way. This was something he had to do alone. This was his fight.

With a chill in the air, summer was grudgingly yielding to the looming winter. Andrew had his visitor's visa extended once and was sure another extension was improbable. He had at best three more months here before returning to Canada. He needed to intensify his search for facts about Lalita. But no one in town was willing to talk or they pleaded ignorance. His only option was to go to the authorities and question them. But he needed a convincing story to request such information. A story that hadn't even begun to take shape.

He decided to spend a few days in the confinement of his hotel room and work on a draft outlining a story based on what he already knew. This way at least he would have something to show to the authorities to convince them that it was a legit project. He ordered room service and spent hours on the first day writing and was so absorbed in his task that he did not notice the vivid colors of the setting sun and the streetlights below beginning to illuminate the old cobblestone streets.

His mind was tired and he stopped writing and decided to go out for a walk. Sunsets were his weakness and he could not waste a sunset cooped up in his room.

A long walk would allow him to reflect on his time to date in Manali and also give him the luxury of wallowing in his newfound happiness in Jyoti's friendship. After walking aimlessly for an hour he found himself strolling down a rather empty road with the wide-open vista of the valley. He stopped and gazed at the golden hue settling over the peaks of distant mountains. He smiled.

Suddenly and out of nowhere a small Ambassador car with its headlights off appeared and came to a screeching halt. The back door opened and a man with his face covered came out. He grabbed Andrew's arm, twisted it back and shoved him in the back of the car and then the car sped away. After about twenty minutes the car stopped outside a small farmhouse and the man pushed Andrew out of the car and through an open wooden door into a small stone house. He shut the door behind him. The man lit a candle and placed it on a small table next to a chair where he forced Andrew to sit. He tied Andrew's arms to the armrests of the chair with pieces of ropes that were lying in a corner. Andrew was still a little dazed by the speed with which this was happening.

Suddenly he remembered what Ajit had endured at the hands of his tormentor and shuddered with fear.

FORTY-FOUR

It was a small abandoned room filled with cobwebs, and looked rather ominous in the flickering candle-light. The man towering over Andrew pulled his scarf from over his face and stared at Andrew with his mouth twisted in anger.

"You don't listen well, do you, Professor?"

It was the same large man Andrew had met before who had warned him to stay away from Jyoti and her friends.

Andrew swallowed hard and in a half-choked voice responded, "I don't know what I have done wrong to upset you? I mean no harm, I am simply here as a tourist."

"A tourist," snarled the man, grinding his teeth. "Tourists don't go around asking questions about twenty-year-old murders. They don't meet with the activists everyday plotting something sinister against the landlords. Oh, I don't think you are a tourist but I am going to find out who you really are. The time has come for us to be properly introduced."

He took out a cigarette and lit it with a match. He inhaled deeply, making the cigarette end burn fiercely. The large man grabbed Andrew's hand, forced his palm open and buried the burning end of the cigarette into it. The sizzling sound and acrid smell of burning flesh filled the small room.

Andrew's face contorted in pain and he involuntarily let out a scream. The night—its silence—its rest, was rent by his sharp, shrill scream that ran from end to end of the small room. Andrew's pulse almost stopped: but then his heart pounded in terror; his stretched arm was almost paralyzed. He looked at the blackened burn mark with wide-open eyes. He was in shock and he stared at the man and his cruel smile.

"That's right," said the man, letting go of Andrew's hand, "you scream as loud as you like. There is nobody here for miles to hear you."

"I don't know what you want?" cried Andrew loudly. "You have mistaken me for someone else. I am not plotting anything. I am writing a book."

"Oh, you know exactly what I want," said he, lighting another cigarette. "I told you before. I want you to leave Manali and go back to your country. This time I will make sure that you listen." This time he burnt Andrew's forearm, making Andrew squeal in pain and cry out, begging him to stop. After ten minutes of torture and several burns later, the man said, "Now I am going to give you forty-eight hours to pack your bags and go home. If you go to the police, I am going to find you again and next time I will not be so lenient and will cut off your fingers."

After the car dumped him back where the tormenter had abducted him, Andrew walked back and first went to a pharmacy to buy painkillers, therapeutic burn cream and bandages and then to his hotel to tend to his burns. He decided not to go to a hospital for treatment for that could have got the local police involved. He was still in shock, as he had never faced violence or this much pain in his life. Fear gripped his soul and he kept wondering what his life would be like without fingers.

He entered his room but did not switch on the light. Instead he found a few candles that he lit and placed them on a table by the window. He looked at his empty suitcase sitting in a corner and wondered if he should start packing. He sat by the window and gazed at the silvery darkness and outlines of floating clouds outside. As he looked up at them, the moon appeared momentarily in the part of the sky that filled their fissure; her disk was blood-red and half overcast; she seemed to throw on him one bewildered, dreary glance, and buried herself again instantly in the deep drift of clouds. The wind ceased around his hotel for the leaves on trees were still; but far away over wood and water, poured a wild, melancholy wail: it sounded of sadness, and he dozed on and off sitting in his chair. The painkillers were taking effect.

As he came out of his intermittent sleep he noticed that the treetops were swaying and struggling in a strong wind. The moon had shut herself wholly within her chamber, and drew close her curtain of dense clouds: The night grew dark; rain came driving fast on the gale.

He dozed off again and it was a while later that, when he opened his eyes, he experienced a strange feeling as if someone was inside his locked hotel room. Perhaps he imagined this due to the trauma and exhaustion from the day's events but he could have sworn that he heard someone breathing in the room. The sound lingered on only for a few seconds and then ended. It was not a frightening experience. On the contrary, it was rather pleasant. He remembered when he was a little boy he often felt the presence of his late mother around the house, especially at night when he was alone and scared. She was back. Back to give him courage and to guide him. He needed her.

The candles, wasted at last, went out; as the light expired, he perceived streaks of grey light edging the window curtains. Dawn was approaching. He blinked his eyes several times wondering, where did the night go? He had no idea that he spent all night sitting by the window. It was chilly outside as the morning dew accumulating on the windowpane began to form tiny rivulets that chartered their individual paths of destiny controlled by gravity.

Faint daylight began to revivify the room; it was dawn lighting the eastern sky, and the beclouded night, though ebbing, was choking the twilight. He heard the rain still beating continuously on the window, and the wind howling; he grew by degrees cold as a stone, and then his courage sank. Suddenly he felt angry at being so weak. His habitual mood of humiliation, self-doubt and forlorn depression felt damp on the embers of his decaying ire. Then his thoughts turned to Jyoti. He wondered if he could ever forgive himself if he were to retreat now like a coward. He admired Jyoti's courage and that of Ajit and wondered why he could not be like them.

FORTY-FIVE

As the daylight took hold and drove the darkness away, the rain finally stopped and the sun came out. A curious sense of what he could not call courage, but more, determination rose in his heart and he felt that the intimidation he faced yesterday was exactly that—intimidation. He must be getting close to something or someone for them to regard him as a viable threat. He should have expected this. It was a positive sign of his progress. With the increasing sunshine his inner glow grew and he, with strengthening will, went out to find Jyoti and Ajit.

Later that morning he met up with them. He hadn't seen Sunil for a while.

"You look tired," said Jyoti, "and why the serious face?"

He rolled up his sleeves and turned up his palms.

"Ah, what on earth are those? What happened?" She had a sudden sharp intake of breath. "Who did this to you?"

"Perhaps the same person who tortured Ajit."

"Who?" cried Jyoti, as if trying to pry a secret out of Andrew.

"Oh, just some paid thug. But the better question would be who ordered him to do this. I guess someone threatened by us is keeping an eye on us, and sending a warning."

Andrew explained yesterday's event but without giving too much detail.

"I've asked you this before and will ask again. Are you thinking of leaving us?" asked Ajit in a tone that neither showed concern nor urgency.

"Actually," responded Andrew, "I must admit that the idea of leaving did cross my mind but this event has made me more determined to stay and finish my book. I am making progress and will not retreat." His voice was firm and heart resolute.

"You're a dreamer," said Jyoti, "you need to reconsider. This is not your fight." She paused, and then added, with a sort of assumed indifference, but still in a marked and significant tone, "You are a foreigner, Andrew; and I should say, a little out of touch with the facts. Perhaps all you care about is an interesting story that will help you write a book. While you've been dreaming your passion, we've been fighting for our very existence. Now that this has happened, I am not sure if your stay will help or hurt our cause."

"I've not been dreaming," Andrew said, with some heat, for her brazen coolness provoked him. Again she looked at him with the same scrutinizing and conscious eye. He could not lie to her, his heart chastised him, and he relented and confessed, "Yes, you're right. I've been dreaming of a story and must admit know precious little about the plight of the untouchables in India. I cannot find a single fact about Lalita. But I would like a chance to get to know you all, and to help you in your fight. Look, your fight isn't organized; it ought to be based on a certain strategy that you can manage. I think I've found new courage from this wretched experience last night."

He smiled, knowing she did not understand. A silent twilight was gathering over the valley and rising darkly from the mountains. Fate, with wide wings, was hovering just over them, ashen grey and black, and like a carrion crow, had them in its shadow. Yet she took no notice. She did not understand. She sat beside him, concerned but careless, which only distressed him more. They were alone on the smooth hills to the east. Andrew looked at the day fading away into the darkening sky, leaving the permanent structure of the night. It was his turn to suffer from genuinely being concerned for someone, which comes after years of lonely living.

The rosiness died out, a remnant of the sunset, as embers fade into thick ash. In himself, too, the ruddy glow sank and went out. He would get her hurt, he mused. The earth was a cold, dreary color; the sky was dark with grey ash; and he himself pale and uneasy. "Don't you see," he said finally. "Whoever it is out there against us wants to teach us a lesson through fear. Sunil was lucky being out of town or he would have got the same treatment as Ajit and I did. But I can see what is coming next. They are going to hurt us where we are most vulnerable."

"Vulnerable?" she asked inquisitively, "we have nothing to lose, what makes us vulnerable?"

"You," said Andrew mechanically, "they are going to hurt you next to get to us. You need to be in a safe place and away from us. Perhaps take a few days off and go stay with your Baba."

"I think you have it wrong," said Jyoti, full of resolve. "That is exactly what they want us to do—run. I am not going to slink off. We need to do exactly opposite of what you are suggesting. We need to up the tempo and put more pressure on them. The Facebook and Twitter campaign is working and this is the most support I have seen in a long, long time. Maybe we ought to organize a protest march?"

It was an oddity of Jyoti's that her face in speech was like a lighted window at night, but her silent pause followed by her speech immediately drew the curtain. The occasion for reply allowed by her silence was never easy to take, for one never knew the message her silence imparted. The often mysterious and contemplative look on her face gave her listener little help to read her mind. "We didn't ask you to come to hear what it isn't—we asked you to come to hear what it is," she said, offering no help to Andrew as to how to respond to such a question, if indeed it was a question.

FORTY-SIX

Andrew couldn't be sure if Jyoti's answer held a veiled challenge or was it a test that she was putting him through. He always felt that in her company he was under a microscope, being examined minutely and from every angle. He had to come up with an answer, a real answer and not question her question.

But in the moment of his obvious discomfort, Ajit came to help. "Don't be too impossible," Ajit blurted out and paused for a moment. "We lost Sunil and perhaps need Andrew, now more than ever, to build momentum and recruit others to join our cause."

"What happened to Sunil?" asked Andrew.

"Nothing," said Ajit, "his father who works for ONGC received an unexpected transfer and the family has been moved to some town in central India. No prize for guessing what caused it."

She again raised her eyes to him, and this time there was something of consciousness in her expression. She seemed to examine him warily; then she said, "You need more than courage to get involved in our fight, you need faith, and I am not so sure you will find such faith by simply getting to know us." She paused for a moment, as if thinking up an answer that would confuse him; and then she fell silent, as if she were letting him off easy.

Andrew was now beginning to understand who the real leader was amongst them and he realized that she was the person he had been searching for to help him accomplish what he came to do in Manali. Lalita was gone but Jyoti was here. He articulated, "I hear you, Jyoti, and I remember you once said that having such beliefs, true or false, gives strength when one needs it. But to be honest with you I don't care about that, and I ought to warn you, I have no faith, not like you have. But isn't it enough that I am here and I am willing to give it a try? We can't let them drive us out of town one by one."

Jyoti said nothing for a moment, but then asked, "Why should you care?"

"Oh, I care because it is so good to see a woman, especially in the developing world, leading a group of men and taking the fight to those who think themselves invincible. I think what this group needs is more women, women with drive, with passion, women like you."

Ajit looked at Andrew with a puzzled look. A hesitant silence fell between the men and the woman.

And when Andrew said, with a little sigh, "Ah, I love the people of Manali," something in her resonated, and something in her spirit stiffened in resistance: stiffened from the terribly physical intimacy his tone seemed to have implied, and from the peculiar haste and ease with which he made the comment. And this time the sharp wit she possessed did not force her to respond.

But oddly, he smiled apologetically as if he had perhaps been a shade too candid. His discrimination seemed
to mark a possible, a natural reality, a reality not wholly
disallowed by the account Jyoti had just given of her
own intention. There was a difference in the air, even if
none other than the supposedly usual difference in truth
between a man and woman; and it was almost as if the
sense of this provoked her.

She began to cast about, and then she went back
resentfully to something she had allowed to pass a minute before. She was ready to take up rather more seriously
than needed the joke about the comment of her being
the leader. "Men are at the core of what is driving this
prejudice, even the educated ones. You didn't understand
just now why a woman needs to lead this fight, but it must
also be with the help of men, as it wouldn't be right for an
all-woman group to band together against this prejudice.
It quite likely would be perceived as an approach based on
predisposition. This is not my group, we are a team."

"You have misunderstood me. But do you suppose,"
Andrew continued as if it were suddenly important for
him, "do you suppose that the passive role assumed by
the majority of women is just as responsible for this
prejudice?"

She said nothing—she kept that up; it might even
have been to let him go further, if he was capable of it,
in the way of paucity of spirit.

"It's your impudence to say so: I expected it of you;
I sensed it in your behavior the first time I met you," said
Jyoti, with a faint smile flickering on her lips.

"Did you? You're very perceptive."

"I am; and I also have a moral sense of decency toward my fellow human being. It is not too late for you to flee. Anytime you want to bail out, just say so and you will have no complaints from us, okay?"

"Okay." After a brief pause Andrew said, "But it is not bailing out that is on my mind. Like you said, we are a team, and I believe that the time has come for us to take the upper hand."

"How to you propose we do that?" asked Ajit, who had been listening to the banter between Andrew and Jyoti with some apparent interest.

It didn't take much computation, but he nevertheless had to think a moment, consciously, as he was already guessing the sense of his appeal. "I'll let you know as soon as I have firmed up my plans. I think that ONGC could well be the common denominator. I need to give more thought to what the next step ought to be. But I promise that you will be the first to know."

Hearing no objection to his proposal, Andrew thought it was the right time for him to exit.

FORTY-SEVEN

A couple of days passed, with Andrew busy writing within the confines of his hotel room and Jyoti busy with her work. He made sure not to go out after dark and especially not on his own, just in case there was danger lurking around. One late morning while he was sitting in the hotel lobby, Jyoti arrived and said, "Where have you been hiding for the past two days? It is beautiful out there. I am going for a walk by the river, would you like to come?"

"I sure would," said Andrew, "it would help clear my head."

She nodded and together they made their way to the river. They wandered along the riverbank quietly, lost in their own worlds, and finally decided to rest for a while on a bench.

She moved her lips as if contemplating something. And as she looked at him she sighed. Thrice she sighed, each time more deeply than the last. Then she knelt down and picked some of the flowers growing wild by the riverbank, and let her hair out of her ponytail. She did more, indeed—in his dream—she put flowers in her hair, she took her shoes off, and then she glided through the air. The dream ended thus, though he wished that it would go on, and he felt as though it had gone away too soon, as such visions do.

Awhile later, he awoke quite suddenly, and opened his eyes. There, near to him, glittering in the full light of the brilliant sun, sat the woman of his dream, only now with her head buried in a book, she was reading intently. Two butterflies, both white in color, fluttered up and down in agitated little leaps, around him. Instinctively Andrew put his hand forward to touch them.

"Ah, you are awake," she said, lifting her head from the book. "I thought you had fallen asleep."

Andrew said something that she could not hear.

A waft of wind came sweeping down the steep slopes of the Himalayans, and trembled through the boughs of the pine trees. The nightingale's song was then the only voice of the hour: listening to it, they both smiled. Andrew sat quietly, awaiting her answer. Some time passed before she spoke; she at last said, "I'm sorry, what was it that you asked?"

Andrew gazed at her as an expression filled with solemnity drifted across her face like a dark cloud casts a shadow on a sunny day; slowly it faded and she relaxed. A twinkle appeared in her eyes that transformed into a faint smile that crept down to her lips and she gave a short laugh. But it did not escape his attention and she asked again, "What? What did you ask?" She insisted now.

Andrew said, "What I asked was that we have known each other for sometime now and I don't even know your last name. What is your family name?"

"To be honest with you," she said, and then paused for a moment as if struggling to find a way to finish what she had started to say. She then responded, "I don't really know. Does that surprise you?"

Andrew laughed. "What do you mean, you don't know? Is it a funny sounding name that you don't want to tell me? Come on now," he coaxed. "Tell me. What is your family name?"

She gave him a look, a certain sentimental look. Lately he had noticed that sitting alongside her in cafes, he was surprised to find how easily she interacted with him, ignoring the semi-sarcastic attention of the surrounding public—hateful looks did not mortify her, nor did taunting remarks trouble her, not anymore.

Noting her silence he asked, "What's wrong? You're not kidding when you say you don't know your family name, are you?"

She let out a sigh and, as if in a trance, said, "When I was a little girl, only six years old," she paused and sighed again as if solving some specific unresolved issue in her head, "I one night heard Baba say to the lady who lived next door to us that my parents were working in Dubai as laborers and they were sending money, enabling him to raise me. I always knew that he could not afford my education and had help, but why did I never hear from my parents if they were living and working in Dubai? What he said about my parents might have left my memory, had not a circumstance immediately followed which served to indelibly fix it there."

"What happened, what incident?" asked Andrew. He had occasionally wondered what sadness she was hiding behind her perpetual smile. He had often seen sadness in her eyes but never imagined the turmoil she hid in her soul.

Andrew waited and wondered if she heard him for his question went unanswered.

Jyoti finally explained, "Well, it was the following week when Baba registered me at a local school, the teacher asked about my parents and he said that my parents had died in a road accident when their rickshaw was run over by the city bus. Since then I have heard many different accounts of the death of my parents."

"It seems to me," Andrew drew a big breath, "that your Baba is trying to protect you; it's only natural, for I'm sure he obviously loves you very much. I mean, after all, you're his only living family and hope for the future."

"Oh, I know that. But don't you see? It was strange, a little odd that I carry my Baba's last name and not that of my father's? I don't even know what his last name was."

Jyoti suddenly fell silent as if lost in thought and Andrew found he was feeling sorry for her. *How could a person not know who her father is?* he mused.

FORTY-EIGHT

Moments drifted by and when Jyoti looked up, Andrew was looking at her with affection. She smiled and said, "What are you thinking?"

"I can't imagine your not knowing anything about your father. Did you ever try asking Baba? Maybe your father was of a different cast? Maybe it was someone your Baba didn't like?"

"Oh, asking him about any of it is impossible. Whenever I did ask I saw Baba shudder: a singularly marked expression of disgust, horror, and hatred warped his countenance almost to distortion; but he only said, 'Come, be silent, and never utter such gibberish again: don't ever repeat it. You'd make your mother's soul unhappy up in heaven.' And that's it. He knows that bringing my mother into the discussion will shut me up."

"Oh, come on," said Andrew, shaking his head from side to side, "you're in your twenties, you are old enough, an adult, you are not a child anymore. You've every right to ask your Baba about your parents. Don't just ask; insist on it. You can't go on not knowing anything."

"Look at you, Professor," she laughed suddenly, "now you are full of helpful advice. And what was it the other day that you told me, that you haven't talked to your dad in the last twenty years and have very little knowledge of your mother's early life? How come you haven't resolved any of your own issues?"

It seemed to Andrew that Jyoti had read his unspoken thoughts with an ability that to him was incomprehensible. In the present instance he took no notice of her abrupt vocal response; but he gave her a certain smile he used only for rare occasions. He seemed to think it too good for common purposes: it was the real sunshine of his feelings—he shed it on her now and said, "Touché." He raised his hands up in surrender. "Point taken. You are right. These are not easy subjects to tackle. Perhaps one day we both will find the answers to our questions."

A tear dimmed his eye while he looked—a tear of disappointment and impatience—ashamed of it, he wiped it away. He looked up at her to read the signs of struggle in her face, now forlorn and melancholy. He put his hand on her shoulder and turned her around to face him. As she looked up to meet his gaze he put both his hands on her shoulders and said, "Give me your confidence, Jyoti." Seeing puzzlement in her face he continued, "I know you want to share more. Relieve your mind of any weight that oppresses it, by imparting it to me. What do you fear? That I shall not prove a good listener?"

"That is furthest from my thoughts," she said, gently removing his hands from her shoulders. "You always seem to be there ready to listen. You already are a good friend."

He looked at her intently and in a faint voice said, "I'm sorry. After the other day when I was tortured, I began to trust in providence, and believed that events were working together for your good and mine. It was a rather difficult night for me, but the calmness of the air and sky that came with the memories of my late mother forbade any apprehensions for your safety. I sat by the window in my hotel room all night thinking of you; and I beheld you in imagination so near me, I scarcely missed your actual presence. I thought of the life that lay before me—your life, Jyoti—an existence more expansive and stirring than my own. I wondered why moralists call this world a dreary wilderness. For me it is filled with prom-ise, provided one has faith."

Jyoti smiled a smile that showed appreciation for his boldness and openness, and he let out a sigh of relief when, rather than abruptly running away from him, she said, "I am always happy to hear that you care about me. But I know you're a dreamer and came to Manali to follow your true passion—writing a novel. And these dreams weigh on your spirit now, Andrew, my work is distracting you. You by now already have enough mate-rial to return to Canada and write your masterpiece. But if you need to be further inspired, then who knows, you may find your inspiration and the subject for your novel in my work. You want my advice? Forget the visionary woe, and think only of real happiness."

Andrew listened with amazement. He had thought he was struggling to separate his various and conflicting emotions to deliver the right message, but it seemed that she knew exactly what his heart wanted. He was relieved and remained silent for he felt she had more to say.

After a momentary pause she continued, "I see happiness in your eyes when you talk about fighting for the rights of the Dalit. So work with me. You say you care for me, Andrew: yes—I will not forget that; and you cannot deny it. Those words did not die inarticulate on your lips. I heard them clearly, expressing a thought too solemn, perhaps, but sweet as music—I think it is a glorious thing to have the hope of working with you, Andrew, because I care for you too."

Heavy clouds were hanging from the edge of the peaks of the mountains as if bowing in awe. Most of the sky was pure and stainless: the clouds, now trooping before the wind that had shifted to the west, were filing off eastward in long, silvered columns. Unperturbed by the threatening dark clouds, the sun shone peacefully, for it knew that its eventual victory was certain.

"Jyoti, I needn't tell you how to live your life but it scares me to think what you have embarked upon. I want you to leave this to me so you can have a safe life," he said, and his unsteady voice warned him to curtail his sentence.

The look on her face was that of a mix of disappointment and anger when she countered, "Then you condemn me to live as a coward and to die accursed? I don't know what you call it, I don't call it life," her voice rose. "Like you, I wish to live free, and I hope to die one day of natural causes, not at the hands of an angry mob."

The sudden realization that he'd underestimated her power and will made him smile. Then a sharp burst of laughter made him throw his head back and he looked again at her and this time with appreciation and a wider grin.

"Now what are you grinning at," she asked, shaking her head indulgently.

"I'm sorry," he said, now in a firm and steady voice, "every time I get closer to understanding you the emotional part of my heart diverts me to another path. But I know now. Let us work together. Let us give those bastards a run for their money. What do you say?"

"I say you are on," she smiled and shook his hand.

As they walked back, even though they exchanged few words, Andrew felt that a deeper understanding between them was established. Not a feeling of comfort but that of solidarity through a common struggle. She had gained a place in his heart like no other woman ever had.

From that moment on she was to him not merely a friend, but his only soul-mate; she was not in his heart a woman who takes that place by being sensuous; but rather she was his soul itself. She was the answer to his prayers, became to him a reason for which he could live, the secret cause of resolution with a promise to save him, the support of his future. Yes, she inspired a new life in him, which would show the path of life to those who were lost souls; she became his guiding star.

BOOK IV

The Circle of Life
Winter 2012
Manali, Himachal Pradesh, India

FORTY-NINE

A knock on the door startled Jyoti, for she never had a visitor to her small one-room apartment this late. She sat on her cot still hoping whoever it was would realize that he or she was at the wrong address and go away. Again there was a knock, this time louder and a weak voice called out, "Jyoti, are you in there? Come on, *beta*, it is *Baba*."

Jyoti opened the door and Baba, carrying a small travel bag, entered her apartment. They embraced in silence.

"You should have called, is everything okay?" asked Jyoti, wiping stray tears of joy at seeing him.

"Everything is fine, *beta*. It is just that I have not heard from you for a while and I worry about you in Manali. I don't like small and remote towns like these. They are not safe for people like us."

"I am fine. You worry too much. I am not a child anymore. I have many friends here, including one from Canada."

Baba, who was about to sit on her cot, remained suspended mid air for a moment and then gradually sitting down, asked, "Who? Who from Canada?"

Jyoti laughed, saying, "What? You know everyone in Canada now? He is a professor of English, here spending a few months writing a book." Jyoti deliberately hid Andrew's specific interest in Lalita's murder and the book's subject on the Dalits.

"I'd like to meet this friend of yours," said Baba, after several moments of measured silence. "I don't like your getting involved with foreigners. I don't trust them."

"Well," she said, still laughing, "he wants to meet with you. Where will you be staying? I don't have room for two here. If you had told me you were coming, I would have arranged somewhere for you to stay."

"Oh, don't worry about that. I have a friend here in the Dalit colony who is away for a while and he gave me the keys to his house. I'll be staying there."

Jyoti went out and brought back some food from an Indian takeaway shop. As they were eating she said, "Baba, lately I have been thinking about my parents again, and have a few questions for you. I know you don't like talking about them but I am grown up now and need to know. Do you understand?"

She hated prodding him about things that he disliked. And yet based on recent talks with Andrew, deep inside, a sense of injustice, of being defrauded, had begun to burn in Jyoti. The physical sense of injustice is a dangerous feeling, once it is awakened. It must have an outlet, or it eats away at the one in whom it is aroused. Andrew taught her that. Poor Baba, he was not to blame, she mused, as she watched Baba contemplating his answer in deep silence. His was the greater misfortune. It was all part of the general catastrophe. And yet was he not in a way to blame?

"I don't know, *beta,* what to tell you," was his brief response as he paused and then slowly gulped another handful of chicken biryani.

This lack of communication, holding back the truth, being secretive, was he not to blame for that? He was never really open, nor even mature in his thinking, only thoughtful and considerate, in a well-meaning way. But never warm, as a father can be warm to a child, as a grandfather he could have been truthful and treated her as an adult. But Baba was not like that. His entire race was not like that. They were all inwardly hard and separate, and warmth to them was a luxury that belonged to the upper classes.

A sense of rebellion smoldered in Jyoti. What was the good of it all? What was the good of her sacrifice, of devoting her life to fighting for the cause? What was she serving, after all? The cold spirit of vanity that seemed to be a part of the upper castes left Jyoti with a sad feeling and she wished she were not born of untouchable cast. Why shouldn't equality be everyone's birthright?

Something echoed inside Jyoti: "I have a right as an adult and we have a right as Dalit to know our past. Condoning the casting as untouchable is sin. Give me the democracy of equal status, the designation of a just system. Don't try to justify the caste system by accepting it. A just caste system would be no caste system." She didn't at all know what her outburst meant, but it comforted her.

Baba ate his meal in one-sided silence and Jyoti finally abandoned her argument. After the meal she walked him to his friend's place and helped him get settled in the small, one-room house. With a heavy heart she returned to her apartment and went to bed.

FIFTY

Andrew saw Jyoti rushing through the crowd of tourists as if on a mission. As she hurried past him, he shouted, "Hey, Jyoti, slow down. Where are you rushing off to?"

"As a matter of fact I was coming to see you. I have news for you. You so much wanted to meet Baba. Guess what? He turned up last night. He is staying at the house of an old friend of his who is away. So if you like I will take you to meet with him. But I must warn you that the house, like us, is very poor and in the Dalit colony."

"Oh, Jyoti," he responded with an excited voice, "I look forward to it. But not right now. I am not sure after all that has happened in the past couple of days that it is a good idea to get your Baba involved. These could be dangerous times for all of us."

"Oh, would you stop being so concerned about everyone's safety. You must, must, must," she repeated like a little child. "I'll never forgive you if you don't come with me tonight to meet Baba. Mind you, I must warn you that when I told Baba about you being not being one of us, he was not pleased. Not because of you, oh no, it is just that he doesn't trust foreigners, especially the white ones. But I'm sure when he meets with you he will change his mind. Please come tonight, won't you?"

Andrew obeyed, because it was evidently useless to resist. It was by this time half-past four, and the sun was on the point of sliding behind the mighty mountains, but he found the town still active.

That evening Jyoti came to his hotel carrying a plastic bag filled with food and, pointing at it, she said, "Sorry, no time to cook, so I bought some lamb curry and biryani rice. I hope you like it." Together they walked to the old house where Baba was staying. It took them only about twenty minutes of a leisurely walk to arrive.

The front door was not locked. She opened it with as little noise as possible. The small yard was quiet, but the door to the bedroom stood wide open, and then they heard a small groan as if someone was waking up. Like the scent of a perfume, the stillness of descending evening spread everywhere. Little birds were twittering in the blossom-laden couple of trees, whose boughs drooped like white garlands over the wall enclosing one side of the yard. A small cat meowed time to time, hoping to catch Jyoti's attention, hoping perhaps for some milk: all else was still.

"Come inside the bedroom, we'll wake him up," she said, smiling, and lifted the curtain at the door. They entered a small bedroom where Baba was awakening. Baba rose up in bed, he bent forward: first surprise, then bewilderment, came over him; and then the blood drained from his face as if his blood now crept cold through his veins. He looked like a man whose sky has just come tumbling down. He tried to smile but it was a pathetic smile, more like an effort to smother a cry. Andrew smiled back and offered his hand to shake, saying, "Andrew, Jyoti's friend."

As he spoke Baba grabbed his hand with both of his as if trying to find some support to hold himself up, then as his teeth started to grind, he gave Andrew's wrist a convulsive grip; the flicker of smile on his lips froze: apparently a spasm caught his breath.

Andrew realized that perhaps the old man had never met a white man before and may be uncomfortable having such a person as a friend of his daughter's. He tried to reassure him and said, "You have a very special daughter. I have never known anyone like her, and can hardly imagine anyone more unlike myself; yet, from our very first meeting a deep understanding established itself between us. She is such a good friend and I am very happy to know her."

"Donavan *Sahib—Chote sahib*?" he said, in the tone one might fancy a speaking automaton to enounce its single words; "Donavan *Sahib—Chote Sahib*?" he reiterated; and he went over the syllables three times, growing, in the intervals of speaking, whiter than ashes: he hardly seemed to know what he was doing.

"Yeah," was all Andrew could say, as it was his turn now to be totally surprised and bewildered. No one but his driver used to address him as *'Chote Sahib.' So who is this old man*, wondered Andrew?

FIFTY-ONE

He could not place him and noted something very strange in him; a light in his eyes as though of intense feeling—perhaps even thought and intelligence, but at the same time there was a gleam of something like fear and sadness.

Jyoti, who looked at the two baffled faces, said, "*Baba*, this is Andrew Donavan from Canada. The one I told you about, but you already seem to know him. How do you know him and why are you calling him *Chote Sahib?*"

Baba looked up at her anxious face and her perpetually sad eyes—opaque in tenderness, indissoluble to tears—and knew that she was resolved to consider him good to the last; because to believe him bad would give her no anchor to hold on to: only a sense of mortification. How much could he tell her? Could he find the courage to tell her the whole ugly truth? Would she be able to stand it?

As Baba continued to stare at her and Andrew alternatively, Jyoti was floundering helplessly in the heavy seas of Baba's intricate hesitancies, surrounding her, drawing her into unchartered waters, where she somehow knew that silver-footed ironies, veiled threats, tiptoed malice, were waiting to explode into a huge embarrassment to shatter her world. She had never seen Baba so scared, so lost and so helpless.

Andrew felt awkward not knowing who this man was and what he knew about him. *Is he related to the driver and through him, knows what my dad and my dad's friends did to Lalita all those years back?* If he was, then Andrew did not want Jyoti to find it out through him. He must tell the whole truth himself to Jyoti, for he knew that transparency was paramount for their relationship. He decided there and then that he would tell her everything tomorrow. But for now he knew that he had to get out of this difficult situation. He said, "Look, you seem to be upset. Let me come some other time. I will leave you with Jyoti and we will meet again. I will come back tomorrow with Jyoti. Okay?"

The old man's grip on Andrew's wrist tightened and he cried, "No, no, no, *Sahib*. I beg of you. Please, you mustn't see her again. Ever."

"*Baba*," asked Jyoti in a raised voice, "what is this? What are you talking about? Let go of Andrew's hands. You are not making any sense. Tell us what you know."

The old man slowly loosened his grip on Andrew's wrist and finally, as his hands dropped in his lap, he let go. His eyes welled up and tears ran down his wrinkled cheeks. He whimpered, "How do I explain to you what karma has done to us? I've had this secret buried deep in my soul corroding away the very core of it. But I did not mind, willing to let it lie there, for exposing it would bring untold damage that I could not bear. *Sahib*, she is my only family and I'd do anything to protect her. I beg of you to please let her be and don't shame us by going around with her in public. Please go back to your country and leave us in peace. No one will ever know. No one should ever know."

Andrew faced a dilemma. He could not leave her now. Honoring Baba's wishes would mean betraying her, for he'd promised to support her unashamed in public and fight alongside her for the rights of Dalit people. He only wished that he knew what the old man was babbling about. Perhaps he had him confused with some other white man. Poor people in India refer to all white men as *Sahib*. They even refer to rich Indian men as *Sahib*. *It is a common-enough term*, he mused. While he contemplated his response, Jyoti came and sat next to Baba and cried, "What're you talking about, *Baba*? What secret and what does it have to do with Andrew? How do you even know him? No more secrets, no more lies. Please tell me what you know."

"Don't ask," he implored her with appealing eyes that were moist at the corners, and in a hesitant voice added, "why do you have to come back to Manali to find work? Why? Why could you not find work in Delhi? We're doomed. It is not safe for any of us now. *Hey Bhagwan*, what shall I do now?"

"Come back?" she repeated in a questioning tone as her brows narrowed. "I thought you told me that I have never been here before. You've said I was born in New Delhi. When my mother and father attempted to enter a

Hindu temple to thank god for my birth, they were killed by an angry mob who thought that the temple had lost its sanctity by untouchables entering it. You also told others that my parents died in a road accident or they died overseas. I don't know what to believe anymore. None of it makes sense. What's the truth? I want the truth, *Baba*."

"All lies, they were all lies," he said loudly and then averting his eyes, added, "to protect you, to save you. I could not lose you, my baby, you're my only family. They would have killed you too."

The truth was more obscure now than it ever was before. *Why would anyone want to kill me?* Jyoti wondered if she would ever get the truth out of Baba.

FIFTY-TWO

T hen Baba fell silent as if choking on his surging emotions and tears again started to roll down with his silent cries. He broke into little sobs and then started to shake as he cried, "I cannot lose you. I cannot tell you anything, I've promised. Because once you know what I know then your soul will be burdened like mine forever."

"*Baba*," Andrew tried this time, addressing him like she did to show respect. "Why would going out with me put her in danger? I can assure you that I am not here to get anyone in trouble. Please tell her what you know. She deserves the truth, we all do."

"Don't call me *Baba*," he shouted and then gradually stopped crying as if finding a little courage, composing himself by wiping his tears away with the back of his hand. He paused for several minutes as if deciding to face the consequences for some past deeds and Baba's next words chilled his ardor: "Look closely at her; she is of your blood, *Chote Sahib*. Remember Lalita? Look at her, look at her eyes. She is Lalita's little girl." His voice was harsh and his tone, bitter.

Andrew involuntarily blinked his eyes several times and in his mind felt a sudden explosion of an image of the blood-soaked baseball bat in the hands of his father like a bolt of lightning revealing the secrets of a dark night. "Oh, my god," he whispered. He suddenly felt dizzy and as he stumbled a couple of steps back, his extended hand felt a wall and he leaned against it to support his body. He remembered the night he laid with Lalita and it had never occurred to him that she could have become pregnant in a single, short and interrupted sexual encounter. "Please god, it can't be," he cried. If Lalita did become pregnant that night, Andrew tried to focus in his mind, then the baby born nine months later would today be the exact age as Jyoti was now. The sea-green eyes; just like his, a genetic clue for sure.

"No, no! It can't be, no!" Jyoti cried aloud in desperation, as though she had been stabbed. "God would not allow anything so awful. Lalita could not be my mother."

"But, perhaps, there is no God at all," Baba answered with a sort of malignance, as he laughed and looked at her. Jyoti's face suddenly changed; a shadow passed over it. She looked at him with unutterable reproach, tried to say something, but could not speak and broke into bitter, bitter sobs, hiding her face in her hands.

Andrew saw Jyoti's gaze boring into him. She was backing away from where Baba sat in the little room, pressing her hands against her chest; her lips were parched and her breathing came in nervous broken gasps. Her eyes glittered as if with fever and looked about with a harsh, immovable stare. And the dim light of the single bulb hanging from the ceiling in the middle of the room made her look like a person suffering from some acute sickness.

There was a curious sensation in Andrew's head that was growing bigger, bigger and bigger. He realized what it was; he was slipping into shock. He daren't utter the word—father. He was a father. For twenty years now he had been a father and he didn't know it. Then a sudden thought like a shooting star exploded in his head. "Oh, my god," he whispered, all this time he had those mixed and confused feelings towards Jyoti, his own daughter. He was filled with shame and guilt and thought he was going to throw up. *My daughter, my own flesh and blood, is it possible?*

He was face to face with it now, with the bond of blood; the consciousness of it was what he seemed most clearly to have 'come into responsibility' with, by the secret revealed by her Baba. The comprehension of his situation to him was still as inexplicable as it was at the time of her mother when he could not understand why god would punish the kind hearted. But this was not punishment, a thought in his whirling mind surfaced, this could be a blessing. But how to embrace it, accept it when so much remained unexplained?

He looked at Jyoti, who was now sitting on the floor against a wall with her head between her legs. He felt her pain and wondered what was going through her mind, considering she had no clue that she was involved in the investigation of her own mother's murder. He wanted to hug her, to take away her pain, but was unable to control his own swirling emotions.

There was a long pause of silence, a cold silence. And in obvious grief, tormented, she began to weep. Andrew did not know how to console her. The storm of weeping swelled and shook her, and shook him.

Andrew felt it was best if he left. There was nothing to be said, nothing to be accomplished now. He had to think, to decide, what next? He needed time alone to find composure, to find sanity. If he stayed here any longer he knew he would go mad. He started to withdraw and turned around to leave.

"Don't. Don't go. Don't leave us. Don't leave us like this. Don't you have anything to say?" she cried in blind frenzy, not even knowing what she said, and clinging to him with uncanny force. It was from herself she wanted to be saved, from her years of suffering and inner turmoil, from her own inward anger and resistance. Yet how powerful was that inner resistance that possessed her, which she could only feel but did not know?

He was silent. But she could feel the black void of despair inside him. His confused heart was surrendering to his weak mind. That was the death of all affection, the death of all friendship: this despair that was like the dark cave inside men when their spirit is lost. She knew she could no longer trust him, but he was all she had, and he had always told the truth.

She was protesting against his existence.

FIFTY-THREE

He did not know when and how he stumbled out of the little house, ignoring Jyoti's cries to stop. He moved, seemingly at random, from alley to alley; he stopped for no reason and remained idle; he sat down in a chair in a café and ordered a coffee and then when the coffee arrived, he moved to a booth; after several minutes he paid for the coffee without drinking it and walked about again. He was so utterly confused that he could not decide whether to return to where he had left Baba and Jyoti or go to his hotel room to cry, to scream.

If he were to return now, he mused, he might say something that may take Jyoti away from him. Living without her was now equally impossible as living with her. She could both raise his spirits and dash his hopes. Her statements of truths were often wrapped in a veiled threat of harsh realities. She had become the meaning of his life that was now gradually draining him of his life. It was an ordinary story of an extraordinary friendship of two people who unknowingly complicated each other's life. Hard to admit, but perhaps it was the story of most good friendships. But this now, he mused, was more than a friendship. He was her father.

The moon was full above the town. He looked at it as a man in abstraction watches some clear thing; then he came to a standstill. It was useless to hurry to his hotel. He needed open spaces to breathe. He was in a kind of trance, his consciousness seeming suspended.

He wandered on the edge of the town by the river and sat on the bench. The night air was calm and cold. He drank it in thirstily. On the road again, he lifted his face to the moon. It seemed to help him; in its brilliance amid the blonde heavens, it seemed to transcend to tranquility. It would confront the whitecaps of this raging river with silver shields as they crashed on protruding boulders, and Andrew, looking at the river, waiting, wrung his hands in anguish. He sighed, and the moon sighed alongside him, through the black masses of the trees.

Again he wandered aimlessly through streets and an hour later found himself in his bed in his hotel room, emotionally exhausted and physically shattered. He lay in his bed, motionless and breathing slowly.

His imagination lay there, curled up and silent, a taciturn sleeping being, and at the slightest notion of what he felt sensitive to—the sound of rain, the coolness of night, thinking of Jyoti—it stirred in its sleep, and then took wings to swirl around his room, gradually turning imagination into the visualization of fear, a bleak future and utter despair. What he needed was the ability to reject such imaginations, to bury them in the deep recesses of his mind, with another imagination that in the past had already completed his life. There was, however, no such imagination today that his mind could adhere to for he felt that his world was collapsing around him.

Hours melted and Andrew's mind remained in a state of blankness. Myriad thoughts in his head smashing into one another resulted in nothing but a state of vacuity. He flitted in and out of disturbed sleep through sheer exhaustion, emotionally drained.

His fists were tightly clenched, his fingers closed over his thumbs, which were pressed bloodless. He got up and paced nervously in his room and once again lay down on the bed.

His head was peculiarly numb; at the back it felt heavy, as if weighted with lead. He could think only one detached sentence in intervals. Between his thoughts was a blank, grey sleep.

That night, towards two o'clock, there came a violent storm of thunder and lightning. Andrew started up in bed at the first clap, waking to an empty room. The room palpitated with white light for two seconds; the mirror on the wall glared supernaturally. Andrew, leaning against the headrest, clutched at his blanket. All was dark again, the thunder booming now in the distance.

There came another slash of lightning. The night seemed to open and shut. It was a pallid vision of a ghost-world between the clanging shutters of darkness. Andrew slowly stepped out of his bed and stood by the window gazing out towards the horizon. A questioned hovered in the back of his mind and unwittingly slipped through his lips like a whisper, "Wasn't the night my mother died like this—" His thought was interrupted as his answer was extinguished by another clap of thunder. He took a step back from the window as if to move into a safe zone.

In spite of his feeling of disquiet, the thunder impressed him with a sense of fatality. The night opened, revealing a ghostly landscape, instantly to shut again with blackness. Then the thunder crashed. Andrew felt as if some secret were being disclosed too swiftly and pugnaciously for him to recognize it. He had this curious sensation that something had happened to Jyoti after he left or was going to happen. Gradually the brutality of the storm withdrew. The rain came down with a rush, persisting with a bruising sound upon the earth and the leaves. He leaned against the window shutter and let the spray from the rainfall drench his face.

He leaned forward over the balcony, trying to catch something out of the star-studded night. He felt his soul like tendrils stretched out, anxiously reaching for the stars to grasp hold. What could he hold to in this great, hoarse-breathing night? He held his breath as he suddenly saw a star falling. It seemed to burst into sight just across his eyes with a bright white flash. He looked up, unable to discern whether he had seen it or not. There was no gap in the sky.

FIFTY-FOUR

Outside the darkness receded, yielding to a faint light gathering strength in the eastern sky. The rays of the morning sun brightened up the pink balcony as if someone had repainted it overnight. Andrew was awakened finally by his own perspiration. He was terribly hot. The pillow, the bedclothes, his hair, all seemed to be moist with increasing dampness, while his body was bathed in sweat.

At dawn the darkness retreated, yielding to the growing susurrate of life springing up in the morning. He was now awake, and his brain was petulantly active, but his body was a separate thing, a terrible, heavy, hot thing over which he had little control. A ray of bright sunlight shot through the partly open curtains of his window. Immediately he shut his eyes again and lay still. He felt a piercing pain in the back of his head.

Andrew lay still, his eyes closed, enduring the exquisite torture of the trickling of drops of sweat. First it would be one gathering and traversing its irregular, hesitating way in his hair and then into the back of his neck. His every nerve responded to it, yet he felt he could not move more than to stiffen his jaws. While the nerves in the wake of this drop were shuddering, raw with sensitivity, another small drop would start from under his chin, traversing off the side of his smooth chest, and trickle sideways and then downwards among the tight muscles of his side, to drip onto the bed.

It was like the crawling of a spider or the grip of an octopus over his sensitive, motionless body. Why he did not get up and wipe himself off he did not know. He lay still and endured this horrible sensation, which seemed to gnaw deep into him, rather than make the effort to move, which his mind didn't allow him to do.

His nerves were shredded by outrage and vivid apprehension. It became insufferable. He felt that if he endured it another moment, he would cry out, or suffocate and his head would burst open.

He sighed, pressing back his forehead as it ached with increasing pressure. His legs, too, ached with irritation, while his mind seemed to be hissing with irritability. He sat up in bed and leaned against the headrest. For a long time he sat with clenched teeth, merely holding his body in check. He knew he could not stay in his room all day. He had to get back to Jyoti to face reality. But how and what would he say to her? In his present state everything that occurred to his mind stirred him with dislike or disgust.

With more will than effort he came out of the damp bed and walked up to the window and closed the curtains. Moments later he flung open the curtains and let the bright Himalayan sun wash over his naked body. In pieces, his consciousness like an old memory returned and he in his mind's eye saw yesterday's events like a faint rainbow on a rainy day—disintegrating yet offering faint hope.

It could be salvaged, he mused, only if he could draw strength to face the facts. Suddenly he thought of his mother, which he often did whenever he felt helpless, for her memories evoked a stronger resolve in him. He needed that now more than ever. Jyoti could be the light he had been seeking all his life, he contemplated. He must take responsibility where responsibility is due and accept the fact that he was her father. His facial muscles tensed as a feeling of determination shimmered in his soul.

Daydreaming and reflecting on last night's events, he washed up, slipped into a change of clothes and came downstairs to the lobby. Conflicting and guilt-ridden ideas that haunted him all night had begun to crystallize and took form while prudence dictated his next move. He realized he must get back to Jyoti and assume his responsibility towards her.

That singular idea began to wash his mind of other cluttered thoughts. He had a feeling that her shock must be unbearable, finding that her struggle to fight the injustice done to a relatively unknown woman she never knew, that woman turned out to be her late mother.

He at last understood why he always had that great affinity towards Jyoti without experiencing any sexual feelings. Yes, affinity was the right description of what both felt. A sharp current went all the way down his spine and he shuddered at the very thought of the sexual considerations he once entertained.

FIFTY-FIVE

He hesitated at the top of the stairwell. Suddenly he thought of his father. His distant father, his naked ambition to put business before family, was a disquieting figure in his mind that caused the chord of discontent to vibrate. "If he could be here now," he murmured to himself. Realizing that he was standing at the top of the stairwell for a purpose, he started to climb down the stairs to the hotel lobby. His father may throw a fit knowing that he was a grandfather. A child of an untouchable woman was his grandchild. What a waste for the family to grow this way, would be his father's thoughts. "Why do I dislike him as much as I dread him," he muttered, lost in his own world.

As he came into the lobby he saw Jyoti sitting quietly in a chair. She sat in a large wing chair looking tired, drained and exhausted like dry wisps of clover. But on her face was a determined yet anxious look. He froze. He would have preferred to talk to her at her place and in front of Baba.

He came to her as she stood up. He could see in her swollen eyes that she had been crying all night. His heart filled with emotion and he could not think of anything to say to her. She waited. *She hates me,* was the thought that started to reverberate in his head. How could he ever apologize to her? Explain to her what his father did to her mother? Explain his twenty years of absence, neglect and irresponsible behavior.

All this passed vaguely and fleetingly through his brain, but looking at her more intently, he saw that the desolate creature before him was so humiliated that he felt suddenly sorry for her. When she made a movement to retreat in terror, it sent a pang to his heart. "I did not expect you," he said, hurriedly, with a look that made her stop. "Please sit down. You come, no doubt, from hearing the whole story from Baba. Allow me—not there. Sit here next to me on the big sofa—"

He held her hands and she let him. He swallowed hard. His eyes apologized and his lips twitched but he could not form words. She slowly released her hands from his. He nodded for he understood her dilemma. Then inexplicably and unaccountably, something remarkable happened. He had no idea where the sudden impulse came from, but he simply spread his arms and hugged her. Hugged her first softly and then tight, like he would never let her go. She did not respond but also did not resist. That melted the ice barrier he felt existed between them and his emotions flowed unashamedly through his tears. He felt rejected by her irresponsiveness but somehow still acknowledged an undeniable certain warmth in the embrace.

After several moments he let his embrace loosen and finally found his voice, uncoupling his arms and holding her hands again, saying in a vacillating voice, "I have so much to say but don't know how to make up for the last twenty lost years."

She gave him a puzzled look. "You don't have to say anything and that is why I'm here. *Baba* explained it to me last night. He told me everything. It is hard for me to say this but I'm going to say it anyway, for I cannot think of any other way for us than to be absolutely truthful to each other. I am not overjoyed by finding my family in you for *Baba* could not bear it and I could not accept a family that is somehow connected to the murder of my mother."

He treated the explanation as needing no reply. Andrew for the first time noticed that she was dressed altogether in black, which gave an even tone, by contrast, to her clear face and made her hair more harmoniously dark. Outside, in the bright sunshine, her eyes showed as soft brown; within, inside the hotel lobby, they showed almost as black.

He could feel that she tried to be sad so as not to be angry, but it seemed that it made her angry that she couldn't be sad. He waited a little, but when she spoke again it was clear, "My family is *Baba* and I'm now more committed than ever to bring my mother's murderer to justice for her sake, for my sake and for the sake of every untouchable woman who has been brutally victimized by a tradition-shackled society of Indian men." She paused momentarily, looking exhausted, and after swallowing to moisten her throat, seemed to have found a new resolve as she added, "I hold no personal grudge against you for you are a victim of your own circumstances. But you can see, can't you, I must work alone? I came to say goodbye and ask you to leave me alone and leave India. Maybe one day in the future and under different circumstances we'll meet again. But for now I wish to be left alone."

Fragments of his heart reflected in his welled up tears and he blinked them away for he did not want to plead mercy through his broken heart. He wanted to be strong-willed from now on if he was going to work his way into helping her, to make her see he was on her side. To make her feel that they were a family and families always stick together.

FIFTY-SIX

They were both by nature passionate. But the nature of each of their passions was opposite. Hers was the raw, primitive, violent flux of the blood, emotional and undiscriminating, but wanting to mix and mingle. His was the sentimental, confused, vulnerable, unchangeable, but wanting recognition and appreciation. She was the spark and he the dry forest. By bringing the two together, they could destroy each other. For the next minute a perfect silence prevailed. It seemed that the place was in a suspension of time, as if forgotten by God and unknown to men.

Nothing less than the whole truth would create a bond of trust between them, so he stated, in a steady and measured voice, with a pensive gaze on her, "I understand what you are saying and appreciate your feelings. I can understand why you want be alone. I'm so sorry about running away last night like a coward. I don't really know where to begin and how to apologize for so many horrible things that happened to you because of me. I don't deserve you. But I would like a chance to explain some of that which you ought to know. Let us get back to *Baba*, for there are matters that we must discuss in detail. Besides, I owe him an apology, too. If after all that you still want me to leave then I'll leave, you've my word on it. But please give me a chance to explain my side of the story. I am ready to tell the whole truth."

She glared at him and her lips twitched. He spoke again. "Before you say anything," he said, in a voice shaken by the throbbing of his heart, which could be heard in the deep silence that surrounded them, "we need to talk in the presence of Baba for me to purify my memories of the past."

She looked straight into his eyes as if measuring the sincerity of what he just said and then slowly nodded in the affirmative. "Okay," she said in a trembling voice and repeated for emphasis, "okay."

They walked together silently and after a short walk they entered the small house, where he could feel the tension in the air. Baba sat in a chair sipping on tea and looked as if he had shrunk overnight from a small to a minute figure, almost non-existent. Andrew expected outrage and screaming, but Baba was surprisingly calm. When everyone sat down, Andrew looked at Jyoti and in a deliberate voice said, "Twenty years ago when I was fifteen I came to Manali with my father. I had a short affair with your mother and one day my father caught us in bed."

He paused for a moment as if recollecting the memory of that day and then, his face contorting in hatred, he added, "My father was very upset and we argued. That night my father and some of his friends got drunk, they went over to your mother's house and I believe they badly beat up your father and maybe your mother too. Soon after that event we left India and returned to Canada.

My father never spoke of that night and never explained what really happened. But I'm sure it was pretty bad as he fled the country to avoid the Indian police and any criminal proceedings that might have been brought against him. But it would not have been for murder charges, for it happened several months after we had departed for Canada. But whatever did happen, I'm here to face the consequences. I'd like to right the wrong, at any cost, and not just to help you but also for my own salvation."

Andrew looked at Baba and again at Jyoti and, feeling oppressed by their silence, urged, "I am so sorry about all this, *Baba,* and I want to apologize to you. Please say something. I know I am guilty. I deserve to be punished for I know that there is nothing I could do now that would pay for all your sufferings."

"I can't believe," she said slowly, as if lost in a contemplative mood, "that all this time I've been fighting for justice for my own mother and I didn't even know it. I had thought it was just some poor Dalit woman who was brutalized." She paused for a moment and then uttered, "She was murdered, my mother was murdered. Whatever your father did to my grandfather and to my mother, he will have to come here himself and make things right for *Baba.* I don't know why your having a fling with my mother makes you feel guilty of anything. But you are the son of the man who brutalized my mother and I cannot forget that. Like I told you before, I'm more committed now than ever before to find her killers. That is all I can think of, want to think of."

"Jyoti," Andrew responded in an anxious voice and then failed to find other words as it occurred to him that she was more concerned about the murder of her mother than finding her father. He understood her feelings but he felt disappointed. It caused a tightening in his chest as if someone was softly squeezing his heart. After a few minutes that seemed inadequate, he said, "I may be the son of a terrible father but I myself don't want to be a bad father. If you give me a chance to accept my responsibility as your father then I promise you that we'll fight together to find who killed Lalita. I've a feeling—"

"What?" Baba interjected, suddenly looking alert, before Andrew could finish his sentence. Color rose in his face, his eyes widened in surprise, and he hurriedly added, "What're you talking about being her father? You're not her father. Who told you that?"

Andrew with a perplexed look on his face stared at him and stuttered, "But you, you said yesterday that she is of my blood, and has my sea-green eyes, and, and—"

Baba cut in again before Andrew could finish his sentence and cried, "Not you, *Chote Sahib*," he shook his head vigorously and continued, "the *Bara Sahib*. It was your father. Jyoti is your half-sister, your father's daughter; your blood. When I said your blood what I meant was that it is your father's blood that runs through the veins of you and Jyoti. Did your father never explain to you what really happened that ill-fated night? What he did to Lalita while the other beasts held her down?"

There was a shocked stillness as if all the air had been sucked out of the room, and it appeared as if Baba regretted his bluntness.

FIFTY-SEVEN

The courtyard trembled under Andrew's feet as if the whole place was hit with an earthquake. But it wasn't an earthquake; it was shock and fear that jolted Andrew. "Stop," cried Andrew, "just stop." Andrew leaned back in his chair and threw his head back to stare straight up as if in search of clues to solve this complex puzzle. *Sister? Not my daughter?* He had not fully recovered from yesterday's shock when he was led to believe, or so he thought, that Jyoti was his daughter and now he was being told that she was his half-sister.

He was preoccupied by two thoughts, each in turn shoving the other aside: that he no longer had a daughter, and that Jyoti was his sister. He looked at her vacantly for the numbness following the first shock was passing away and all the agony of his loss began to fix its fangs upon his heart.

His eyes were dry and wide open but could not focus on anything in particular: eddying darkness seemed to swim around him, and reflection came in as black and confused as a recurring nightmare. Self-abandoned, overwrought, and dazed, he felt as if his body was floating in the Bea River rushing down through the great mountains and a torrent was rising in his soul; to move, he had no will; to speak, he had no strength. He felt faint, longing to be dead.

One idea only still throbbed life-like within him—a remembrance of his mother. It begot an unuttered prayer: 'Thank god she is not alive to endure this'; these words went wandering up and down in his deadened mind, as something that should be whispered to have some meaning, but no energy was present to express them. He was utterly stunned by this new revelation.

He closed his eyes and felt a loss of consciousness come over him so immediately opened them again. He held his head in his hands and slowly lowered it by placing his elbows on his knees. From the corner of his eyes he saw Jyoti. She walked over to him and, standing next to him, said in a voice laced with anger, "Last night *Baba* explained all this in a little more detail to me. I'm not sure what to make of you being my half brother but I'm sure as hell that I will never ever forgive your father for what he did to my mother. He is a rapist and he too like any other rapist deserves to be punished for his crime."

"Listen to me," said Andrew, in a half agitated and half exasperated voice. "I can still help you if you give me a chance."

"How could I," she said in a raised voice, "can't you see that you are the son of a rapist who raped my mother. We can no longer work together." She stood there shaking with rage that was now apparent in her voice.

Andrew saw the hurt in her eyes and said, "I'm not sure anymore what to believe. It could be all true but," he hesitated not knowing his own further thoughts, and then shaking his head, managed, as if in surrender, "I know I must return to Canada and face my father. You were right when you said I must get back to Canada. He has some explaining to do."

Baba stood up and they all clustered in the small courtyard. For a moment they were all still as if afraid to bring an end to what seemed to be the beginning of a dreadful sequence of events. Baba walked towards the front door and then stopped and turned around to face Andrew and Jyoti. He seemed to be reorganizing his thoughts and then said, "After yesterday's event I knew things would unravel rather fast and be damn confusing for both of you. I might as well tell you the rest of the story. Jyoti *beta*, I didn't tell you everything last night."

'What next' was the confused expression written on the faces of both Jyoti and Andrew. They looked at each other and then at Baba. Andrew's mind was in a whirl but somehow in all this upheaval, standing next to her, he felt the curious sense of strength of having a sister right next to him. They went back to their chairs and dropped down in them.

Baba cleared his throat and in a clear voice, as if clearing his conscience, too, said, "After Lalita gave birth to Jyoti she threatened to go to the press to make public the events of the night when I was beaten up and she was raped. She wanted justice so one could explain to Jyoti about her father, and compensation to give Jyoti a better life. *Bara Sahib*'s friends, especially Harish *Babu*, threatened her with dire consequences if she did any-thing foolish." Baba stopped but no rejoinder came from his listeners, so he continued, "This made Lalita even more determined to go public but before she could do anything, she was found beaten to death and her body thrown in a well. I felt concerned for Jyoti's safety so I ran away with her to New Delhi, hoping nobody would find us in the crowded big city."

Feeling impatient and confused, not knowing where Baba was going with his story, Andrew asked, "Why did you not contact us in Canada?" Soon after Andrew blurted out his outrage he realized that his own father was on the side of the murderers, so he hurriedly added, "Sorry. I am so sorry, *Baba*, please go on."

Baba simply nodded and said, "Well, as you can imagine, it was impossible for me to raise Jyoti the way Lalita would have. I know she wanted Jyoti to have an education, go to a university and become a professional. I've no means, no education and then New Delhi is an expensive place. For this and a whole host of other reasons, I contacted your father."

"You did?" Andrew exclaimed, jumping up. "So he knows about Jyoti?" He slowly slumped down, feeling betrayed, feeling as if he'd wasted his life. What else had he not been told by his father? He felt as if he was buried in a grave of secrets.

FIFTY-EIGHT

Baba wanted to unburden himself by disclosing all the secrets that had been gnawing at his soul. He sighed heavily and resumed, "He did not respond for a long time. I wrote to him many times and pleaded for him to help his own daughter. Finally and suddenly, one day he turned up in New Delhi. First he apologized for what he did to Lalita. He said he was upset but insisted that he knew nothing about who and why someone would kill Lalita. He promised and I believed him that he had nothing to do with Lalita's murder. He apologized for how he put us in an unfortunate position and offered money basically to shut me up. He said he was working on the advice of his attorney and asked me to sign some papers."

"I hope to god you didn't," said Jyoti, breathing heavily, "and I trust you didn't take his money?"

Baba looked exhausted, like a marathon runner at the end of the race. But at the same time there was a sense of relief that showed in his eyes. He continued, "I explained I did not want money for myself but for Jyoti, his daughter, to give her a proper education. He wanted proof for he thought I was making up a story to extort money from him. So I agreed and he contacted some local doctor and did some tests, I believe you call it a paternity test, and after that test his attitude changed completely. He was a different man. He became generous, sent me money every month, and that helped me to put Jyoti through school and also to keep her away from Manali, but as fate would have it here we are again back in the place where our lives could be in danger, for Lalita's murderers are still out there."

Andrew tried to remember if his father ever said anything in the past twenty years about going back to India. He could not recollect any such memory but then he stayed out of touch most of the time so he didn't really know what his father did.

The very thought of his father churned a sickening feeling in his stomach and in an almost inaudible voice he said, "Sounds like he was more paying for his guilt than helping his daughter." The bitterness in his voice was apparent and he added, "Otherwise he would have told me about Jyoti. I believe the time has arrived for all of this to come out in the open. I'm going back to Canada to drag him out here if I have to for him to explain this to all of us. We're all his victims."

"You don't have to go," said Baba, in a mysterious tone. "He is coming here. I called him yesterday and explained about you being here. Everyone was upset and I thought it was the best if *Bara Sahib* was present. He told me he was very busy but would soon make arrangements and be here in the next couple of days."

There was no sound in the room. The morning sunlight shot rays through the slits of the blinds. Jyoti stood trembling with rage, her fingernails pressing into her palm.

"No," she said. "The man who brutalized my mother has been invited by you to visit us? Is this some kind of a sick joke? Or some kind of a trick?"

Baba paused before he answered: "Neither, I hope. I hope it may be a prophecy." There was a curious warning in his voice.

"Couple of days," said Andrew, standing up and then looking at Jyoti. "Busy, that is my father, business always came first for him. I don't think I can take anymore of this. I might as well wait till my dad gets here. I need to clear my head, I'm going for a walk by the river."

He left the house and walked towards the river in silence and when he reached it, he found the bench where he sat down, and quietly gazed at the water. The river shimmered with flickers of waves scurrying across her belly. A riot of leaves blew across the riverbank and the swirling wind wrapped them around a large tree trunk while he breathed in its stillness. The wind whipped the few remaining leaves on the trees into an eerie, spinning frenzy, and in the sunlight he could see the occasional leaf give up the fight and escape by floating away with the fast moving current of the river. The air smelled of fresh snow on the mountains across the valley, and suddenly he remembered the snow-clad mountains of Banff and the emerald-colored Bow River. The two worlds were so far apart not just geo-graphically but also in their prejudices, and yet so simi-lar in their nature.

FIFTY-NINE

Time passed slowly and a strange silence surrounded Andrew. In the chatter of his mind he could hear nothing recognizable. It's astonishing what you hear when you're alone in the blackness of your mind. A sound without shape or color seems strange. To be blind is to hear. He didn't know why but felt that nowhere more than in India does a human being feel his weakness and insignificance.

Andrew studied the rocks on the riverbank where in the dark, jagged stones he spotted one small, yellow flower with faint brown lines on it and began examining how many petals it possessed, and how many lines on each. He felt his arms and legs as lifeless, as though climbing a tall mountain had exhausted them. He did not attempt to move, but stared obstinately at the flower. His heart felt hollow and empty.

When confusion subsides then through undiscerning suffering, men know fear, and if that fear can provoke a will to act for the good, then it is the most divine emotion. It is the stones for altars and the beginning of sagacity. Unlike his mother's Hindu gods that are worshiped in flowers and chants, Andrew knew that his gods required sacrifice.

Half an hour later he saw a young girl timidly and noiselessly making her way down the path towards him. It was Jyoti. When she joined him, she said nothing, sitting next to him. She clenched her fists, seeming to be seething. Finally she spoke. "Nothing has changed, you understand? I wish, I truly do, that I could find it in my heart to accept you as my brother but I cannot get it out of my head that your father is somehow responsible for the death of my mother. Any man that raped my mother is not my father. A rapist is a rapist, you understand?"

In the thick fog of her undefined existence, there were parts doubtless magnified and parts certainly vague. But now, more than ever, she knew what she wanted. A moral standing in society, and as terrified as she was, she was willing to pay any price for it. The singular reason for this was perhaps that in her soul such a stand represented all events alike, the dim and the distinct, an existence and more importantly, eventually, death with dignity. It was perfectly clear to Jyoti that in her quest for freedom she might be devoured, and in that pursuit she compared herself to a child suffering from acute hunger, who, upon watching a rich family devouring a sumptuous meal, suffers more from the indignity and the injustice of it than the actual hunger pangs.

Andrew remained quiet and said nothing. He was deep in his thoughts. He heard what Jyoti said but didn't listen hard enough to respond. He rubbed his chin as if contemplating some deep theory. He grunted in response to his internal struggle of conflicting thoughts. Suddenly he turned towards Jyoti and said, "I've an idea."

As she glanced at him quizzically, he added, "Listen, I'm going to help you to put away the murderers of your mother. And I promise you if my father was implicated in this murder then I will not get in your fight for justice for your mother. If he is guilty then I'll help you put him behind bars. I've a good idea who is behind the murder, though, and I think I'm going to pay him a visit and have a chat with him. I believe he is involved and if he did not do it himself then I've a feeling he would know who did."

"You're still the son of my mother's rapist," she screamed, and in a trembling voice added, "he is your father so I am sure that you want me to forgive him, but I cannot forget the wrong. And if I cannot forget then how could I forgive." This logic stopped all argument until she spoke again, "How could I believe that you are going to be on my side?"

"I will not take anyone's side," he pleaded, "I want to be on the side of justice, the truth. I owe this to myself. I don't know how to explain this to you, but I need it for my own sanity. By helping you I am doing no favors to you, but you could do me a favor by letting me help you fight for Lalita, to allow me to atone. To me it is about myself and not about my father." Andrew somehow knew that if parted now then they might meet again only in dreams, just like one finds a dried-up flower with its extinguished memories pressed in an old book. He wanted resolution now. "Listen," he said, "what is one's life, detached from the once-in-a-lifetime special friend with whom fate happens to have joined to that life? We will be friends first and my relationship with my father will not come into it."

SIXTY

Andrew also knew that this was his last chance to find what he had been looking for all his life, but struggled to convey it to Jyoti. After a silent pause he, in a soft and meditative voice, said, "I am living a promise I never made to my mother. And I know it is going to be hard and even dangerous, but I must deliver. Because if I don't, my life will have no meaning."

"It is a good reason," said Jyoti, "but is it the real reason?"

Andrew turned towards Jyoti and then, lowering his head, responded, "I was wakened to conscious life by the two tremendous forces of love and truth, both imparted to me by my mother. My mother used to say that every person is born twice; once through natural birth and second through conscience. The former gives physical life while the latter yields a meaningful life. I now know my destiny."

"But your father?" said Jyoti, letting her unfinished sentence be finished by Andrew.

Andrew nodded as if he understood well what she meant and countered, "I have known all my life that the ability to make something of my life came chiefly from

my mother's side, and I also know that when my mother
was alive I hoped that one day my father would acquire
meaning under her influence. But that day never came
because vanity absorbed him, and I have always wondered what stifled cravings once germinated in him, and
what manner of man he was really meant to be. That
he was lonely, haunted by something always unexpressed
and unattained, I am sure. I don't want to end up as a
lonely old man. I don't want to become my father."

Jyoti closed her eyes, as if weighing options in her
heart. She was feeling mixed emotions of anger, hate,
vengeance, and love. Yes, there was a hint of love for
her brother. She certainly wanted to negate such a feeling, for she felt guilty loving someone from a family who
had abused her mother. But then Andrew was innocent
and he wanted to put things right. Was it fair for her to
persecute him for his father's misdeeds?

She lowered her face into her cupped hands and
pressed her hands against her face. The pressure on her
eyes felt good and she saw floating images under her
closed eyelids. The feeling of a brother's love took a
definitive form in her heart and something inside urged
her to accept his offer. She parted her hands and her
face, glowing with renewed hope, emerged like a struggling sun when it reemerges from the parting clouds.

"Who do you think is responsible for my mother's
murder? What do you know?" asked Jyoti.

Andrew, in an excited voice, responded, "The friends
my father had that evening who beat up your Baba.
Remember what your grandfather said, that after you

were born Lalita went back to one of them and he had threatened her with grim consequences. He mentioned the name Harish, and I know that man. Yeah, I think that is where I'll start." Andrew's resolute voice and clenched fists clearly supported his intention but his distant tone indicated he was talking to himself.

"I'll come with you," said Jyoti inflexibly. "I want to continue my mother's fight and I want those bastards to pay for what they did."

Andrew looked at her as if it was the first time he laid eyes on her and then, gathering the gravity of what she'd just said, he responded, "Oh no. This could turn ugly if you were with me. They would not suspect me of anything. Remember, they are friends of my father's. They might divulge something useful to me if I go alone and under the pretense of a friendly visit. I'll come around to your house after my visit to my father's friends and tell you everything I learn. I'll not hold back anything from you and will keep you fully informed. Okay?"

Once again it was unclear what she thought of either his offer or his wish that she should stay safe.

"You misunderstood me," she said, looking back at him with unyielding eyes, "I'll not hide anymore from danger. I am not alone, I've friends."

An uncomfortable silence prevailed. She was so strong in her self-possession, in her passion of fighting for the rights of the Dalit and of dreams, that Andrew knew it would be hard to persuade her to his will. Her agitated response provoked emotional sentiments in Andrew and he responded, "I know you have friends.

These last two days haven't changed anything for me, you're still my best friend."

Because it was the last thing she expected him to say, she stole a look at him out of the corner of her eye. He was smiling at her, and when he caught her gaze, he extended his hand. She timidly offered her hand to shake his.

He would have a better chance on his own of finding useful information and besides, she could become a liability if things got worse, so finally prudence took hold and she reluctantly complied. She said she wanted to get back to Baba and Andrew promised to see her soon.

After Jyoti left he felt a curious sense of renewed strength. He walked back to his hotel slowly and deliberately, feverish but not conscious of it, entirely absorbed in a new overwhelming sensation of life and strength that surged up within him. This sensation might be compared to that of a man suffering for years from a serious illness suddenly given a new lease on life through a wonder drug.

"Strength, strength is what one wants, you can get nothing without it, and strength must be won by strength—that's what they don't know," he muttered proudly and self-confidently as he strode with determined footsteps from the river toward the town. Pride and self-confidence grew stronger in him; he was becoming a different man. What was it that worked this revolution in him? He did not know himself; like a man clutching at straws, he suddenly felt that he, too, could live, that there was still life for him and that his life had not died with the old memories. Perhaps in the past he had not given himself the chance he deserved.

His soul began to expand, to exult, with the strangest sense of freedom, of triumph, he'd ever felt. It seemed as if an invisible bond had shattered, and that he had managed to break through into unhoped-for liberty.

An overwhelming, unaccountable prompting drew him on.

SIXTY-ONE

And when he woke up again it was sunny, it was morning on the hill opposite, though the river deep below ran in shadows. The morning sea of silence broke into ripples of bird songs, the flowers swayed in a gentle breeze beneath his window, and the wealth of gold was scattered through the rifts of the clouds while the people of Manali busily went on their way and paid no heed to the beauty around them. To him, the magic of Manali was dead, gone forever.

He thought of the previous night. God knows what efforts he made to weaken the decree that condemned him. What hopes, long cherished with eagerness of soul, were doomed to perish in a moment? But his life was not over. He had undertaken a task that he must finish, and made certain promises that he must keep. He sprang to his feet like a startled horse.

An hour later he went to the regional offices of ONGC for he remembered that his father's friends used to work for this company. At the reception desk he found an Indian lady desperately trying to look like a western woman of the sixties with ruby-red lips, mascara-laced eyelashes, rouge-coated red cheeks, a bob-cut hairstyle, short skirt, and she was chewing gum. She smiled broadly at Andrew and asked, "How can I help you, sir?"

"I don't have an appointment but if it is convenient, I would like to see either Mr. Harish or Mr. Dinesh. I am sorry I don't know their last names, but they ought to be your senior executives."

"Hmm," she scratched her head with a pencil and with a perplexed look on her face said, "I don't believe we have any executive called Dinesh but we do have a couple of gentlemen with the first name Harish. Which one would you want to see?"

"Well, he was a friend of my father's. It was all about twenty years ago—"

"I see," she interjected, "you mean Mr. Harish Kumar Singh, he is the President of this office. It is rather difficult to see him without an appointment. He is very particular about that. Let me call his secretary and see if he could make an appointment for you. What is your name, sir?"

"Donavan, my name is Andrew Donavan."

While the receptionist got busy with the phone, Andrew found a sofa and made himself comfortable, expecting it to be a long wait. He sighed; he was born to wait.

His mind was in a whirl. The images followed one another, swirling like a hurricane. Some of them he liked and tried to clutch at, but they faded, and all the while there was an overwhelming oppression within him, sometimes it was even terrifying.

He did not have to wait for long as a young, smart-looking man in his late twenties approached him with a big smile. "The President will see you now," said the young man, extending his hand to greet Andrew. He escorted Andrew to the penthouse floor and opened the doors of a small room with comfortable sofas surrounding an oval-shaped coffee table. "The President will be with you shortly, may I get you some tea?" Andrew said no and thanked him.

This conjecture had begun to grow strong the day before, in the midst of all his alarm and despair. Thinking it all over now and preparing for a fresh conflict, he was suddenly aware that he was trembling—and he felt a rush of indignation at the thought that he was trembling with fear at facing that hateful Harish. What he dreaded above all was meeting that man again; he hated him with an intense, unmitigated loathing and was afraid his hatred might betray him. His indignation was such that he ceased trembling at once; he made ready to go in with a cold and arrogant bearing and vowed to keep as silent as possible, to watch and listen and for once at least to control his overstrained nerves.

He looked around the room. The walls of the room were adorned with large pictures of Rajput warriors and a large chandelier hanging from the center of the ceiling spelled opulence. About ten minutes later a large man walked in with the young man in his wake. This man's appearance was at first sight very strange. Nothing like the Harish he remembered from twenty years ago. The approaching man stared straight before him, as though seeing nothing. There was a determined gleam in his eyes; at the same time, there was a deathly pallor in his face, as though he were being led into a deadly game. His brown lips were twitching.

The thick curly hair that looked unnaturally black for his aging body failed to give him the appearance of a young man. The little tufts of gray mingled with black were visible around his temple. His face bore a vague resemblance to that of an aging wolf with blood about its muzzle, for his nose was inflamed and his face had marks of fading pox, signs of a life poisoned at its springs.

His forehead, too short for the face, and transversely wrinkled in crooked lines, gave signs of a life filled with experience, but not of any mental activity; it also showed the burden of constant misdeeds, but not of any efforts made to surmount them. His cheekbones, which were brown and prominent amid the general pallor of his skin, gave him an air of importance. His hard, dark-black eyes fell upon Andrew like the gathering darkness at dusk, bright without warmth, anxious without thought, distrustful without conscious cause. His mouth was violent and domineering, his chin square and strong.

Andrew had a sinking feeling that nothing good was going to come of this meeting.

SIXTY-TWO

The approaching man suddenly smiled and squeezed Andrew's right shoulder with his left hand and shook his right hand vigorously, "It is so good to see you, Andy, my boy. You have grown into a fine man. How is your father? I haven't heard from my old friend Tom in what, over twenty years. I hope he is well."

His whole air was one of simplicity, joviality to a certain extent, as if two old friends were meeting after a long absence. But Harish was no friend to Andrew. Two emotions filled Andrew's mind, hatred and fear—hatred for he could see the devil in Harish's face, and a vague, but real fear for he knew what this devil was capable of doing. There was something disturbing in the constantly twitching lower lip of Harish.

Andrew looked uneasily at him. There was nothing peculiar in his simple questions but his body carried an aura broadcasting that he was not a man to be trifled with. "He is fine," said Andrew finally, shaking his hand. "I came out here on holiday and thought it would be a good idea to say hello. You were such a good friend of my father's."

"Indeed," said Harish, gesturing for him to take a seat. "Are you sure you won't take some tea?" He was suddenly changed. His tone of assumed arrogance and defiance was almost gone. Even his voice was now amiable. He tried to smile a genuine smile, but there was something arrogant and incomplete in his pale grin. He dismissed the young man with a sweeping gesture of his hand.

"Your father and I had some fun together, you know real fun, especially the night we went hunting together, and it would have been nice to see him again," said Harish, wetting his thick lips with his tongue and swinging his arms as if holding an imaginary baseball bat. And suddenly a strange, surprising sensation of a sort of bitter hatred for Harish passed through Andrew's heart. He met the man's inquisitive eyes fixed on him; there was malice in them; his hatred intensified like a gathering storm. Andrew knew what night he was referencing.

"Actually, I just learned that my father is coming here soon. Apparently twenty years ago he was involved in a disastrous incident with a Dalit girl and I believe that is the night of unfortunate circumstances you are remembering. Anyway, he is coming back to set the record straight with the local authorities. You would not know anything about how she was murdered a year or so after we left for Canada, would you?"

As soon as he had said this, the same familiar sensation of anxiety and fear froze his heart. He looked at him and all at once seemed to see in his face the visage of a monster. Andrew strained to listen to what Harish had to say.

The sparkle, which began in the corner of his eyes and trickled leisurely down to his twitching lip, showed that his answer was ready. His face was expressionless when he responded, "Her name was Lalita; you can say her name. You remember her, she was the girl who took advantage of your young age and your father's money." He laughed as if he had said something quite amusing. Then, assuming a serious look, he said, "Tom is making a grave mistake in coming back and talking to the authorities. Besides, everything has been taken care of and he need not worry about what happened all those years ago. This is India, my son, and here it is not what but who you know. You ought to inform your father he should cancel his trip or some people are likely to get hurt."

"Are you threatening me and my father?" he said, tightening his facial muscles to bring some gravity to his tone. Harish gave a short burst of laughter first and then snorted loudly. "You are so naïve," he said, wiping his moist mouth with the back of his hand, "this is just friendly advice. I am on your side, always have been. There are a lot of people in this town, in this province, in India, and I mean violent people, who hate and despise Dalit lovers more than Dalit themselves. What your father did, we did, is admired by these people and we are here to protect you, not threaten you. It is for your own safety that you and your father are to stay away from Manali. Do you understand me?"

Andrew felt he had learned enough for the first meeting to be convinced that Harish was either involved himself or knew who was behind Lalita's murder. It was not enough to go to the authorities with but that was not why he came to see Harish. He was there to shake him up so he would make some foolish move that could yield desirable results.

"I understand completely," replied Andrew, "and will keep in mind your advice. I don't want to keep you but will see you before I leave. Thank you for seeing me."

He stood as though lost in thought, and a strange, humiliated, half senseless smile strayed on his lips. He went quietly out of the room.

Andrew returned to his hotel rather than going to see Jyoti, to contemplate what his next move was going to be. He wondered how he was going to face his father. Unpleasant for sure, but he was determined to bring everything to the surface and once and for all get his father to admit the truth.

BOOK V

Atonement
Winter 2012
Manali, Himachal Pradesh, India

SIXTY-THREE

Strings of sunlight scaled the window of his hotel room in Manali and the morning glow with its gentle warmth woke Tom up to a new day, to a new life. The winter morning in the Himalayan mountain town was fresh and fragrant with its pine scent, and he felt confident of a new day filled with new promises. There was no conflict in his mind as to what he intended to do but he was anxious, for he might be endangering other's lives. It was a risk but necessary to achieve the desired results.

On the horizon was always the majestic radiance of the mountains, and there was the enigmatic, crystal-clear river rushing through its pink shoals into the mysterious darkness of the pinewoods; there were always the ice crystals in the thin air, and the rush of roaring water. And the luminosity of snow on distant mountains was vivid with timeless immunity from the flux of encroaching life.

It was his second day in Manali, the day he both dreaded and eagerly anticipated. He had not yet informed his son of his arrival, as yesterday he had to finish a couple of errands before facing Andrew and Jyoti. He got out of bed and stood in front of the bathroom mirror.

As he turned, he saw himself like a ghost reflected in the mirror. His hair still grew thick and dark from his brow: he could not see the grey at the temples. His eyes were soft and tender, and his mouth compressed in perpetual struggle, was full of determination.

He squeezed some foam out on his fingers and covered his unshaven face with it to start shaving. If there was something that was causing disquiet it had to do with certain critical information he was withholding from his son. He wondered if he should ever tell Andrew about what he had recently been told.

Tom always carried in his wallet an old picture of his late wife carrying in her arms a day-old Andrew. So many years had lapsed since she had gone and he could not understand why he could not let go of that picture. Today as he came looking for his grown-up son, he could see that one of its uses lay in preserving a few fond memories he had of his son when he was a baby, for such memories were like drops of an old and rare vintage wine, to be savored by a wine connoisseur in order to be truly appreciated; and he wanted to atone for his unappreciativeness by trying to revive that faint memory. But perhaps he was unconsciously trying to atone for his culpable neglect of his duty as a responsible father and a role model, which he had long disdainfully held far from him, fatherhood eclipsed by his naked ambition of pursuing business probity, and imposing his values on whoever lapsed from them.

Tom looked in the mirror and a surge of guilt showed in the eyes of his reflection. The black snake of wounded vanity had been gnawing at his heart for a long time. He needed to make peace with the man in the mirror. One can never hide the truth from one's own reflection. He was afraid to search his own soul for answers but was condemned to peer into that heart of darkness.

After he arrived in Manali, he knew that this was a culminating point where his life would change, even though it was the most complex byzantine labyrinth to survive. It was like one moment you were in a soothing warm Caribbean blue ocean rejuvenating your soul, and the next, drowning in it. Lying under water, suffocating slowly, you watch helplessly air bubbles rising as your life slips away. He has been drowning for a long time in an ocean of his own misery.

As he shaved he was daydreaming and remembering events of the last few days. Lately he had been feeling discomfort in his upper abdomen and he blamed it on indigestion. When the discomfort persisted, he reluctantly visited his doctor, although he detested doctors after his bitter experience of fighting against the medical system. He still believed that it was negligence on behalf of the doctor that had claimed his wife's life.

The doctor insisted and Tom grudgingly agreed on performing an endoscopic needle biopsy test and when the results came, it was not good news for Tom. He was diagnosed with pancreatic cancer. The doctor explained that the pancreas lies deep in the abdomen and doesn't have nerves that can send pain messages to the brain. As a result, the tumor in the pancreas had grown quite large without Tom having any symptoms, besides mild abdomen pain. Tom was not convinced and sought a second opinion, but it did not alter the outcome.

Tom saw a specialist who too confirmed that the tumor was large and recommended an immediate Whipple procedure, a surgical treatment involving the head of the pancreas. The specialist explained the procedure as a pancreato-duodenectomy, in which the pancreatic head would be removed together with the curve of the duodenum. This would make a bypass for food from the stomach, a gastro-jejunostomy, attaching a loop of jejunum to the cystic duct to drain bile.

The specialist warned that such a procedure could be performed only if the patient survived major surgery and the cancer was localized without having invaded the local structue or metastasizing. Listening to the almost incomprehensible logic of what was being proposed, Tom remembered asking in an exasperated voice, "What are my chances of survival?"

"It varies—" explained the specialist but Tom interjected harshly, "does it work, this procedure?"

"Rarely," he answered and added matter-of-factly, "but you have run out of options. My recommendation is that we waste no more time and admit you immediately for the procedure."

SIXTY-FOUR

The following day came the news from Baba and he realized that Andrew could be in grave danger. He must go to India to protect him. He was the only family he had. But even that perception was being challenged lately by his conscience. Jyoti was his family too, and he had to come to terms with the reality that she was his daughter. What must he do, was the question his consciousness was asking. There was something almost ritualistic in this. The question came regularly and imperiously; and though, when it caught him at inconvenient moments, he would struggle against it consciously—for he was beginning to become a very conscientious grown man—the struggle was always a losing one.

Then one day as he was driving to home he saw a dog run into the middle of the road into oncoming traffic in an attempt to save her pup. The pup survived as the cars came to a screeching halt after fatally hitting the dog. It struck a chord. Suddenly he realized that the specialist was wrong; he did have an option. He could right the wrong and earn his son's respect before succumbing to cancer. Dignity could only be earned through courage, for courageous hope is the last thing to die.

He finished shaving and took a hot shower. Wrapping one towel around his waist and rubbing his hair with another dry towel, he walked back into his room when he heard a loud knock at the door and it broke Tom's reverie. It was room service bringing his breakfast on a trolley. He let the waiter in and asked him to leave the trolley by the window. After tipping him twenty rupees, he shut and locked the door behind him and put on a clean white shirt and blue jeans.

He took delight in finishing his breakfast, like a condemned man enjoys his last meal. Then he sat by the window with the morning newspaper in his lap reflecting on his past. So many years had gone by, and that old world of his youth had been so convulsed and shattered that as he looked back, and tried to recapture the details of particular scenes and conversations, especially the ones that took place when he was in Manali twenty years ago, they dissolved into obscurity. But in any case, he was not too concerned with the past today. Today he was concerned with what he was about to do and as a result, what the future may hold for the ones he loved.

In his career he'd had many human rights organizations approach him for his contribution, but none of them made an impact on him during the brief time he had to spare for them. One feels, in looking back, something premonitory in this impatience, this thirst to slake an insatiable curiosity to accumulate huge wealth, almost as fervent as his moral ardor. He wondered if because Jyoti had her roots in the untouchable class, that reality had finally awakened his conscience. Answers to such questions, he realized, were of no consequence. Well, not any more because now he was willing to give everything up just to make a dent in eradicating the very concept of untouchables. His passion was absolute and his mission was clear.

He needed a plan. Lurking in some corner of his imagination, hinting at regions perilous, dark and yet lit with mysterious fires, just outside the world of copybook axioms, he knew that the old restraint and deference remained in his blood; and even the hint of these was useful—for a businessman of meticulous planning. But this time he needed a different kind of plan. A plan so simplistic in its execution, that it was almost elegant in nature. He kept going over and over in his mind details of his plan and hoping and praying that it would work.

The hours slipped away and the noon hour approached. Tom realized that no longer could he procrastinate and the time had come for him to act. He dialed the number of the hotel where Andrew was staying. Luckily he was in his room and answered in a voice laced with bewilderment, "Hello, who is this?"

"Andy," said Tom in a voice filled with resolve, "it is I, Dad. I am in Manali."

"You?" Andrew answered. "How did you get my number here? When did you arrive?"

"Jyoti's grandfather informed me where you were staying. I drove in yesterday and have been busy with a few things. Anyway, that is not important. What is important is that we all meet now, and hear me out as to what I have to say, for time is running out for all of us. Can we get together in the next half an hour?"

"Next half an hour? What is the urgency?" demanded Andrew. "What have you done now?" There was an abrupt silence on the other end as if Andrew felt the rude accusations of his latter question.

He should, if he had deliberated, have replied to this question by something conventionally vague and polite; but the answer somehow slipped from his tongue before he was aware—"Well, nothing yet, but I am about to do what I should have done a long time back."

"Are you finally here because of what you did?"

Tom nodded in an empty room as if half expecting Andrew's disappointment to show in his aggressive questioning but continued, "It is not only what I did, it is what you have started."

He had put it as a truth more than as a question; but there had been plenty of truths between them that each had contradicted. Andrew, however, let this one pass, only saying in response, "Why are you really here?"

"I am here because I wanted to be here. Look, I am pleased that you are here too but son, your approaching Harish was not a good idea. He is a dangerous man. I will explain when we meet. Meet me with Jyoti where Baba is staying. I know the house and will be there in thirty minutes."

"What's the hurry?" Andrew's voice was inquisitive, "why can't we meet first? You can tell me everything before we see Jyoti and Baba."

Tom took a deep breath and realized that Andrew had little trust in him and what he had to offer. But he could not explain everything on the phone so said, "Listen Andy, I know that I've made enough mistakes to last a lifetime and I've now for the first time found a way to redeem myself. Don't look back to your past for a path to the future. Don't look for fortune by venturing into the recesses of your mind. We all are caught in a whirlpool seemingly going round and round but in effect, being invariably drawn into its centric vortex, for no one can escape their fate. Destiny catches up with us all, eventually. I have come to meet my destiny. Don't judge me, please, and hear me out, what I have to say."

"But we could meet first just for a short while to make sure whatever you have to say is not going to upset Jyoti and Baba more than they already are. I could come to your hotel—"

"No, I am sorry, son," Tom interrupted Andrew. "It has to be said in front of everyone. Be there in thirty minutes. I've got to go now." Tom replaced the receiver and let out a heavy sigh. His plan had to work; otherwise, too many lives were at risk.

SIXTY-FIVE

No sooner had Tom finished replacing the receiver back on the cradle than the phone on his bedside table rang. It was the reception clerk confirming that his taxi as requested was waiting for him. He told the receptionist to tell the taxi to wait for five minutes.

Suddenly there was a loud knock on the door. Tom cursed under his breath. The taxi driver was supposed to wait downstairs and should not be knocking at his door. He opened his door and said, "What—?"

His words choked in his throat as he saw two police officers standing at his door. "Mr. Donavan," said one of them, dangling handcuffs in one of his hands, and in a stern voice, stated, "you're being detained for questioning. Come with us to the police station."

Tom's heart sank with a sense of horror. *This can't be happening.* He never imagined that the young police officer twenty years ago had meant his warning advising Tom never to return to Manali. "There has got be some mistake, I can explain," he said hesitantly.

"There is no mistake," growled the officer, "turn around and put your hands behind your back. You can explain everything to the magistrate when you see him in a couple of weeks."

Couple of weeks, thought Tom nervously, *in a couple of days everything will be over*. In his mind he saw his plan crumbling into a heap of dust.

"Please," he said politely, "let me make one phone call to my son."

"You will get your one phone call at the station. Now no more questions or we will drag you out of here."

He put his jacket on and came down the stairs with the officers. They shoved him in the waiting police car and drove it to the local police station.

At the station they locked him up. An hour passed and Tom sat in a small cell in isolation. He wanted to call Andrew to let him know what had happened and warn him of impending danger. But he was helpless. He knew that this day that began so badly with the interference of the police was destined to end in a nightmare. Redemption, what he had hoped for, now seemed far away. At that moment, everything did.

An hour and a half later a policeman arrived and escorted him to an interrogation room where a senior police officer was leaning against a wall and waiting for him. The policeman gave Tom a chair to sit on.

"Remember me," he said in a harsh voice, "I was the young inspector Tiwari when I saw you twenty years ago, now I am the Superintendent of Police. I did warn you not to come back. Why are you here?"

He was pale, his brows were sullen; he was as distant as a far off star. Policemen were all alike. Tom saw the determination in the hard face of the SP and after a momentary pause in which he quickly decided his next move, he said, "My son is here and he is in danger. Look, I'll confess to my previous crime and you can lock me up for as long as you like. All I want is a few hours with my family. I am not going to run away, you can keep my passport. Just a few hours to right the wrong that I did so many years ago."

"I'm afraid it is too late for all that. We have procedures to follow. We will have to detain you for a day, if necessary two days, while we conduct questioning and if we must, then prepare our charge sheet, and after that you can make your appeal to the magistrate."

"I do not have that time," pleaded Tom. "Okay, please just listen to what I have to say and then make up your mind about me. I'll do whatever it is that you want me to do, just give me a chance to tell you my side of the story. But to you and not other strange officers." Tom was banking on the fact that Tiwari was sympathetic to him twenty years ago and may still treat him with some leniency that he may not get from total strangers.

"I don't have time to listen to you. I just wanted to see you one last time to make sure it was you. You will have to stay here and soon other officers will conduct your interview. You ought to have come here first as soon as you arrived in Manali then I would have listened to you."

"Yes, I ought to have done that, oughtn't I?" he said, as if regretful.

Outside suddenly the valley was covered in diffused light as fog rolled down the slopes of the mountains. The fog was cold. It seemed to rob him of his courage to talk further. He suffered an agony of disillusionment. Would his first attempt of redemption be in vain? Was this his just punishment? In the gloom facing him he could see the projection of his soul. He took in his breath sharply. There was an awful blank future before him.

Moments before bathing in sunshine, the valley was now yielding to the oppressive, heavy, dark clouds. There seemed a ghost-glimmer of greyness in the open spaces of the valley.

SIXTY-SIX

Tom stood up and Tiwari let him. He walked towards Tiwari as if walking away from himself, but after a couple of steps he turned around and sat back down in his chair. He was too confused to think. But in the recoil of his confusion, he was determined to deliver his message to Harish. He would not be stopped.

The day had greyed over; the heavy bellied clouds were poised low on the valley and a haze of rain was fast approaching from the mountains; there was a raw cold in the air as Tom sat in the stillness of the interrogation room. It was going to rain. All grey, the world looked worn out. And time was running out for Tom.

"I came here not just to see my son," said Tom slowly and then he raised his head. "I know there is an old unsolved murder, that of Lalita, currently getting too much attention. I believe I can help."

The time passed with dream-like slowness, and Tiwari did not answer. Tom had only half expected him to listen but had hoped that since Tiwari was involved with the case he might be interested in what Tom had to say. He took his silence as a positive sign and continued, "You know what happened twenty years ago?" Encouraged further, he changed his tone, "You know without asking that what I did was foolish but in no way was I involved in any murder." Which was true and Tiwari knew it. He walked up to the table and sat across from Andrew and said, "Go on, I am listening."

"Based on what I know I am almost sure that my old friend Harish Singh was responsible for that murder and I am the person who could make him confess. All I need is a few hours."

The SP listened for about ten minutes to what Tom had to say and then rubbed his chin with his cupped hand, as if determining Tom's fate. Then it seemed the light dawned on him. "Wait here," said Tiwari in a contemplative voice, "you might get your wish yet."

Tom heard the curious satisfaction in his voice. Tom caught his lower lip between his teeth, in fear and excitement. And Tiwari hurried from the room.

Five hours later Tom was rushing in a taxi to Baba's place. He wondered if Andrew and the others were still waiting for him. He wished and prayed that it was not too late.

He hadn't seen Harish for twenty years and when he went to see him yesterday evening at the office, he was told by his secretary that he was in New Delhi on a business trip and would be arriving later that night. She promised to inform him of Tom's visit. Later in the evening she called Tom at the hotel to advise him that Mr. Singh was delighted to hear about Tom and had requested the presence of both Tom and Andrew the next evening at his residence for a drink. Tom had accepted. Tom looked at his watch and saw he had only an hour left before going over to Harish's house. He wondered if it was Harish who informed the police of his whereabouts.

When Tom arrived at Baba's house, Andrew, Baba and Jyoti were all still there. Tom let out a big sigh of relief. Jyoti had a perplexed look on her face; her eyes were burning with anger and hatred.

"Oh, you all are still here." Tom half-raised his hands, as if to imply the fatuity of the question.

"You never did care about anyone else's time and priorities, did you? Was it another business acquaintance that detained you?" said Andrew in a bitter tone.

He watched his son. His child-like indifference to consequences touched him with a sense of the distance between them. He himself might play with the delicious warm surface of life, but he always reeked of the relentless mass of cold beneath—the mass of life, which has no sympathy with the individual, no cognizance of him.

Tom nodded his head as if he read the sentiments of Andrew, answering as if its import had been spoken as well as imagined. "Yes, yes, you are right," said he. "I have plenty of faults of my own: I know it, and I don't wish to palliate them, I assure you. I am here to stop you from whatever it is you are doing."

Andrew felt a pang of aversion in his heart for he saw, as he had never seen before, how material things spoke to him. He held that he had a right to sadness and stillness.

Storm clouds gathered above and raindrops started to fall. Nobody made an effort to move out of the courtyard and into the tiny old room.

"It is a little late for that," answered Andrew continuing with his unpleasant tone.

"You do not know how dangerous these people can be. You could die out here."

His response, when it came, was cold but distinct. The world was different—whether for worse or for better—from his rudimentary readings, and it gave him the feeling of a wasted past. "Could I? It seems to me I've died once or twice already. Yet here I am, carrying on, and in for more trouble." He was thinking hard, yet listening to the storm. "And weren't you happy in this world, when you were without me, without a family? Free to do whatever you wanted?"

Again he was stern, his face sullen. Outside there was thunder on distant mountains.

"It's not quite true," Tom whispered. "It's not quite true. There's another truth." He felt he was bitter now partly because he was leaving his son forever, deliberately going away from his life. And though immersed in his own sorrows, this half pleased him.

SIXTY-SEVEN

Tom looked at his watch, time was running out. Confused, Tom couldn't imagine what he wanted to say to Andrew after all these years, especially when words of affection were so foreign to him that he couldn't form a single coherent thought of what a loving father should say to his son.

The sky was gray and hanging low against the weight of innumerable skeins of promised snow. A cool dampness infused the air and hung in mists among the barren twigs of sleeping trees. Tom held out his hands and let the almost-winter afternoon poke fingers of blessing across his stooping frame.

Andrew braced himself to face a terrible and unknown ordeal. At times, he had longed to fight it out with his father and extract the truth out of him. The truth about what happened between him and his mother, the truth about what happened to Lalita, the truth about why they couldn't have a normal relationship like a father and son should. This anger was what he dreaded from the beginning and it ate at his soul. The moment of that anger with his father culminating in his determination to know the truth had finally arrived. He felt that his parched lips were burning and his heart was throbbing. But he was still determined not to speak till the right moment. He realized that this was the best policy in his position, because instead of saying too much, he would be irritating his father by his silence and provoking him into speaking freely. Anyhow, this was what he hoped.

All except Tom, who remained standing against a mud wall, sat down in the courtyard. Andrew sat next to Jyoti as if declaring both his defiance and allegiance. Tom allowed the silence to prepare those present for his declaration, or confession. He said, "I know what you all think of me." He looked up and saw two pairs of angry eyes staring at him. Jyoti hadn't said a word yet. Baba was sitting with his head bowed as if regretting all this. Tom continued, "I am not here to present any justification for any of the unfortunate things that you all had to endure because of me. All I ask, request, is that you hear me out."

In the next few moments, he neither spoke nor moved. But time was pressing on him and he knew these matters amongst them had to be resolved. He dwelt on it with gathering dread. Then after an awkward pause and in a slow voice, he said, "When you commit a heinous crime like what I did, it kills a part of your soul. But it keeps living within you and over time that dead part of your soul begins to corrode the rest of your soul. When you kill someone like I did by brutalizing Lalita, a little bit of you dies too."

Andrew had a grudge and a grievance: that was obvious to Tom. He had always loved Andrew but didn't want to say anything to upset him more than he already had.

So instead of sharing his real feelings, Tom said, "I died when I violated Lalita, my love for life was lost, my hope to be a role model for you, Andy, was quenched, my faith death-struck, hanging above me like a sword. I betrayed the trust I gave to your mother. That bitter hour cannot be described: in truth, the poison came into my soul; I sank into deep mire: the devil robed me of prudence; minute by minute in that hour it all attacked my soul till I was void of the humanity within me. I became the devil."

Unimpressed faces ignored his plea and continue to stare at him. Still there was no response, but Tom took their silent fury as an opportunity to have his say.

He willed himself to utter the words he came to say. They came almost as if they had been waiting eagerly behind a locked door and toppled out hurriedly when the latch was released. "My conscience has tortured my soul for what I did to Lalita, what the uncontrollable monster evoked by anger that possessed my soul that fateful night did to that poor, harmless girl and often I wanted to return to India to confess my sin and atone. But I was weak. I was a coward. Then, when I heard that you have returned to Manali, a voice within me averred that you may end up paying the price for my iniquity, and I should find the courage to do the right thing. I wrestled with my own resolution: I must admit that I wanted to be weak that I might avoid the awful passage of further suffering I saw laid out for me, for the Indian police are known to be notoriously harsh; and conscience, turned tyrant, held my soul by the throat, taunting me, if I did not act morally now then destiny, with its arm of iron, would thrust me down to unsounded depths of agony, forever."

He stood immobilized with appealing eyes. Suddenly he turned away, with an inarticulate exclamation, full of passionate emotion. He strode through the courtyard towards the door, stopped, turned around and came back; he stooped towards Jyoti as if to kiss her forehead, but hesitated.

The storm had abated and the golden hue of the setting sun filled the valley and the courtyard of Baba's house with a tawny light that was both calming and serene. But it was not serene for Tom, for he was suffering from tumultuous thoughts. He had not yet told his son that he has just arrived in Manali with a greater objective. He wanted a few hours to himself to collect his thoughts. But all he had now were a few minutes. He took a few deep breaths and in an attempt to calm down, he reminded himself of the importance of the day, for he was going to pay his long outstanding dues to humanity. Failure, he mused, was not an option.

SIXTY-EIGHT

A perfect silence descended in that dwindling light in the courtyard. Andrew was startled as Jyoti suddenly stood up and walked up to Tom and in a voice that sounded more like hissing, she said, "Have you come to apologize to Baba and expect all of us now to simply forget about your heinous crime? What are you expecting from us—a family welcome? I am not your daughter, and I will never be your daughter. You may not have killed my mother but she died anyway the day you took her dignity away from her. We heard what you came to say and now we would like you to leave us in peace. I am going to put away my mother's murderer and I don't need any distraction. So, goodbye."

Tom collected the bitterness of her scorn as he has been collecting pain in a dreary little pile in his heart—a contemptible altar to the god of his own demise—and somewhere deep in his heart he muttered the apologies that he would make if he were a better, stronger person.

Tom wanted to reach out and embrace her, hoping the love of a father and daughter might rise above the hatred she felt towards her mother's violator. Then he realized that was never going to happen. He smiled sadly and responded, "I know all about Andy facing up to Harish and you two trying to make him reveal the name of the murderer. But you don't know him as I do. The real reason I am here beyond apologizing to all of you for your sufferings at my hand is to make the wrongs right. Leave Harish to me and I will get him to confess, if he was the culprit behind Lalita's murder. You two should stay away from him, leave him to me."

The thread of emotion—anger, misgiving, and anguish—that had held Andrew back from speaking his mind finally snapped and he retorted, "We are not playing any of your games." Andrew walked over next to Jyoti as if showing his unequivocal support for her and gave further support to her objection by saying, "It is our fight and we will follow through on it."

It was clear Tom understood the direction this was going. Tom could see the struggle in his son's head and his heart. But he could not give up now.

"But," Tom resisted with the persistence of a child, "listen to me now if only for the first, the last, the only time in your life. One day you will see that man owes his debt to the society he chooses to live in through a thousand differing ways. Trust me when I tell you that this is not a game, you have got to let me do this my way." Tom insisted now, looking imploringly at Andrew, clasping his hands in dogged entreaty, as though it all now depended upon him. Andrew stared quietly trying to decipher the meaning in his eyes. A minute passed. The old man was sitting down with his hands and his head hanging in terrible sadness as if feeling the burden of this unfortunate day.

Tom tapped at his watch nervously. "We have no more time."

Andrew stood his ground and in an unwavering tone said, "I know, but you are not doing this on your own."

Tom said, "Okay, we will do it your way. But at least allow me to come with you two. I am meeting with him this evening, in a few minutes, and if you must insist then come with me. If I fail to accomplish what I have set out to do then go ahead and do what you feel is right. One chance, that's all I ask. Let me do the talking."

It was finally agreed that Jyoti and Andrew would go with Tom to Harish's house. There was a sparkle in Andrew's eyes for this was the first time he had triumphed over his father. His resolve had defeated Tom. But in his defeat was a kind of triumph that he and only he understood.

A few minutes later they were on their way to Harish's house. Tom could see nervousness in both their faces, as they remained quiet during the short journey. To lighten the mood, Tom asked Andrew, "How did you find Harish? I haven't seen him in twenty years, was he hostile towards you?"

"I wouldn't know how to go about proving it but it is written all over his face that he is guilty. When I confronted him I began to feel uneasy. I am not used to such situations, and there was something ominous in the atmosphere. It was just as though I had been let into some conspiracy—I don't know—something was not quite right; and I was glad to get out. But I am sure of one thing, and that is he was shaken by my presence here and definitely didn't want to see you in Manali."

As they arrived, Tom paid the taxi driver and told him to come back in about an hour and wait for them.

On the outskirts of town, Harish's house was built of large blocks of stone and wood. The house looked relatively new and its vast, surrounding gardens were well manicured and stocked with summer flowers. The two stone pillars outside the large entrance were covered in jasmine creeper and its hundreds of tiny white flowers with orange stems against deep-green leaves looked like millions of stars in the night sky. The front door of the house was large and made of teak. It showed carvings of the Hindu deities Lakshmi, the goddess of wealth, and Ganesh, the symbol of good luck. The border around these deities was carved with the images of elephants, another symbolic expression of wealth and fortune.

Tom glanced around and the mountain opposite was so still that his heart seemed to halt in its beating as if it too would be still. Overhead the sky was half crystalline, half misty, and the air was chilled and vibrant with rich tension. He noticed that up above the snowline, in the diminishing light of the sky, a frail moon had put forth its appearance, like a thin, scalloped film of ice floating gently on the slow current of the coming night. And a conch sounded in some far away temple.

SIXTY-NINE

Tom rang the bell and immediately the door opened and a servant dressed all in white stood in the doorway and first briskly saluted them, followed by his bowing deeply at his waist, gesturing for them to enter. Inside was a large drawing room with a spiral staircase on both sides leading to the bedrooms upstairs. In the middle of the room, hanging from the high ceiling was a large and brightly lit chandelier made of cut glass. The whole setting was emblematic of some famous Bollywood star or rich industrialist as it exuded wealth.

As they stood among the various crimson-colored, crushed velvet sofas they saw Harish with arms wide open and a broad grin on his face descending on the spiral staircase. Tom had not seen Harish for twenty years and almost did not recognize him. Harish was now a person of copious, malleable visage, with a nose in a cylindrical bulge, an ample, fluctuating mouth, and a pock-marked face. His obese figure leaned to embonpoint; his large limbs accentuated this inclination.

The man descending from the staircase looked at the people below with the vagueness of a child, but with the queer blank cunning of an old man. As he came down

and his gaze fell on Jyoti, his smile turned into a frown
and he said, "Who let this bitch in the house. We'll have
to wash and fumigate the whole place now." He then half
turned to look over his shoulder and shouted, "Balram,
get this filth out of my house."

At this juncture two things happened simultaneously.
Andrew saw Balram with his moustache waxed, pointing towards heaven, a saffron-colored turban tightly
wrapped around his head, as he was stepping out of a
back room and looking fiercely at Jyoti. Andrew recognized Balram. He was the torturer who had burned him
with cigarettes and threatened to chop his fingers off
next time he saw him. And Tom marched right in front
of Harish and in a firm voice said, "Jyoti is my daughter
and nobody touches her. I mean it."

This checked Balram who, with a puzzled look on his
face, looked at Harish with inquiring eyes. Harish with
his hand gestured him to step back and, grabbing Tom's
right hand as if greeting him, said, "Tom, don't be foolish. It is this kind of behavior that has filled the heads
of this class of people with stupid ideas that they are
equal to us. You had your fun with Lalita and as a result,
this thing," as he gestured with his eyes towards Jyoti,
"this creature was born, but you are not to concern yourself with it. One day she will meet the same fate as her
mother did. They don't matter and besides, they deserve
such treatment. Like I said, I will take care of her. But let
us not talk of it." Something peculiar betrayed itself in
the intonation of his voice.

Considering the matter settled and with a grin returning to his face, he asked, "How are you? I haven't seen

you for a long time. I have heard that you have become a very successful and wealthy industrialist in Calgary. Good for you, my friend. Maybe we could be business partners one day? You always were an inspiration to me. Here, have a seat." He gestured towards a sofa and at the same time gave a stern look to Jyoti, implying that the invitation excluded her.

"That is okay, I prefer to stand," said Tom, keeping an eye on Balram.

"I know this man," shouted Andrew, "this is the man who tortured me."

Harish smiled apologetically and looking at Andrew, said, "It wasn't torture, just a warning. It was for your own good. Because if you continued working with Dalits then like I warned you before, there are some people who will get rid of you. Permanently."

He then turned towards Tom and said, "You and your son are in my house for the first time. Please, please, take a seat and let us have some whisky. She can stay if you like." He turned to Balram and in a harsh tone barked, "Tell the girl to sit on the floor and get the servant to bring us some whisky."

"You come and sit next to me," Tom implored, as he gently held Jyoti's hand and made her sit between him and Andrew. Harish's mouth involuntarily contorted into a grimace as if he had swallowed some bitter medicine, but he quickly regained his composure and once again gestured to Balram to stay calm.

"Look Harish," said Tom, "I haven't come here to fight. Actually I've come here with a purpose. I would like you to know that I've made up my mind to confess my crime of violating Lalita to the local police and give them a sworn statement of the facts, what actually transpired that evil night, and even though Lalita is gone now I fully expect to be charged with a criminal offence and serve a sentence. This is something I ought to have done years ago for it will clear my conscience. To tell you the truth I feel quite at peace doing the right thing."

Harish looked left and then right as if finding it hard to believe such an incongruous statement and said, "What? You've found religion now? Come on, what you did, what we did that night was just a bit of fun. Dalit girls get raped and killed every day in India. Who cares? They are Dalits. They are not like us. They are used to such treatment. Who knows, maybe Lalita enjoyed what you did to her?"

Andrew felt Jyoti's hand in his tighten and he squeezed it gently, as if asking her to remain calm. Jyoti reserved her questions and anger for a better occasion and tried to control her trembling, evidently in a state of suppressed rage.

SEVENTY

And for a moment it seemed to Tom as if he was buried in a vast grave full of unspeakable secrets. He felt an intolerable weight oppressing him, the smell of the damp earth, the unseen presence of the devil, the darkness of an impenetrable night. He continued looking straight at Jyoti's face that now burned with fiery eyes, and an expression of wistfulness and hate. He made no answer to Harish for a few moments, but saw an expression on Harish's face, an expression of indefinable meaning, and his colorless lips twitched convulsively.

Andrew stood up and was about to speak when Tom said, "Sit down, Andy, please. You'll get your chance but let me finish first." Andrew, gritting his teeth, sat back down.

"Do you not," Tom said, gasping, as if the words had been torn out of him by a supernatural power, and he repeated in a painful voice, "do you not remember how mercilessly you beat her father and now you are telling me you got rid of her by murdering her? Don't you feel anything? Any remorse, any pain?"

It was a dark and stifling evening. Threatening storm clouds continued to gather like a conspiracy over the sky. There was a clap of thunder, and the rain came down like a waterfall. The water fell not in drops, but beat on the earth in streams. Flashes of lightning came every minute and each flash lasted to the count of five before it was followed by a clap of thunder.

"Look," said Harish steadily, "we started on the wrong foot. Let us all have a drink and please, let us forget about this ugly topic and talk about something pleasant. I mean, it has been such a long time and we've so much to catch up on."

"We'll have that drink soon, Harish," said Tom and added, "but first we need to put an end to this poor girl's suffering. You owe her an apology for what you did to her father using Andy's baseball bat and then just amongst us you need to explain what happened to her mother. Trust me, you'll feel better, and then Jyoti can find closure too. She just needs to hear the truth, we all do."

Harish neglected his question, because his attention attached itself more and more to the untouchable girl, sitting in his house and now demanding through Tom an explanation and an apology. He wished not to show any interest in discussing her or her mother.

"You're treading on some very dangerous ground, my friend," said Harish in a grave voice. Wearing a grim expression, he continued. "Leave all this to me. Neither of you know India nor its ways. I know how to take care of this situation. I'll teach her the same lesson I taught her mother. You don't know how to deal with this kind, I do. There is only one language they understand and this time I will shut them all up for good."

As his eyes gleamed with some horrible intent, Tom remained silent for he knew that now he had touched the right nerve. Tom deliberated, and it was perhaps the very truth of his own bold claim of a pending confession— it's not being negligible—that sharpened his focus on what he had come to accomplish and thereby also sharpening his wit. He articulated, "You're blasé about what you call 'these kind of people,' and their rightful place in modern society, because you're not civilized. You're under the false impression of being familiar with everything, but conscious really of nothing. What I mean is that you've got to learn to change with the times. Rather than fighting it, you could be contributing by supporting the Dalit movement. But like me, first you must come clean. We all must pay for our misdeeds before we can think of continuing on. It's the right thing to do."

"I wish you'd keep your business out of my life," said Harish, in a tone of savage expostulation. The host laughed abruptly, a bark of a laugh that he seemed to bite and kill in his mouth and added, "I did what I had to do to keep these low-caste people in their place. These people are not like us, Tom, but I don't believe you'll ever understand that. They mean nothing, nothing, you hear me? They are dirt."

Tom had not noticed before that Harish had a small greying moustache that stood out horizontally on each side of his face, and his pock-marked features were expressive of nothing much except certain insolence. Suddenly Harish shouted, "What the hell do you want? Why are you here?"

Tom felt his ears glowing. This was quite ineffectual. He tried another tack. "What did you accomplish by killing Lalita?" he asked in a challenging tone. "I know what

I did was wrong and I will pay for my crime. But I'm no murderer like you. You killed that innocent girl for no good reason. All she wanted was some support for a child that was forced into her young life through a brutal act of violence. Why did you have to kill her?"

Harish looked at Jyoti and a flicker of a smile played over his lips. His position in society, his influence with the authorities, and arrogance that came with the superior cast he was born into gave him his shield, behind which he felt invincible. He spread out both arms as if making the obvious known and said, "For you, my dear friend. Don't you get it? I did it for you. We care for our friends. This little trash was being claimed as your child. No untouchable is going to be recognized as a child of my friend, especially an important friend such as you. You ought to be thankful for what I did."

"But killing her?" Tom stressed every word as if encouraging Harish to divulge more.

Harish blew out his cheeks, and his eyes were eloquent of his casual air. Shrugging his shoulders, he said, "What do you care? You had your fun with her your way and I enjoyed it my way. She knew that one day she would end up face down in a well anyway. If it wasn't me it would have been another man of our civilized society who knows how to rid our world of this curse."

He paused for a moment with visible frustration on his face, and looked intently at Tom. "I don't really know what you need. But I will let you know what I don't need, I don't need a lecture from the likes of you; especially when you're standing in my house where I could have you all disappear overnight and no one would ever know.

Lalita wasn't the first one for me and mark my words, she wasn't the last. You should all get out of my house before I ask Balram to throw you out."

SEVENTY-ONE

Jyoti could not keep quiet anymore and fixed on him her deeply expressive eyes. "What in the world is the matter with you?" It had a sound of impatience, hatred and held a challenge. Choking back her tears, she cried, "Be a man and admit it; did you kill my mother or not? I don't think you have the guts to be a man. You're a coward and you hire thugs like Balram to do your dirty work. I despise you and hope you burn in hell." Jyoti was trembling with rage and her words were not far from releasing her tears.

His evil eyes took somehow unpardonable liberties staring at her, and he said in a voice that sent chills down her spine, "That, I think, is enough from you." Harish spoke with that irresistible air of finality he could assume at will, and in a voice that carried an open threat, said, "she cried and whimpered like you're doing now when I strangled her first and then threw her half-dead body in the well. She drowned, okay? I should have done the same with you when I had a chance. You better learn to keep your mouth shut and better still, go back to New Delhi, for here it is my town, I own the police, and I'm the law for I'm a *Thakur*. You get off my sofa and get your filthy body out of this house and never show your face here again." He was screaming and a spray of saliva flew from his mouth as he stood up, his body shaking with anger. He pointed his finger towards the door and shouted, "Balram, drag her out of here and throw her out in the street, the filthy bitch."

Suddenly Harish sat back down, raising his outspread hand towards Balram as if needing a moment to decipher something. "Oh I see," he said contemplatively. "Oh, I can see now." Suddenly he laughed. "I think I have seen this in a movie. I know what you are up to. Oh, how very clever of you, Tom."

He nodded as if feeling satisfied with his insight to why and what was happening in front of him. "I get it now," he laughed, "you are trying to set me up. You think getting my confession is going to free you." He then stood and staring hard at Tom, said, "I was informed that before you came here you were arrested by the police. What happened there, Tom? Did you make some kind of deal with the police? You are wearing a wiretap, aren't you? That's it, isn't it? You think your little trick is going to get me trapped." He laughed again.

Tom showed just a hint of fear that did not escape Andrew's attention. "Yes, I was at the police station but not to plot to trap you. I was there to confess my crime. It is up to you to do the same," answered Tom.

"Really," shouted Harish, and he rushed towards Tom and grabbed the front of his shirt with both hands and ripped it open. Three broken buttons fell to the ground and Tom stood there bare-chested, looking perplexed. There was no wiretap; he was clean.

"So, you are not that smart after all," said Harish with a tinge of disappointment in his voice, "for a moment I thought you had me trapped. Me and my big mouth, but anyway, no harm done for you were telling the truth after all. You missed a great opportunity, my friend, which you could have built into a pyramid of evidence."

Tom responded, "But from now on the police will be very suspicious of every move you make, especially after we tell them what we have heard."

"Tom, Tom, Tom," he shook his head and said his name with due politeness, but there was a threat of menace in his expression. "As the English proverb goes, from a hundred rabbits you can't make a horse, a hundred suspicions don't make proof." Harish laughed at what he thought was a clever statement, and continued, "Balram, you may want to throw these people out of my house now. But not the girl, she is mine. I am going to teach her a lesson like I did her mother."

Tom moved between Balram and Jyoti. Both Tom and Balram stood still and gazed at one another, as though measuring their strength. But at this moment a strange incident occurred, something so unexpected that neither Harish nor Tom could have imagined such a conclusion to their confrontation.

Balram took out a long, sharp, and serrated knife that was strapped to the side of his ankle and instead of moving towards Jyoti, he stood in front of Harish. In a deep and trembling voice he said, "For years I have been following your orders like a dog and doing your dirty work. But all that is behind me now, it is all over. I am going to finish you."

Tom, Andrew and Jyoti didn't move a muscle, mystified by this unexpected and sudden move from Balram. Tom in his plan had not allowed for this contingency and was not adequately prepared to respond to it. In his discussion with Mr. Tiwari at the police station he had assured them that he would get Harish to confess. He was convinced that once Harish knew that Tom had made his confession and given a sworn statement, then Harish would see that it was better for him to make a deal with the authorities to secure a lenient sentence by confessing to his crime. He wanted Harish apprehended alive.

"You ungrateful bastard," said Harish, grinding his teeth, "you too have developed a conscience now? What is wrong with this day?" His lower lip was white and quivering and his big black eyes flashed like fire. Tom had never seen him so spiteful and hateful. Before Balram could bring his raised arm up to strike Harish with his knife, Harish pulled out a handgun from the inside pocket of his jacket. He took a step forward and a shot rang out. The bullet grazed Balram's shoulder and flew into the wall behind him. Balram collapsed like a tree falls after a lightning strike and hit the floor hard.

Harish turned his gun towards Jyoti and said, "And it is your turn now. Say hello to your mother for me." Harish's voice broke and he seemed unable to articulate the words clearly. He raised his eyes and turned a gloomy sinister look at Jyoti. Tom sprang forward with rage, finally showing all his latent hatred for Harish, especially for what he made him do that fateful night. Over time he had suppressed these deeds, pushing the memories deep into the dark recesses of his heart. Tom thought of rushing Harish and grabbing his gun. But he knew that an irrational act in response to another irrational act usually spells tragedy.

So, without a moment's hesitation, Tom quickly stood with his arms spread out in front of Jyoti, covering her with his body. "Stop this, Harish," Tom shouted, "I would rather die than any harm should come to my daughter."

"That can be arranged, my foolish friend," said Harish, raising his gun and pointing it at Tom's head, "say goodbye."

SEVENTY-TWO

But before Andrew could make a move or Harish could pull the trigger again, heavy footsteps approached, running heavily, and the front door flew open violently, and Mr. Tiwari with his gun raised and a few smartly dressed policemen, waving their batons, shouting and screaming, rushed in.

Tiwari saw Harish moving his gun around and shouted, "Don't move or I'll shoot you where you stand. Put your gun down."

Harish lowered his gun and put on his charming smile and said, "Mr. Tiwari, *Sahib*, why are you shouting so much. We're not doing anything, just a few friends having a drink. Shooting Balram was an accident. I was handing him my gun and it went off accidently. Tell them, Tom."

"Not Mr. Tiwari, but Superintendent of Police to you," he shouted again. "I'm here to arrest you for the murder of Lalita, battery and assault on her father, the shooting of Balram and threatening behavior towards Jyoti. Put your weapon down on the floor and kick it towards me."

"You've no proof, SP *Sahib*," said Harish defiantly, but also maintaining respect for Tiwari's position as a senior police officer. He slowly put his gun on the floor and kicked it towards Tiwari. Tiwari took out a handkerchief and picked the gun up carefully, making sure not to smudge the fingerprints. He passed the gun to another officer who collected it in a bag as evidence.

With a sense of indignation rising in him, Harish shouted, "Do you know whom you're dealing with? I'll call the Police Commissioner and have you removed from your post. I don't care what these foreigners may have told you, you don't have a shred of proof for any of your allegations."

"Actually," said the SP, "we do." He walked up to where Balram was lying on the floor holding on to his bleeding shoulder and carefully opening up the top three buttons of his shirt. Pulling out a wiretap, he continued, "We've your confession and I have several witnesses to it."

Harish's eyes narrowed as if trying to comprehend the seriousness of the situation he was in. In a hissing voice he said, "You can't just knock down my door and barge in. Where is the warrant?" He protested with an apparent panic rising in his eyes.

"You'll get knocked about a great deal more if you don't shut up and come quietly with us," said the Superintendent of the Police, handcuffing Harish, and Harish abruptly became silent but only momentarily. In a bitter tone, he retorted, "You'll regret this." He eyed his interlocutor, and then glanced about him.

As the police escorted a handcuffed Harish out of his house and towards a waiting police van, an ambulance arrived and Balram, moaning in pain, was taken out of the house on a stretcher. Tiwari turned to Tom and said, "Sorry I could not let you in on my plans. When a few weeks ago Balram discovered that we have been mounting a case against him for torture and kidnapping, he voluntarily approached us offering his help to trap Harish for murder in exchange for us showing leniency towards him. Since then we have been waiting for the right opportunity, and we made the deal. You provided us with the perfect opportunity when you came to see us last night and gave us your confession and told us that you intended to confront Harish and make him talk and convince him to confess to Lalita's murder. Now you will have to come with us too but take your time saying goodbye to your children and I'll wait for you in the jeep outside." He then smiled at both Andrew and Jyoti, turned around and walked out of the house.

Andrew looked into Tom's eyes and said, "Dad, what have you done. You've confessed to your crime without any legal assistance. You could spend years in jail here. From what I've read the Indian prisons are horrible and the system is corrupt."

Tom could not help shedding two small tears of happiness. The way Andrew called him Dad and showed sincere concern made him feel that he was redeemed. He had accomplished what he came to do. Well, at least partially, he thought, for it seemed to him that Jyoti had not yet forgiven him. He bowed his head in contemplation and then, raising his head, a smile appeared on his lips. He placed a hand on Andrew's shoulder and said, "Did you know that Jyoti means light and she is indeed a shining light like that of a rising sun that turns the darkness of night into the brightness of day?"

He paused for a moment and then meditatively continued, "I know that laws and principles are not for times when there is no temptation: they are for such moments as that ill-fated night, when my body and soul rose in mutiny against their rigor; inflexible. I know the laws and I also know that I broke them, and I deserve to be punished. Otherwise what would be their worth?"

"But," Andrew hesitated and then repeated, "but this is the Indian police and their horrible prisons. Dad, you must have legal representation from Canada and maybe even the help of the Canadian embassy and the Premier of Alberta. I'm sure they could exert enough pressure in the right places to help you. You assisted the police in apprehending the murderer of Lalita and I am sure that would not go unrewarded."

"I've already made a deal with the Police Commissioner and he gave me his word that the system would be lenient as I have voluntarily turned myself in and aided them to apprehend Harish for the murder of Lalita. I'll be out in a few years or even less. This is nothing compared to the suffering I've caused Jyoti." Turning around to face Jyoti, he continued, "And I hope you will find forgiveness in your heart for me? I have been foolish, negligent of my duties and have done wrong to you like I have done to Andy. I hope in him you'll find the love and support I could never give you. He is your family now."

Andrew stood in silence and ruminated. The thunder crashed outside. It was like being in a little ark in the flood. Then a thought exploded through him like lightning charring a rotten tree: had he just begged him to

forgive his lack of care in the past? Did he just hear an
apology? He felt a twisted knot loosening in his soul.

It touched her, the way he atoned and looked at her,
as a father should at his daughter; and the fact itself that
he placed on her same the importance as he did on his
son came to her as so precious that she yielded to the
wish to get more from it. "I'm proud of you and hold no
grudge against you, not anymore. You gave my mother
and all of us justice and in doing so risked your life. I'll
visit you in prison and make sure they're treating you
right. We'll not abandon you."

Tom gently patted her head as if she was a little girl,
and becoming sentimental said, "All humans seem to
have an ambition to live forever. I guess I am no different and often wondered what I could do to at least live
longer, a lot longer than the average age so I could spend
some time with you. But I am not unhappy as I chose to
live a lot longer through my legacy—my children. You
will understand one day what I am saying."

He had fared so long on the thin diet of hope
deferred that for a moment or two his heart vacillated
and queried. Then, like violins reaching the end of a con-
cert swelling to a crescendo, it swelled to bursting, and he
knew his vision now had a real chance to be realized. *Yes,*
he thought, *I shan't remember all this except as a golden blur of
emotion.* But the time left for him to relive this moment of
emotion was enough.

Epilogue

A thin smile flickered on Tom's lips as he viewed the sad faces of Andrew and Jyoti. He let out a sigh and in trying to lift their spirits, he said, "As I have known, life can be the gloomiest thing there is, next to death. But it doesn't have to be that way." He added, in a voice that hinted at the pain in his heart, "There are always new hopes to foster, moments to enjoy, in your case perhaps new fights to win."

He looked away and paused for a moment as if to reflect on past memories and then continued, "Don't be so sad. You know in the sea of humanity surrounding us there are thousands of injustices and our fight must never cease to irradicate the world of such evils. But do take time out to enjoy the little daily wonders that surround us, to marvel at and rejoice in them, and those magical moments when a sudden realization of the simplicity of nature brings not despair but delight."

He stopped and this time laughed, a genuine laughter filled with relief that comes from the sudden release of pain and he persisted, "Look at me. I am babbling on about nothing. You two have a life full of challenges ahead of you. What I really wanted to say was that in the past twenty years I have accumulated a little wealth and a beautiful house in Calgary. I have put everything in a trust with you two as equal beneficiaries. Working closely with international immigration lawyers, I have almost completed all the paperwork for you to take Jyoti with you to Canada and for Baba to follow under your sponsorship. Anyway, upon your return to Canada, contact my lawyers and they will walk you through all this."

But almost at the same instant a serious and careworn look came into Tom's face; to Andrew's surprise he saw a deep sense of sadness in it. He had never suspected such a genuine expression would appear on his face. This was a different man, the father he always yearned for. "Can't accept this. None of this is necessary," interjected Andrew, "we are staying right here till you come out of prison. As a reward for what you did for the police, I will see that justice is done for you. We will plan our future together."

"Your future is before you; but no one in the world can make his way unaided. Therefore, make use of the house; it is yours now and its doors are open to you; I am convinced that the life you will create for yourselves under its roof will serve you both in a hundred ways." As moments of silenced prevailed, Tom let out a sigh.

A shadow of sadness flickered fleetingly in his eyes. Again a wave of the same feeling surged into his heart, and again for an instant softened it. He paused and sank into thought. "I wish I could have been a good father to you—God knows I do." He said this as if he spoke to a vision, viewless to any eye but his own; then, folding his arms, which he had half extended, on his chest, he seemed to enclose in their embrace the invisible being. "Now," he continued, this time addressing Jyoti, "I believe in higher justice—no sooner did I confess my heinous crime, than I've been rewarded the greatest gift of all: you. You truly are a new light in my life."

She glanced at him again, with her wonderful, expressive eyes that were like the heavens, pure and filled with innocence, or like two wild flowers that were open unblemished and hidden. She simply stared at Tom with admiration but due to surging emotions could not utter a word.

Tom raised his hand, stopping Andrew from saying more, and responded, "Your work with Jyoti to fight for the rights of the Dalit people is important and your voices need to be heard both in the eastern and the western world. Use my resources and your energy to continue your fight but give your struggle a chance to succeed by using Canada as the platform. Do it, if not for your own sake, then for the sake of your cause. Do it for Lalita."

Andrew felt a surge of pride and embraced his dad. He held him tight. The long embrace in which they held each other was the culmination of a lifetime of longing, and he took from it the certitude that what he had from him was real. It was stronger than a spoken vow, and the name he was to give it in afterthought was that he had been always been a loving dad. That was all he asked—love making a basis that would bear almost anything. This settled so much, and settled it so thoroughly, that there was nothing left to say to him. Oaths and vows apart, now they could coexist in harmony, and it seemed only now that their lives in earnest could begin. Andrew let go of his dad and looked at Jyoti, his heart filled with pride.

They wanted to speak, but could not; tears filled their eyes. They were both pale and thin; but those sick pale faces were bright with the dawn of a new future, of a full resurrection into a new life. A bond of friendship renewed them; the strength of relationship rejuvenated them, the heart of each held infinite sources of life for the heart of the other.

And now the incredible had happened, Jyoti suddenly found her voice. "We have a saying that when a lost person finds the way back to his home, he is not called lost anymore. You're, we all are home now." Jyoti blinked her eyes rapidly to suppress yet another rising emotion in her heart and, with her head tilted to one side, she simply spread her arms out and embraced him. Tom let out a huge sigh as he embraced her back. Andrew squeezed his arm as if to say they would wait for him and hope to receive him soon back in Calgary.

Tom lowered his head half in dejection and half in embarrassment. All the brilliant words he had just proclaimed seemed to him like dead leaves now, crumpling up and turning to dust, meaning nothing, blown away on a gust of wind. They were not the words of an exuberant life, lively with élan. They were the fallen leaves of a life that is ineffectual. He knew he was not coming back.

Tom held his breath and stiffened, then breathed again. He reluctantly had to leave the rest of his soliloquy as he was flooded by emotion. He simply nodded, turned around and started walking out of the room. 'Goodbye,' was the cry of his heart, and at the door he stopped and turned around to look for what he knew was the last time at both Andrew and Jyoti, as the truth in his soul added, 'forever.'

A slip of moon waning in the sky reminded Tom of the fragility of life.

-- The End --

About the Author

Narendra, published author of several books, writes mysteries, memoires and misadventure stories and has lived in England, Canada, Saudi Arabia, United Arab Emirates, India and the USA. Having traveled to more than seventy different countries has allowed him to gain an insight into diverse cultures. He finds inspiration from his travels and life experiences and through his novels invites you to join him on a journey of life, adventure, mystery and intrigue. He lives in Canada and the USA.

www.narendrasimone.com
www.facebook.com/AuthorNarendraSimone

Other Books by Narendra

1. Desert Song
2. Tuscan Dream
3. 1001 Arabian Nightmares
4. Kismet, Karma & Kamasutra
5. Cry of the Soul

Other Books to be published soon:

6. Temple of Hope
7. The Last Goodbye
8. The First Dawn
9. Long Way Home
10. The Unholy Ghost
11. Unbroken Line

Praise for Narendra's Books:

Desert Song – "Reading *Desert Song* is what I imagine a few evenings to be like of listening to a master story teller take us through the descent of Beowulf. Medieval in its proportions, gruesome in its verity, raw in its necessity, *Desert Song* exposes the sinister triangulations of politics, religion, and law in a world wrought with dark forces. Our hero, Matt Slater, witnesses unimaginable crimes in his desperate search for a lost child. Startling ironies erupt on each page as Simone's first thriller hurtles us through a journey both disturbing and authentic. Before you read any other book on the Taliban, read this book first."—Almeda Glenn Miller, author of *"Tiger Dreams"*

Desert Song – A Brilliant Story Masterfully Crafted – "Right from the beginning I enjoyed Narendra's style ... the picture was drawn and I stepped right into the set ... he cleverly interweaves his characters and gives his reader intrigue and interest in learning the dangerous world of Arabia ... Once I started reading it I could not wait to finish it." – Praveen Gupta, Published Author of 14 Books

The Last Goodbye – "In his riveting story, The Last Goodbye, Narendra Simone skillfully portrays the soul of a mother/son relationship in a culture that remains an enigma to so many of us." – Mike Sirota, author of *"Fire Dance"* and *"The Burning Ground"*.

Tuscan Dream – HIGHLY RECOMMENDED – "Narendra is a widely travelled author with an eloquent writing style. Artistic descriptions of the beautiful city of Florence, creates an enriched backdrop for the characters and plot of this novel of romance and intrigue. I began reading this story and could not put it down as it transported me to a culture of great beauty, architecture and art, through the eyes of captivating characters." – Elaine Fuhr, Allbooks Reviews